MELLOW SUBMARINE

A NOVEL

MICHAEL ATCHISON

www.michaelatchison.com

Publisher's Note: This is a work of fiction. Names, characters, places, and incidents are a product of the author's imagination. Locales and public names are sometimes used for atmospheric purposes. Any resemblance to actual people, living or dead, or to businesses, companies, events, institutions, or locales is completely coincidental.

Book Layout ©2013 BookDesignTemplates.com
Cover design by Grant Pace

Mellow Submarine/Michael Atchison. -- 1st ed.
ISBN-13: 978-1534966727
ISBN-10: 1534966722

For Kurt and all of my friends from places that are gone

ONE

Whe Mike McAfee opened his mother's front door on that Tuesday morning to find the perfect circle of a TV camera lens looming just past the tip of his nose, he knew that they had found her body. He studied the circle, huge and black like an eclipsing moon, and felt it cast darkness over his world. It blocked out the reporter, the house across the street, his ability to recall Jenna's face. He felt neither grief nor relief in that instant, just the awful feeling that it was all about to happen again. The tabloid smears, the police interrogations, the fear that innocence might not be enough. He squeezed the door knob to keep his knees from buckling.

He had come here, a thousand miles from Denver, to get away from the round-the-clock insanity. The opposite of the childhood fantasy, he had run away from the circus to go home. Looking at the camera, he saw that the circus had come back for him.

Before the reporter could speak, Mike began to formulate sentences in his mind, to note that he had not yet heard from the authorities but that this was the sad day everyone feared would come. He considered reaffirming that he had nothing to do with Jenna's fate and no knowledge of how she came to meet it, but he thought better of any immediate declarations of innocence. Today is about her, he thought. I'll begin fighting for my life again tomorrow.

And so when the sunny blonde reporter emerged from the shadow of the lens and asked "what is your reaction to the news that Jenna Kaye has been found alive and well in Reno, Nevada?" he had no words for her. He could not speak of what he could not believe.

Back inside, Mike discovered that he would have learned the news earlier had he not silenced his phone in an effort to get a little extra sleep. He found a string of text messages, missed calls and voice mails from ecstatic friends ("Dude! OMG!!") and scoop-seeking reporters ("pls call asap").

As he scrolled through messages, the phone buzzed in his hand. *Edward Kaye* lit up the screen. *Edward Kaye*. Millionaire, entrepreneur, philanthropist. The man who hired Mike, promoted him, groomed him, anointed him, blessed his intentions, and shared in his shock before suspecting him, accusing him and firing him.

"Hello, Edward," Mike said.

"Good morning, Mike. I assume you've heard by now."

"I found out just a minute ago. A TV crew rang my doorbell."

"Mike, I'm so sorry," Edward said. At first Mike thought Edward was apologizing for the way the news was delivered.

As they spoke, Mike turned on the television. CNN showed a picture of a police station and the banner headline "She's Alive!"

"Have you talked to her?" Mike asked.

"I'm here with her now."

"Is she OK?"

Edward paused. "She has not been harmed by anyone."

"I can drive to St. Louis and catch a flight. I could be there by late afternoon."

"I would send a plane if it were a good idea for you to come."

Mike paused to consider all of the messages contained in that statement. "So I take it the wedding's off?"

"You deserve better," Edward said.

♦ ♦ ♦

The Reno cop thought she looked familiar, but the face didn't quite register, nor did the identity on the license, Stella Driver, which seemed like an ironic name for one who swerved between lanes with so little apparent care. It started like a routine traffic stop until he ran the license and considered that the sweet thing behind the wheel looked pretty good for being eighty-four years old. And dead.

Things began to crystallize for Officer Riley an hour later in a conference room back at the station when the platinum blonde with the pixie cut and the banging body confessed her true identity. In that moment, Riley saw his future unfold. By morning he'd be on the *Today* show, by noon he'd have an agent, and by night they'd have a deal for a book, a TV movie and a line of action figures depicting the chiseled physique of the courageous cop who had rescued America's missing angel. He took a moment to ponder whether he should immediately resign in an effort to cleanse himself of the department's prohibition on officers accepting million-dollar rewards.

And then Jenna Kaye pitched forward and puked all over the conference table and Taylor Riley's dreams.

"Fugghgh," she said, and rested her forehead in the puddle.

♦ ♦ ♦

By the time Edward Kaye finished talking, the loop of TV images included video of a guy in a doorway sporting a Ramones t-shirt and a bad case of bedhead. Mike recognized himself as the slack-jawed man, but just barely. He was more interested in the graphic that identified him by name in big letters, with smaller type that declared "Did not kill Jenna Kaye." Mike assumed he spoke for all of America when he muttered "no shit."

Still, it was no more absurd than the words that Edward had spoken. Though Jenna had many details yet to provide, the rough sketch is that she had attended her ten-year high school reunion shortly before vanishing, and had become reacquainted with her senior-year boyfriend, Craig Doolittle, who possessed the most fitting name Edward could imagine. Mike had not attended the reunion with Jenna because he was downtown in a hotel ballroom, in a tuxedo, introducing Edward as he received the Person of the Year award from Denver's Council of Philanthropy. Apparently while Mike was hobnobbing with Mile High society, Jenna was boot-knocking with a high school loser who had migrated to Nevada, where he dealt cards in a casino and Chinese Viagra on the internet. Whatever Jenna knew of Doolittle's vocation seemed not to bother her, at least not enough to dampen her rekindled passion or her unstated desperation to escape her life. Doolittle was savvy about the perils of leaving digital breadcrumbs, so he and Jenna communicated by mail over the next few weeks, burning each letter after reading. She quietly stockpiled thousands in cash, no sweat for a child of such wealth. Then on that fateful Sunday, Craig Doolittle pulled up to the curb and she hopped into his Camaro with only the clothes on her back and the money in her bag, leaving her phone behind to preclude any electronic tracing. It sounded like "Thunder Road" meets *Breaking Bad*, Mike thought. Jenna and her old new flame were in

Reno by Monday morning, and no one knew to talk to Doolittle because no one knew that she had any ongoing relationship with him. She chopped her lustrous chestnut hair, bleached it blonde, took to wearing oversized sunglasses, and hid in plain sight at Craig's house for months. He procured a counterfeit ID for her in the name of a recently-deceased local woman, which Jenna used primarily for the purpose of buying liquor. She was out shopping when federal agents raided Doolittle's house and seized his implements of online drug-peddling. As she approached the house with a trunk full of groceries, she saw the fleet of law enforcement vehicles parked out front. Without being spotted, she turned left and then turned despondent. Jenna stopped in a bar, looking for a cool place to sit and think, but mostly she just sat and drank, which inspired the driving that caught Officer Riley's eye. At the station, she emptied her stomach and then spilled her guts, never wanting her daddy quite as much as she did right then.

She called Edward. Within an hour he was on a private jet. Within three he was on the ground preparing for a wave of attention that no man, no matter how powerful, could hold back. The list of people who knew that Jenna was alive before Mike did included Edward's general counsel, a crisis communications expert, a Hollywood publicist and the governors of Colorado and Nevada. Edward didn't want to call Mike until Jenna confirmed that he had nothing to do with her disappearance, and by the time she did, it was the middle of the night in Illinois, and so Edward waited until morning.

"At least she won't be charged," Edward said.

"With what?"

"Abetting the distribution of controlled substances. They've agreed to give her immunity in exchange for information about Doolittle."

"What a relief," Mike deadpanned.

"Mike, you have a right to be angry."

"It beats the right to remain silent."

"Jenna is going to have to account for what she's done. I can't apologize for her. But I can apologize for myself and my family and my company. You've suffered terribly and unfairly, and I regret the part I've played in that. I don't expect you to forgive me, at least not yet, but I want you to understand how sorry I am. In a few days, after we get Jenna back home, I want to talk to you about coming back to work."

"We both know that can't happen."

"I know it feels that way today," Edward said, "but there's no telling how it will feel next week. I'll be in touch. Until then, be well."

Mike hung up and wondered what to do with the rest of the morning besides avoiding the swelling mass of reporters he could see through the curtains. Then a text message popped up. *Put on a ball cap and come to your back door. We're going on an adventure.*

TWO

Mike opened the back door and Greg tumbled in, ninja-style.

"Nice somersault," Mike said. "So what are we doing?"

"I have our getaway all figured out, but first, have you made coffee yet? I was up late last night. Still a little groggy. I feel like I ought to be better caffeinated in order to properly execute the plan."

"Use the Keurig. Make whatever you'd like. Make me one, too."

Greg brewed two cups of Italian roast and used the steam from the first to liven his face before taking a sip. "Quality shit," he said.

"So what's the plan?" Mike asked.

"As soon as I finish this cup, we're going to bolt out the back, over the fence, through the Hendersons' yard, and down to Polk Street. We'll be outside the perimeter of the news trucks there."

"There's a perimeter?"

"You have the world's attention, my friend. There are cars parked along Jefferson for two blocks. The previous record for cars parked on Jefferson was a block and a half for the homecoming parade that year the football team was good. Once we get to Polk, we can hoof it down to the shop and you can hang in the office, where we'll discuss phase two of Operation Prairie Storm."

"Was there anyone in the back yard?"

"Nope. All clear. They seem to be adhering to a no-trespassing protocol. But we better run for it before those dicks from TMZ get here. I doubt that they'll be so respectful of your domicile."

"My domicile?"

"My brother the lawyer drops fancy words on me from time to time. Some of them stick." Greg broke into a broad grin as the steam condensed on his beard. "You've been back in my life for a week. Most eventful seven days in ages. Glad to have you home. Also, it should go without saying, I'm glad you didn't kill your fiancée."

"Did you have any doubts?"

"If you were a killer, I'd have been dead a long time ago. Now go throw some decent clothes into a backpack."

Mike came back two minutes later with a bag slung across his shoulder.

Greg gulped the last of his coffee. "Time to slip out the back, Jack," he said.

With that, the two old friends bolted out the door, sprinted across the yard and leaped over the fence, executing ninja maneuvers they had perfected nearly thirty years earlier.

A few minutes later, several blocks away, they sat inside the office as Greg unveiled the rest of the plan. Mike didn't love it, but he knew that he would either have talk to the reporters or hide from them, and with his life so fully ripped open there was little to be gained from seclusion. And, anyway, things had to get better now that he had been vindicated. Have a press conference, answer some questions, get on with life. And if his friend drummed up a little business in the process, so be it.

"All right," Mike said. "Let's do it. I'll rough out some notes while you're gone."

Greg stepped out to the alley behind the shop and on to his vintage Schwinn Sting-Ray chopper with the zebra-striped banana seat. He rode the eight blocks to Mike's house, down shady streets, past old colonials that served as fraternity houses. They must have been private residences at one point, Greg thought, but he couldn't imagine that anyone in Cameron could've afforded such extravagant homes seventy-five years earlier. He envisioned an alternate history for his hometown, a place where railroad barons settled in plantation-style homes, drank 100-proof bourbon, smoked cigars of exotic Caribbean provenance, stocked libraries with leather-bound volumes of Verlaine and Rimbaud, kept mistresses, threw debauched dinner parties and enjoyed raucous dialogues on philosophy, music and politics. Greg wanted to believe that this sort of thing was possible here. He needed to feel that there was some *there* here, some reason to exist in this dead end, something to hope for. Maybe Mike McAfee and his attendant calamity were just what this town needed.

Greg approached the media throng from behind. Seven satellite trucks, twice as many cameras, even more microphones and steno pads. He was never good at estimating crowds. He could be in a high school gym or a pro football stadium, look around, and conclude that one thousand people were in attendance. And so as he got closer to the McAfee house, he surveyed the scene and thought to himself "maybe a thousand."

Greg put the kickstand down, snaked his way through the bodies to the front steps, and shouted until he had the attention of the crowd. Ringed by cameras and microphone flags for ABC, CBS, Fox, NBC and CNN, Greg stood his straightest and cleared his throat.

"Ladies and gentlemen, my name is Glanville T. Allen. I am Mr. McAfee's . . . *au pair*," Greg said as he stood before the crowd in his cargo shorts, Chuck Taylor high-tops and Mr. Bubble t-shirt. "Mr. McAfee is not here. He is at my place of business. And he is prepared to speak to all of you. He would be glad to answer your questions to the best of his current ability. After that, it is our hope that you would allow him his privacy. The information about Ms. Kaye that has become available makes clear that Mr. McAfee has done nothing to warrant your attention. He is merely an innocent bystander."

Back inside Greg's office, Mike watched the scene unfold on television as the graphic "Glanville T. Allen, Mike McAfee's *au pair*" stretched across his friend's girth. "Jenna isn't dead, but fact-checking is," he thought to himself.

"Now, if you will follow me, I will lead you to Mr. McAfee," Greg said. He descended the front steps and the assembled press parted for him. Greg imagined that he was Chuck Heston in *The Ten Commandments*. As the sea closed in his wake, he mounted the Sting-Ray, which he thought of as a chariot, and then considered that he was conflating Heston flicks.

A news helicopter had arrived, and Mike watched through the eye in the sky. It was a glorious day in late May, and his hometown looked more beautiful from above than it had ever appeared at street level. The action was framed by trees so thick with leaves that they looked like broccoli stalks. Greg pedaled his three-speed bike as news trucks fell in line behind him, a slow procession down a small-town street, with oncoming traffic stopped to accommodate a wide convoy travelling at fifteen miles per hour behind a sweaty bearded cherub struggling to propel his bicycle up a gentle incline.

The trip took just a few minutes, but after all the back-and-forth of the previous hour, Greg's thighs burned like he had ascended a French mountain. He parked his bike along the street in front of the shop. Looking at the sign, reporters wondered if he had taxed himself so greatly that he needed to stop for a sandwich. Greg bent over and grabbed the ends of his shorts, panting and sweating. "All . . . right . . . this . . . is . . . the . . . place," he said before beginning to catch his breath. "If . . . you'll gather . . . here on the sidewalk . . . I'll get Mr. McAfee."

Greg took keys out of his pocket and let himself in. He walked straight to the refrigerator next to the cash register, grabbed a sixteen-ounce Diet Coke and drained it with a single forceful pull. He said hello to Alyssa, who was preparing for the day's business. Then he stepped into the office and looked at his friend.

"You said you were my *au pair*," Mike said.

"I said that? Man, I was so nervous. I think I meant *attaché*. That has more panache than saying I'm your friend. Anyway, it's French. No one will understand what I said."

"Everyone understands, Greg. It means nanny. You said you were my nanny."

"Well, that doesn't make any sense," Greg said with a snort. "Why would you need a nanny? Don't worry. They'll fix it in post-production."

"There isn't any post-production. This is news."

"You're being naïve, Mike. This isn't news. It's entertainment. You're going to need an agent."

"I don't need an agent."

"Well, you certainly need an agent more than you need a nanny, but that can wait until later. Come on. You need to do this now."

Mike stepped into the unlit dining area and saw the reporters through the windows. He looked at the television behind the counter and saw the same scene from above. The instant he stepped through the door, the snapping sounds of camera shutters and shouts of "Mike! Mike! Mike!" engulfed him.

The bewilderment Mike felt when first hearing the news about Jenna had given way to other, darker feelings. Ninety minutes after talking to Edward, he tried to calm himself. An inner monologue repeated that it must be more complicated than it seems, that more details will emerge. But he couldn't imagine what they were. His fiancée had ditched him for another man, and had left him as the prime suspect in her disappearance. *Gonna take a shitload of mitigating circumstances*, he thought.

Mike stepped forward and put up his hands like a quarterback quieting the home crowd. "Thank you for coming here," he said, voice quavering. "I'm sorry about avoiding you back at the house, but I wanted to show some respect for my mother's neighbors and not overrun their block."

Greg stood to the side and grinned while the whole nation saw the Mellow Submarine sign glowing behind his friend.

"I don't know much more than you do, but I am overjoyed by the news that Jenna is alive, and I am grateful to know that she seems to be well, or at least unharmed. I have not spoken to Jenna, but I have spoken to her father, Edward Kaye, and we had a good talk. Mr. Kaye was very gracious. As you can imagine, his primary concern is for the safety and health of his daughter, but he also expressed his concern for my well-being. Edward Kaye is a good man. Despite what has been reported over the past few weeks, there is no animosity between us, certainly not anymore."

Mike dropped his head slightly, closed his eyes for a moment, and looked back at the reporters.

"This day isn't about me in any respect, but I do want to take the chance to thank all of the people who have supported me through these past few months, which have been hard. I feared that the woman I loved might be dead, and I fell under suspicion. I understand why that was, but it only served to make an unbearable situation even worse. Suffice it to say that I'm grateful to many good people in my life, including my friend Greg Allen, in front of whose shop we are standing today. With that, I'm happy to answer your questions to the best of my ability."

Mike barely saw faces. He just heard voices.

"Was Jenna kidnapped?"

"My understanding is that she was not, but I have no first-hand information."

"Did she leave Denver of her own free will?"

"It appears that she did. But again, I don't know anything first-hand. Other people will be able to answer that better than I will."

"Did you have anything to do with her leaving?"

"No."

"Did the two of you fight before she left?"

"No."

"Did you have any idea that something might be wrong?"

"No."

"Did she run off with another man?"

"It seems that she did."

"Do you know his name?"

"I have heard a name, but just once, and I'm not sure I remember it correctly. I wouldn't want to give the wrong name."

"Was the name Craig Doolittle?"

"Again, I'm going to leave that to someone else."

"Did you ever hit Jenna?"

"No," Mike said and flinched. "No. No."

"Did you ever threaten her?"

"No. Emphatically, no."

"Did you abuse her in any way?"

"Absolutely not. No."

This was beginning to seem like not such a good idea.

"Why did she leave?"

"I really don't know."

"Are you going to see her?"

"No. At least not immediately."

"Does that mean that the wedding is off?"

"I think that's fair to assume at the moment."

"What's the status of your relationship?"

"I don't know. It's complicated."

"How did you feel when you heard that she had run off with another man?"

"I really haven't had the chance to process that yet."

"Do you still love her?"

Afterwards, Mike didn't remember his answer to the question, or anything that followed. He just remembered the whooshing of blood in his ears and the cold prickling on his face. He asked Greg if he had passed out at any point, and Greg said no, he'd handled it all like a champ.

After ten minutes of questions that grew increasingly inane and repetitive, Greg jumped in front of Mike like a corner man shielding a battered boxer. "OK, folks, we're finished. But I know that you've been at this for hours and you must be hungry. Mellow Submarine is now open for lunch."

THREE

The Cameron he had known was not quite the Cameron that Mike found when he returned. It was the Dadaist version, familiar but rearranged. Walker's, his family's preferred grocer, had been razed and replaced by a Wal-Mart. Easton Elementary, where he attended through fourth grade, became a school for students with special needs. The county courthouse, a castle when Mike was a kid, suffered from the addition of an annex that resembled a big shoebox. Perhaps that was where Lady Justice kept her pumps.

Morgan Park remained, though it seemed so much smaller than when Mike played little league baseball on its lone diamond. In the first days after he came back, Mike would go there and wedge his adult ass into a child's swing and wonder about creation. A cousin who was a Bible literalist once took a trip to a museum devoted to Creationism and then emailed a missive to everyone he knew, claiming to have seen proof that the earth was made in seven days just a few thousand years ago, and that all the science that claimed otherwise was either a hoax or a cock-up in the calculations. The message didn't offend Mike, it just made him sad. If God is all-powerful, Mike thought, surely He is capable of a metaphor, and that's how Mike chose to think of the book of Genesis in the time he thought of it at all.

As he looked at buildings that had gone up in spots where totems of his youth had come down, Mike thought that the world couldn't have been created in seven days because it was still being made, with ice caps collapsing into the Atlantic and volcanoes pumping bedrock into the Pacific, and there was probably some crazy seismic shit happening in the Indian Ocean that he had never even heard about. He thought to himself that the issue was mildly fascinating, and then he thought that nothing could be "mildly" fascinating, only vaguely interesting. And since he found the topic only vaguely interesting, someone else would have to write the book rebunking all of the museum's debunking. He had no immediate plans to get off the swing in the name of science.

Mike had been home a week when he decided to survey the town's ongoing evolution on foot, taking long walks, five or six miles a day. He took inventory of old friends' houses. He retraced the steps he took to the public pool years before. He went in search of familiar tastes and smells. To his delight, Murray's was still there and still serving the nachos with chicken and avocado. The aroma took him back to 1989, which he recalled was a very good year.

During the fourth such excursion, Mike walked up Monroe Avenue and turned left on Van Buren, a leafy street named for a nondescript president. It

drew its heavy shade from elms planted by a long-
dead history professor in honor of the little-known
fact that the nation's eighth commander-in-chief
grew up speaking Dutch. Given that most of the
townsfolk couldn't tell an elm from an oak, and
none knew this piece of historical ephemera, the
reference remained a secret that the professor took
to his grave. In fact, half the people in town still
called the street Van Doren, so dubbed in the 1950s
by teenage boys beguiled by the cantilevered cleavage of a certain Hollywood starlet. If only the president had sported better tits.

Back in high school, Mike walked this street at
least once a week to visit Gould Records. Marty
Gould opened the store in the Seventies, selling
records, eight-track tapes and other implements for
expanding one's aesthetic horizons. Before he had
a CD player, a pubescent Mike McAfee hovered for
hours over the record bins, first flipping through
the hits of the day and then graduating to hipper
fare, including the great alt-rock bands of the early
Nineties. But Marty's influence on the impression-
able boy helped make Mike a young Bob Dylan fa-
natic. Before he was old enough to drive, Mike was
especially fond of the lesser-loved records: *New
Morning, Planet Waves, Street Legal.* To love any Dylan at age fifteen projected depth, Mike thought. To
love it all, well, that projected dimension.

After years away from home, Mike assumed the
shop would be gone, the record store having grown
as quaint as the rotary phone, but he walked that

way just so he would know. And even if it were gone, it could still be his secret and sacred place, a spot for quiet reflection, like a Civil War battlefield. Or it could be a time machine, a place that transported him to his younger self, to a boy who had never heard of Jenna Kaye. Some speck within him felt that if he approached the place from just the right angle, he could wish it true and go back in time, walk into Gould Records, and warn the kid flipping through the bins not to take the job in Denver.

As he rounded the corner from Van Buren to Division Street, Mike felt his heart flutter. And when he got close enough to see that the Gould Records sign had been replaced by one that said Mellow Submarine, he felt both relief and a new sense of anticipation, as if this might be a worthy successor. Could be something. Could be nothing. Could be sandwiches.

Mike stepped through the door, saw the face behind the counter, and felt a surge in his chest that recalled the time he touched an electric fence on a dare from the boy who had grown into the man he now saw. Through the beard and the pounds and the years, there stood Greg Allen. They had been friends. Then they had been rivals. Then they had been nothing. It had been twenty years, more than half his life, since Mike saw Greg in the flesh. But there he was, bouncing his head to an old soul tune and making a sandwich for a pretty young woman. Mike and Greg used to hang out inside Gould Records and pretend not to look at the college girls, with their perfect skin and buoyant breasts. They still pretended not to look, but for different reasons. The girl handed Greg a ten, he handed back change, and then he looked up at the man in the doorway and froze.

Mike never hated Greg. He felt betrayed, aggrieved and confused, for sure. He even felt glints of recognition, understanding and compassion, which he didn't expect at first, but which eventually made perfect sense. When Jill changed from the skinny girl Mike had known since elementary school into the best-looking, best-smelling, best-feeling, best-tasting person in his world, she achieved gravity. He was drawn inescapably to her. Mike might have been able to summon the strength to push away from her ever so slightly, a sort of emotional jumping, but he always fell back towards her soft landscape. And when she exerted that same kind of force on Greg, what was the guy supposed to do? Not fall into her? At age eighteen, at the intersection of emotional infancy and hormonal anarchy, it would be like asking Greg not to hit the ground after falling from a tree.

When Jill released her pull on Mike, he began to drift away not just from her and Greg, but from his hometown, too. He was just a few weeks from high school graduation, and then off to college, and beyond that, who knew? He wasn't going to grow soybeans, sell insurance or teach history at Central Illinois University, so he failed to see much reason to remain tethered to this town beyond semi-annual visits to see his mother. From as early as he could remember he placed special significance on the city limits sign that made it seem like one small wing of the Holiday Inn hung over the edge of town and into nothingness, the region he and his friends called the Wild Prairie Outback, or WPO, site of many a clandestine campfire kegger, the place where he first felt the soft flesh beneath Jill's lacy bra. The population number on the simple green sign that marked the break between civilization and wilderness had stayed pretty steady over the years, and he was always struck by the precision. By the time high school ended, it read "Population 21,238," an awfully specific accounting for a place where no one lived and nothing happened.

Even after drifting out of Cameron's orbit, he still received occasional transmissions from home in the form of phone calls from his mom or clippings from the local newspaper that she would mail to him. She sent stories about the junior high basketball team winning the state championship; about the retirement of Mrs. Baird, Mike's beloved second-grade teacher; about the closing of Papa Anthony's, the town's best pizza place and home of the hippest jukebox around, not one of those modern CD-playing varieties, but an old Seeburg Select-o-Matic chock full of vintage 45s by the likes of Stevie Wonder and David Bowie. Linda McAfee kept stacks of newspapers in her kitchen and would spend some Sunday afternoons catching up on weeks of news. By the time it arrived in Mike's mailbox, the news could seem like history, including one story that was two months old when Mike finally laid eyes on it. His mom had written "I thought you'd want to know" in the margin and highlighted the name Greg Allen in the first paragraph. It recounted how Greg's two-year-old son Luke had been killed when Greg backed over him in the driveway. Mike held the paper up high after his first tear hit the page and began to form a gradually expanding circle. The story said that Greg and his wife Kim, whom Mike had never met or even heard of, each thought that Luke was with the other parent inside the house. It also quoted someone, maybe a prosecutor, as saying it was all a terrible accident and that no charges would be filed.

When he put the paper down, Mike felt an urge to call Greg, but he had no idea what to say. It was too late to send flowers, and Greg and Kim were already weeks into whatever process couples go through to try to heal. Offering condolences at that stage might simply remind them of their loss and amplify their pain, he thought. And in some small sense, the temptation to contact Greg felt selfish. Mike hadn't seen Greg in, what, fourteen years? Of all the names that streamed through Greg's grieving mind, Mike's wouldn't be one. They had been friends long ago, before Mike refused to forgive Greg for a transgression now all but forgotten.

Why should he expect an invitation to the Allen family's lingering wake? In the absence of knowing what to do, Mike did nothing.

A couple of years later, another clipping. It was from the courthouse news. Greg and Kim's divorce was final.

Glanville Allen, the youngest of three children, was born to parents who planned to stop at two. He was not just an accident, but an afterthought, given a name that should have gone to Mark, the family's first-born. Though Jerry and Anita Allen never bothered to do the genealogy, it was understood that Jerry's great-great-great grandfather, Glanville Putnam, enjoyed some connection to Abraham Lincoln back when the Great Emancipator was still a state representative. Some relatives said that Glanville was Lincoln's personal secretary. Some said he crafted the man's hats. And others whispered that the two shared a more intimate bond. Whatever the case, this ill-defined relationship to the nation's greatest president conferred considerable pride on Glanville Putnam's descendants, at least when they remembered it, which Jerry and Anita regrettably failed to do when their first son was born. The oversight struck Jerry only shortly before Stephanie came along two years later, and when she emerged *sans* scrotum he viewed it as a missed opportunity. And though he was unenthusiastic about the birth of a third child, and resentful at Anita's lack of contraceptive care, he was at least glad to be able to grant his second son the name of the family's most celebrated ancestor. Except that he and Anita realized that it was a silly name for a child born in 1975, one that smacked of a certain foppishness. In searching for a nickname that began with G, Jerry and Anita looked no further than the television show that transfixed Mark and Stephanie, and so baby Glanville, the youngest Allen, came to be named for the oldest Brady.

Glanville, an old French name, meant "a settlement of oak trees," which seemed painfully perfect to Greg, who felt stuck in the ground in this shitty little town. He had lived all but part of one year of his life here. Born, raised, escaped, captured, returned, and sentenced to life within the four walls of corn fields that surrounded the place.

After high school, Greg went to the University of Illinois, where the only major he declared was a major affection for weed, and the only distinction he earned was the distinction of being asked to leave. Greg seemed mostly untroubled by being kicked out of school but it infuriated Jerry, who was still grieving for Anita, lost to cancer a year and a half earlier. Faced with the threat of going to work in Jerry's insurance agency, Greg opted to enroll in the culinary arts program at the nearby community college, where he thrived. The idea of making a living by making food unearthed a previously unrecognized passion in Greg. He was especially enthralled by the great sandwiches of the world, the kinds he never found at home – the *Cubano*, the *Bàhn Mi*, the *torta* – and he put them on the menu of the local restaurant where he worked after graduation. In those next few years, Greg saved some cash, married Kim, and hung out at Gould Records. When Marty decided to close the shop because no one wanted to buy music anymore, Greg couldn't bear to see the town's lone record store go. So he bought it and diversified, keeping a few bins of records, but transforming most of the space into a sandwich shop with a few beer taps. He changed the name to Mellow Submarine, in homage both to his favorite band and to the place's history as a head shop. That he quit his job and did this without consulting Kim, who was eight months pregnant, proved unpopular at home.

Mike had been on Greg's mind. On some level, Mike had been on the mind of everyone in America who owned a television or who scanned the tabloids in the checkout line. But it was different for Greg, who still felt the remnants of their long-broken bond whenever he saw Mike's face on the screen, like some phantom limb of friendship. So when Greg spied Mike standing in the doorway of his shop he momentarily believed it was some kind of brain trick, a subconscious conjuring of the person he most wanted to see. But when the realization took hold, he felt the bond regenerate, stronger than before, tempered by the kind of ex-

perience no one else could understand. Greg was
the only friend who could comprehend what Mike
was going through, the suffocating weight of guilt,
suspicion and grief. Greg was not the sort to believe that Mike had been put in his shop for a reason, but circumstances like this could give a man
pause.

For the longest time they did not speak. They
just held on to each other and cried.

Over the next few days, Mike would come into
Mellow Sub in the afternoon and hang out until
close. Then they would adjourn to Max's, the bar
their dads frequented three decades earlier. Mike
and Greg had grown out of the college joints and
into this place, away from cheap beer and young
girls and toward stiff drinks and mature women.
They bridged twenty years with talks in a small
booth in the far corner.

"At first we assumed it was a kidnapping for
ransom," Mike said. "Edward is very wealthy. But
no one made a demand. And so the attention
turned toward me. I did everything the police
asked. I told them everything I knew. They
searched my house, my hard drive. I think they determined pretty early on that I wasn't involved, but
there's one detective, total jackass, who I can't quite
read. Maybe they are still looking at me. They've
refused to rule me out, at least publicly. Still, the
media has been after me much harder than the
cops have. And Edward, I don't know. We were al-
lies at first, trying to do whatever we could to help

find Jenna. But when there were no leads at all he just got desperate. And I think he suspected me because he didn't have anyone else. It got ugly and I went on leave and then he fired me. But the not knowing, that's the worst. It's just awful."

Mike covered his eyes with the heels of his hands, and Greg decided to change the subject.

"How's your mom?"

"Really good," Mike said. "This has been hard on her, of course, but she has been great about it. She retired not long ago. Did you know that my sister is living in South Carolina, married with kids?"

"I had heard the married-with-kids part. I don't think I knew where she lived."

"Anyway, mom had been planning to go out there and visit, spoil her grandchildren. Then she decided to extend her stay so I could have the house to myself. That's been good for me, getting out of Denver. I just got too self-conscious. It felt like everyone was looking at me all the time. Normally, that would seem paranoid. But in my case I think it was true."

"Ever hear from your dad?"

"Every once in a while," Mike said. "He lives in Texas, near Houston. His wife is nice. I haven't seen him in a long time but I still get a Christmas card. What's up with your family?"

"Mark is in L.A. He went to law school at Stanford. Now he's a partner at some gigantic firm. Has money flowing out of his ass. He has to wear special pants just to keep it all in. Stephanie lives in Chicago. She did pharmaceutical sales and then married one of the doctors on her circuit. Now she stays at home with three kids."

"How about your dad?"

"He's, um, not so good. Still lives in the same house. He started to drink after mom died and he never really stopped. It wrecked his business. Been to rehab twice but never tried very hard. He gets out, goes to meetings for three or four months, and then gives up. And it all falls on me because I'm the only one who's close. Mark's a total hard-ass. He doesn't have the time or patience. He just thinks that dad is weak. At one point, dad wanted to move to Chicago and live with Steph, but she said no, and I don't blame her. You don't want to interject that kind of shit into your kids' lives. He forgets. He accuses. He can be a mean old bastard, but every once in a while you can see the glint of the guy he used to be. Then it goes away. I grew the beard because I was starting to look so much like him and I got sick of seeing his face in the mirror."

"That's too bad. He was always nice to me."

"You wouldn't recognize him as the guy you remember," Greg said.

"You seeing anyone?"

"No. Not for a long time. I have no talent for it. My marriage was never very good and it got even worse after Luke was born. I don't even know why we got married. I think it's just what we thought we were supposed to do. Around here, if you reach twenty-five without tying the knot, it's like there's something wrong with you. Kim tried for a while, but I think she finally realized that I wasn't worth it. I had opened the shop. I was stressed, drinking too much. I had a girl on the side for a while, someone who worked at the shop. That's something I've never told anyone before. It sounds so pathetic when I say it out loud. I broke it off after I, um – after what happened with Luke."

Mike didn't know what to say, so he said nothing.

"Now," Greg said, "it feels like I'm married to this town. I always wanted to be someplace else, but I've managed to spend my whole life here and now I'm permanently anchored by my Mellow Submarine."

In the town where I was born lived a man who failed to flee, Mike thought to himself.

"Hey, can I ask you something?" Greg said. "And don't answer if you don't want. But what was the deal with that other woman?"

FOUR

Though suspicion naturally fell on him as the fiancé of the missing woman, Mike escaped the public's full scorn until the day that Maggie Kleinsasser sold her story to a national tabloid. There, on the front page of *The Inquisitor*, a photo of the two of them ran beneath the blaring headline "I Had an Affair With Mike McAfee!" Once that happened, well, things turned very bad indeed.

Yes, he had slept with Maggie. He did not deny it. He wasn't proud of it, but he felt no real guilt about it, either. What he did feel was a scalding embarrassment when the world learned that he'd done the deed with a relatively homely sociopath. The detail with which she described the encounter proved especially excruciating. "He removed my panties with his teeth," Maggie told *The Inquisitor*, "and then dived in head-first like a boy whose hands are tied behind his back in a pie-eating contest." She went on to say that "he treated my body like a buffet, gently biting the meaty flesh of my thighs and nibbling my nipples like sweet cherries." Maggie had no future writing romance novels, Mike thought to himself, but he acknowledged that he was no authority on the subject. He had not foreseen the boom in women's literature that involved sex with vampires and other fanciful creatures, nor the one in which credulous young women do S&M with handsome rich men. Maybe the world thirsted for some kind of chick-lit food-porn. Maybe Maggie would one day become the J.K. Rowling of stories about sloppy cunnilingus and the drunken schlubs who perform it. Maybe selling her story was just the first step in a masterful marketing plan. Maybe he had drunk-fucked a literary genius.

It would be wrong to say that Mike foresaw no negative consequences in sleeping with Maggie. A string of them had flashed in his mind between the fourth and fifth rounds of Maker's Mark. Pregnancy, STD, workplace awkwardness, and worst of all, the thought that he would one day be sober and she would want to do it again. At the far end of the spectrum was the idea, not entirely far-fetched, that they might one day enjoy something of a man-and-his-stalker relationship. Still, this seemed like nothing that couldn't be cured with a restraining order. As a consequence of the pain in which he then found himself, Mike could barely see beyond the night's end. He was going down in flames, and Maggie was a very soft, very wet place to land.

But he could not foresee that one evening of torrid, gelatinous ambiguity with Maggie Kleinsasser could serve as evidence that he had murdered a woman he had not killed and who was not, in fact, dead. Jenna broke up with *him*. That's an important piece of context, he shouted inside his head. Mike had never fully considered the ethics and etiquette of post-breakup sexual escapade but he assumed they imposed no restrictions on the partner whose heart had been stomped upon. Sure, if you did the dumping, decorum somehow dictated that you wait an acceptable period before engaging in third-party intercourse, and however long that period was, we could all agree that it was longer than six hours, couldn't we? Sex that same night would be an act of cruelty. But if you had been dumped, why should any rules bind you? Mike had not asked to be heartbroken and bereft. Jenna, if she had any sense of mercy, would want Mike to find solace any way he could, even if it came between another woman's thighs. She didn't want him to suffer. She just didn't want him.

So why should Mike's lack of obligation be retroactively revoked the next night when Jenna showed up at his door sobbing, saying she had made a mistake, begging him to take her back? It was a sign of his own basic goodness that he had taken Jenna into his arms, into his home, and had held her, told her that it was OK, and had never asked why she left him in the first place. "Let's pretend the last twenty-four hours never happened," he said, knowing that it was a good deal for him, too. Still, the moment Mike took Jenna back, the previous evening's coital misadventure was somehow converted into a betrayal, and that was fundamentally unfair. It made him flash back to his high school civics class. It was like an *ex post facto* law, and this great nation won't stand for those.

Mike and Maggie had come up through the ranks of EDK together. The picture of them that appeared in *The Inquisitor* wasn't really a picture of *them*. No such photo existed. Instead, it was a shot of them next to one another at an office party, with a dozen other revelers carefully cropped out, giving the illusion of intimacy. Maggie had long craved to turn the illusion into reality, but the flame she carried for Mike had only served to scorch a once pleasant and platonic relationship.

Business-bright but socially stunted, Maggie was just *too much*: too loud, too close, too brash, too big. She carried thirty pounds she would never miss, and Mike knew he was shallow to include that on the list of reasons he could never be with her. But in fairness it was way down the list, behind a plethora of traits that had made Maggie a good bar-hopping buddy back in their twenties but poor relationship material in their thirties. She could drink like a fish, curse like a sailor, lie like a rug, and sing like Aretha come karaoke time. But she couldn't, or wouldn't, keep a secret when it came to sex. Maggie wasn't promiscuous, just prolific, and the unsolicited details she provided Mike about her exploits with a series of steady boyfriends seemed funny at first, if only for their startling impropriety. But after a time they grew to seem sad and perhaps exaggerated or even untrue, some kind of distress signal that Mike could never decode.

Still, the two remained friends until the night, a few years back, when Maggie called to say that she had broken up with her boyfriend because she was in love with Mike. "I'd be in bed with him and think of you," she said, failing to understand that this was the sort of thing that people simply do not say. Mike knew that his silence in that moment must have devastated Maggie, but he could think of nothing short of the boldest lie ("I'm gay!"; "I'm dying!"; "I'm moving to Cambodia!") that could possibly paper over her humiliation. Instead, he said "Maggie . . . I'm sorry . . . I . . . I don't know what to say." And before he could figure anything out, she hung up.

In the days and months that followed, Maggie tried to play it all off as a joke but she couldn't nail the tone because it wasn't a joke at all. "Remember that time I called and professed my love and you totally crushed me? That was hilarious!" At first, Mike would smile and play along, trying to tele-pathically communicate that it would be fine just to forget all about it. But he couldn't forget because Maggie wouldn't stop reminding him, so he did his best to ignore her altogether.

Their career paths had already begun to diverge. Maggie was an ace analyst – no one knew Asia like she did – but her rough edges chafed Edward Kaye and ensured that she would never advance further. While she floundered, Mike flourished, earning Edward's trust, Jenna's love and a corner office. When Mike and Jenna announced their engagement, Maggie showed personal growth by telling the kind of polite lie that allows people in pain to get along in the world: "I'm so happy for both of you."

Looking back, months later, Mike could pinpoint the moment when his world began to crumble. He was sitting in their favorite old bar, half in the bag, when he saw Maggie come through the door. He was just sober and decent enough to know that he shouldn't, but just drunk and despondent enough to know that he would. Maggie Kleinsasser had never looked as good as she did right then.

FIVE

D r. Emory, the school is on the line. I think it's the principal."

The nurse lingered as the pediatrician picked up the receiver and punched the blinking light.

"Hello? . . . Yes. . . . . Hi, Dr. Keller. . . . What happened? . . . No, you did the right thing. . . . I don't know for sure, but I have a pretty good idea. . . . I'll be right over. Thank you."

"Everything OK?" the nurse asked.

"More or less. How many appointments do I have left?"

"Just one."

"Would you ask Laura to handle it?"

"Sure."

Ten minutes later Dr. Emory walked down the first-grade hallway at Carl Sandberg Elementary School, stopped in the doorway of Mrs. Tepper's classroom, and saw Liv tied to a chair.

"Hi mommy," Liv said through the gap in her smile where her baby teeth used to be.

"You're tied to a chair," Dr. Emory said.

"Yep."

"Who tied you to the chair?"

"I did."

"And why did you do that?"

"Because I'm like Martin Loofer King."

"You're like Martin Luther King?"

"Uh-huh."

"And how are you like Martin Luther King?"

"For Martin Loofer King Day, Mrs. Tepper told us that Martin Loofer King had dreams and that when bad things happened he would sit in the same place until the bad things didn't happen anymore. And sometimes I have dreams, like the one with the great big hamster, and I'm going to sit here until I don't have to go to daddy's this weekend."

"I don't think you really understand that much about Martin Luther King."

"I think I do. I got a perfect score on my Martin Loofer King Day quiz."

"Martin Luther King would think that you're a silly little girl."

"Do you know that he was a mountain climber?"

"I don't think that's right."

"We listened to him talk and he said that he went to a mountain top."

"That's a metaphor, sweetie."

"What's a metaphor?"

"It doesn't matter right now. Let's untie you and go home."

"No! I'm going to stay here until I don't have to go to daddy's. I don't have any friends there, and I would have to miss Maddie's birthday party, and we were going to dress like princesses, and Christina is always at daddy's, and she always talks about how pretty I am and about how I'm going to be a flower girl."

"You are pretty and you are going to be a flower girl."

"I don't want to be a flower girl. I don't want there to be a wedding."

"Well, there's going to be a wedding whether you want it or not, and you're going to go, and you're going to be good, because we want your daddy to be happy."

"Daddy doesn't want you to be happy."

"Oh, that's not true," she said without really believing it. He chose this. Chose to leave his wife and little girl, to take up with a woman ten years younger, to not give a damn about how it looked or who it hurt. "He wants you to be happy. And he knows that you won't be happy unless I'm happy, too."

"I won't be happy if I have to go."

"Sometimes you have to do things that don't make you happy right now, but that will help make you happy later."

"But Maddie's party," Liv said with a sadness so real that her mom felt it in her own chest.

"Tell you what. Let's call Maddie's mom and see if we can go out for ice cream tonight, and you can give her your present and have your own little party. OK?"

"OK." Liv stood up and the blue yarn fell to the floor.

"I don't know how to tie a knot," she said.

SIX

Greg put in the beer tap and fantasized that he'd have regulars. He'd be like Sam Malone from *Cheers*, but instead of talking about the Red Sox, his regulars would talk rock and roll. Unfortunately, he never got regulars, he just got Jenks. Richard J. Jenkins, sociology professor, know-it-all, putz. Jenks would stop by each day at about three o'clock after a hard day of nothing much, have a High Life, and drown out the records. Greg put High Life on tap only after he'd grown disgusted by every square-inch of his shop, after it went from being his anchor to the thing that weighed him down. The high life, indeed.

Jenks loved music but didn't give two shits about records. Or CDs. Or tapes. "Music is meant to be heard and not held," he said to Greg not five minutes after they first met. In Greg's sandwich shop. Which doubled as a record store.

Unlike Greg, Mike took to Jenks out of a bit of contrarian benevolence. He liked Jenks precisely because he wasn't likeable, and having recently been America's most hated man, he felt a certain bond with Mellow Sub's most pitiable customer.

Two days after Jenna turned up in Reno, Greg cranked up *Frampton Comes Alive*, which a customer had just surrendered for five dollars. He and Mike admired the LP cover with a joy that was only a little ironic. "Do you feel like we do?" Mike asked Jenks.

"What is it with you guys and records?" Jenks asked. "I never even had any. It was cassettes and then CDs and now iTunes. I boxed up all my discs a long time ago. Can't tell you the last time I used my CD player. I just use my phone or my computer."

"That's no way to live," Greg replied.

"It's convenient," Jenks said.

"Microwave sausage biscuit sandwiches are convenient," Greg snorted, "but they're not food."

"They're sustenance," Jenks said. He really liked microwave sausage biscuit sandwiches.

"Is that what you want out of music? *Sustenance*?"

"They're *sounds*, man," Jenks replied. "Why do they have to have some sort of physical vessel?"

"Because you can't know true intimacy with something that doesn't have a tangible form," Greg said, as if Jenks were ignoring some self-evident truth. "Every album you ever loved once had a beautiful body. Then they took that luscious black body and turned it into a little silver thing, and then into nothing. What do people buy now? Fucking electrons or something. You press a button on your phone and the thing's just there. Those files are like viruses, they just hop from one place to another and no one ever sees them. That's why these kids don't think it's stealing when they just take them. No one ever thinks they stole the flu from someone. It was in someone else's body and now it's in yours. The song was on someone else's hard drive and now it's on yours, or even worse, it's in the fucking *cloud* like water vapor. If the thing doesn't have a body it's not stealing. Not when it's just electrons, just *ideas*. Nobody ever steals a record from this place. But the second someone takes one out of here and rips it to his computer, half the kids in America are ready to help themselves. I'm not opposed to progress and options and shit. I have an iPod. It's got 20,000 songs on it. It's convenient. I like to shuffle my songs, make a playlist. But the thing's not a body. It's a soul capturer. All my songs' souls are in there and they can talk to me, but I can't commune with them in the realm of the senses, if you're feeling my vibe."

Jenks paused. Greg's vibe was not being felt.

"Here, I'm gonna show you." Greg stepped behind the counter and returned with a copy of *Mingus Ah Um*. "It's not just about the sounds. Music can be a full-on sensual experience. Or is it sensuous? I get those confused. Do you know?"

Jenks looked at him blankly.

"Look at that cover," Greg said, and Jenks contemplated the modernist painting that comprised the artwork. "It's beautiful. Just like a woman who catches your eye. First thing you notice is her exterior. Then she turns around," Greg flipped the LP over to show Jenks the back cover, "and you notice her posterior. Somewhere along the line we got convinced that inner beauty is what's important, and it *is* important, but anyone who says that the way a woman looks isn't important is talking bullshit. You're never gonna find her inner beauty unless her outer beauty catches your eye. You follow?"

"Sure, I guess."

"Here, take the record," Greg said and handed it to Jenks. "Take it in with your eyes. Gaze upon its beauty."

"Greg, really, I'm not into this part. I just like to listen."

"Stick with me, man. It's time to remove her dress."

"Her dress?"

"The outer sleeve, man. It's a pretty simple metaphor."

Jenks slid the record out and Greg took the empty cardboard from him.

"Now, you see," Greg said, "she's in her panties. I love 'panties.' 'Panties' is a goddamn righteous word."

"The inner sleeve is her panties?"

"Again, simple metaphor. It's the last thing between you and her skin. I like the old opaque ones. The old Capitol sleeves had pictures of all the label's current releases. But this one, as you can see, is just a plain sleeve with a cutout that allows you to see the label. Comparatively, this is like a thong. It doesn't leave much to the imagination. I guess those old Capitol sleeves were like granny panties because they covered up so much. The metaphor breaks down a little here because I'm generally not enamored of granny panties, but I do like a lady's undergarments to leave a little to the imagination."

"So this record is wearing a thong?"

"I suppose she is, but we're going for sensuality here, not pornography," Greg said, growing concerned that they were not affording the record its proper respect. "Now you're going to prepare her for play. The open end is her head. Put your right hand behind her back, support her weight."

Jenks stuck his hand out, parallel to the floor, with the thong-clad Mingus album flat on his palm.

"No, no, no," Greg said. "You're not a waiter. She's not a fucking *tray*. You ever put your hand on the small of a woman's back?"

Jenks relaxed his hand, got the record up on his fingertips.

"Put your right thumb up top, on the edge of her head. Don't touch the surface, just the edge. Now take your left hand and tilt her hips up and slide her out of the sleeve. As you do that, stretch out the middle three fingers on your right hand and place them gently on the label. Keep your pinky in the air and don't touch the skin. Your thumb is on her head. Your fingers, there in the middle, are on her –"

"Don't even say it, Greg!"

"You're a grown man, Jenks. You don't need to be embarrassed by this stuff. Now you're ready to take her behind the counter to the turntable."

Jenks approached the record player as Greg lifted the lid and removed the Frampton LP.

"Support her opposite edge with your left hand and gently lay her down. There you go, that's good. Now you take the needle and drop it into the groove and you let it ride for twenty blissful minutes, and if you have anything left, you flip it over and let it ride until you're finished."

While Jenks stood behind the counter sensually communing with Charles Mingus, the door opened. The gangly kid had been in before. He didn't always wear the same clothes, exactly, but variations on a theme. Tight jeans over bony boy-legs, Vans, t-shirts depicting skulls or skateboards or vintage cartoons. He wore his pimples like war medals.

"You buy and sell records, right?" the kid asked Greg.

Greg flicked his eyes toward the bin of LPs beneath a sign that read "We Buy and Sell Records."

"And you sell sandwiches?"

"Is this a rhetorical question?" Greg asked.

"Can I trade this for some sandwiches?" the kid asked Greg, and then reached into the canvas bag hanging from his shoulder and pulled out a copy of Elton John's *Captain Fantastic and the Brown Dirt Cowboy*.

"Old Reginald Dwight," Jenks said in an accent that was not quite English or Australian.

Greg cradled the record in his hands. The cover betrayed its age only through the faint outline of the vinyl underneath. "Goddamn, this is sexy," he said to Jenks. "Like a nipple poking through a blouse."

Greg slid the record out of the inner sleeve and held it gently by the edges. He lifted it to the light and then pulled it close to his face, tilting it and squinting, a jeweler examining for clarity. "This is like wet lacquer," he said as he studied the shiny, smooth, black surface. He looked at the kid and then back at the record. They didn't match.

"How old are you?" Greg asked the kid.

"Does it matter?"

"No, but if you get to ask if I sell sandwiches, I get to ask how old you are."

"Sixteen."

"Where did you get this?"

The kid's eyes hit the floor and then bounced back up to Greg. "It was my dad's," he said. "He died about a year ago."

"Oh. I'm sorry to hear that," Greg said. "I lost my mom when I was about your age. It's terrible but it gets easier over time. Your dad must have been a good man. He took great care of his records." Greg had known plenty of assholes who treated their records like religious artifacts, but it seemed like the right thing to say.

"Is that a good record?" the kid asked.

"Great record," Greg said. "What's your name?"

"Jacob."

"My big brother had this one. Came out the year I was born, but he still played it a lot when I was a little kid." Greg's memory flashed on Mark's crappy department-store record player and his unkempt stack of LPs. "He treated his records like Frisbees." Greg closed his eyes and heard a faint echo of the long fade of "Curtains," the album's last song.

"So, umm, can we trade?"

"Jacob, I'd love to have this record. The last time I saw a copy was at a yard sale. It had a six-inch gash across the second side. I almost cried. But this record looks like it was special to your dad. It's something you can remember him by. My sandwiches are pretty fucking memorable, but they won't help you keep a piece of your father."

"I don't think it was any big deal to him. I didn't even know he had any records. They were boxed up in the basement. My mom told me I could have them. I don't even know who John Elton is. If you don't want it, I'll sell it for cash on eBay and then come in and buy sandwiches. I just thought we could cut out the middle man."

"Fine," Greg said, "but why don't I just buy it instead?"

"Instead of me giving you a record, you giving me cash, me giving the cash back to you, and you giving me a sandwich, we could eliminate some steps. Plus, since you're paying me in sandwiches, I thought maybe I could get the wholesale rate. What's this record worth?"

"In this condition," Greg said, "probably twenty, twenty-five bucks."

"Shit," Jacob said and smiled. "Record collectors are crazy. Give me thirty bucks in sandwiches and it's yours."

Mike and Jenks looked at Greg and laughed. "You just got hustled," Mike said.

"I think you're right," Greg said, smiling. "Jacob, I either really like you or I hate your little adolescent guts, I'm not sure yet, but I'll make that deal. Do you want all of your sandwiches now or can I set up an installment plan?"

"Could you, like, load 'em on a gift card?"

"Of course," Greg said. "We have the most up-to-date gift-card-loading technology here." He grabbed a business card off the counter, flipped it over and wrote "Jacob - $30" on the back.

"Cool," Jacob said. "Can I get a meatball sub to go?"

"Sure," Greg replied, and then scratched out "$30" and wrote "$25" in its place. He made the sandwich and handed it over. Greg didn't see Jacob leave. He was too busying admiring his new treasure.

SEVEN

S weat dripped from the ends of Maggie Kleinsasser's flame-red spirals as she finished her last set of lunges, which followed her last set of pull-ups, which followed her last set of squat-thrusts. As she stood and faced the mirror at Pinnacle Fitness, one bead of perspiration recklessly rode the edge of her left breast before plunging into the abyss of cleavage amplified by a sports bra one half-size too small.

Maggie felt a sexual charge at the end of each workout, a sensation that intensified with the passing weeks and her shrinking waist. In little time, Maggie's fleshy spread gave way to flat, hard abs and slim, toned thighs. Whenever Maggie caught a glimpse of her new pumped-up, trimmed-down self, she felt a pulsing in her panties and noticed her nipples protruding through her Dri-Fit bra. She could cut glass with those things, she thought, and on this night she leaned forward to test the theory. As the tips skimmed the mirror's surface leaving behind vapor trails, she noticed the slack-jawed reflection of the forty-something man on the chest-press machine, and gave him a wink.

Maggie had banked on being famous, but she hadn't bargained on being infamous, and she was ill-prepared for the national commentary on her appearance. Deep down she understood that she wasn't movie-star hot, but she had never lacked for men willing to fall into her bed. The better looking a woman was, the better-looking the men she attracted. Maggie knew this. But she felt she always punched above her weight in this respect by projecting an out-there sexuality, as if she had "I will fuck you hard" tattooed on her forehead in ink she could make visible to prospective mates through a naturally-selected chemical-biological power, like some desert-dwelling sex lizard. Survival of the fittest really meant survival of the horniest in her book. The future belonged to breeders.

But Maggie discovered that her one-to-one sexual power proved useless once she entered the mass consciousness. Now millions of men knew who she was and what she did and what she looked like, and no matter how hard she tried she could not make her invisible tattoo light up the television screen, and even if she could, she had no interest in arousing those losers. So instead of treating Maggie like an object of sexual desire, a nation of Neanderthal men (and quite a lot of women, too), transformed her into an object of serial derision. And the smaller the medium, the more savage the reaction. The late-night talk-show hosts, disparaging as they could be, kept things within the broad realm of decency (during a week in which Maggie seemed to appear on every cable news channel, and in some questionable outfits, Conan O'Brien quipped that he was no longer the least appealing woman on television). Morning radio jocks across the country did disgusting bits that drew rebuke from the National Organization for Women, though Maggie felt a certain pleasure when Howard Stern spent a week asking guests whether they would rather have a body part amputated or have sex with Maggie Kleinsasser. He started with the little finger on each guest's non-dominant hand and worked his way up to larger and more vital extremities until the answer was "have sex with Maggie Kleinsasser." It pleased her deeply that these famous, mostly handsome men were being prompted to consider her carnally. Artie Lange got all the way to saying he would prefer to have his head amputated, while Ryan Gosling, that sweetie, declared that he would rather sleep with Maggie than lose even one fingertip. Maggie felt the same about both of them.

She could take it from Conan and Howard. It was all in good fun. But she refused to take it from the slithering vermin of the internet, the sleaze bags who bombarded her with photoshopped pictures of her being sexually degraded, who called her "bitch" and "cunt" and worse (yes, worse), and who, if you strung all the epithets together, came to some cave-dwelling consensus that she was a fat, ugly, pasty, sloppy, used-up whore. She began to spend an hour each morning, and then an hour each night, behind her Twitter account, @MagsDontTakeNoCrap, engaging, battling and doing her best to humiliate, emasculate and eviscerate the vile creatures. She retweeted every dick pic, sexist slur and as much personal information as she could gather, and then unleashed her growing army (more than a quarter-million followers at last count) on them until they deleted their accounts and every last trace of their digital lives. She delighted in pointing out every deactivated account with her tagline, which she hoped to copyright, "who's the cunt now, bitch?"

Still, as she stood in the middle of the weight machines toweling off and turning heads, Maggie Kleinsasser felt in touch with her new reality. She knew that she couldn't go back to being a financial analyst, certainly not at EDK, having been fired instantly and in person by Edward Kaye upon publication of the first tabloid story. It was the first time in ages that he had fired anyone himself, which gave Maggie some perverse sense of pride. She knew that her fame flowed solely from the fact that she once copulated with a drunken desperate schmo, which meant that she now lived at the intersection of sex and fame known as scandal. And she knew that she created this new reality when she took a five-figure check from *The Inquisitor*. She was not offended that the most lucrative offer to date had come for a porn video that she had no intention of making. The worst she permitted herself to consider was a spread for *Playboy*, not that they had asked (but they hadn't seen her new bod yet), and the most she had allowed herself to fantasize about was a chair on *The View*. She was famous for having humped Mike McAfee. She didn't expect to parlay it into being elected president.

Maggie stepped out into the cool, dry Colorado night, walked two blocks to her building and rode the elevator to her fourth-floor condo. She locked the door behind her and stripped off every stitch of her sweat-soaked clothes, leaving the heap on the entryway tile. During her transformation into Hot Maggie, she polished every hard surface in the place – picture frames, toaster, TV screen – to reflect her newly-sculpted physique back at her. She couldn't help admiring the pleasing mixture of hard and soft, accentuated by red hair and fair skin. She fed the fish, moved into the kitchen, and blended a concoction of coconut water, protein powder, almonds, kale and mixed berries. She took her shake into the living room, plopped her naked self on the couch, and turned to the cable news show on which she had appeared four days earlier when Jenna was found. There Lacy Nantz, a bleach-blonde former prosecutor and self-styled "victims advocate" was telling the world "what we know at this hour" about Jenna Kaye and why she disappeared in the first place. And it struck Maggie that she was no longer part of the narrative. Now that Jenna was not dead by Mike's hand, their one-night stand wasn't a vital clue in an unsolved mystery. It was just two sad and lonely people dulling their pain in each other's flesh. The oldest story in the world.

In the studio, Lacy interviewed Janet Culp, identified in a graphic as "high school classmate of Jenna Kaye and Craig Doolittle." Lacy probed Janet about the relationship between Jenna and Craig, of which she knew almost nothing, a fact that did not prevent her from talking at length. But her pretty head filled the screen nicely, which seemed to matter most. They discussed the slow drip of facts and innuendo emerging from Reno. Jenna didn't love Mike anymore. Maybe she never did. She felt trapped, duty-bound, pressured. Sources said that Mike wasn't abusive, though Lacy raised her eyebrow at this. She was gonna need some proof. Maggie slid her bare ass to the edge of the couch while they showed soundless video of Mike opening his door that first day as Lacy sneered and said that Mr. McAfee had declined to speak to the media in the ninety-six hours since his press conference ended, a tacit admission that he was hiding something.

Maggie turned off the television and began to cry softly.

"What a shitty thing I did to him," she whispered.

EIGHT

In the days immediately after Jenna was found, Mike, having no real job, made it his work to analyze Greg's business. He didn't go through the books. He just watched how the place operated and noted what worked and what didn't. He couldn't help it. At EDK this was how he evaluated investment opportunities. Did the company have a good product? Did it understand its customers? Was there room for growth? So Mike watched the employees, mostly part-timers enrolled at CIU. There was Trina, a sociology major, petite, sneaky-pretty and great with customers; Robert, who studied English and worked at the campus radio station; and Alyssa, the only employee Greg trusted with keys and the closest thing he'd had to an assistant manager since a guy who may or may not have been named Dave (Greg couldn't quite recall) quit two years earlier. A handful of other college kids picked up hours here and there, but Greg never committed names to memory until they had worked for at least six months. Mike checked a mental box: *management style needs improvement.*

The shop's strength, without question, was its food. Mike sampled a different sandwich each day and always proclaimed the most recent one his favorite. The *Bàhn Mi*, spicy and sweet, blew his mind. The Italian Dagwood, creamy with fontina d'aosta, rocked his world. And the muffuletta evoked a response that was almost sexual, the musky, briny olive salad redolent of hot, tender flesh.

Still, the thing that Mike contemplated most was the concept. It was a word that Greg would have loathed, but you can't choose whether or not you have a concept, you just do. In some cases it's intentional and in some it's pure happenstance. And so Mellow Submarine presented a happenstance concept. Greg made sandwiches. Greg liked record shops. And in trying to produce the former and preserve the latter, he had stumbled into a concept that was, more or less, a sandwich shop that aspired to record-store ambiance. The problem as Mike saw it was that the two sides weren't fully integrated. The record-store part was little more than a side business tucked into the front corner. Aside from the fact that music was always playing, that piece of the concept could be lost completely on a person who just came in for a sandwich. Greg hadn't incorporated album-style artwork in any of the décor (and *décor* was a pretty highfalutin word for Greg's minimalist approach to the shop's visual aesthetic). He hadn't worked the theme into the names of his sandwiches or even into the logo on the t-shirts worn by employees. Mike took care never to force his impressions on his friend, but if Greg should ever ask, twenty pages of notes awaited him.

The thing about the shop that Mike loved unconditionally was the jukebox, the Seeburg Select-o-Matic salvaged from Papa Anthony's. Mike left the Seeburg out of his notes because he felt too close to it to be objective. He loved it because he had known it since childhood, had enthusiastically fed it every last coin in his pocket hundreds of times. Mike did a rough calculation of how much he might have earned had he invested those coins instead (he couldn't help it), but was glad he didn't save them. The musical education had proven too valuable. He recalled how the selections always seemed five or ten years out of date but somehow timeless, as if Anthony knew better than to be fooled by flash-in-the-pan pop sensations. As a kid, Mike's favorite record to spin was one that came out before he was born, the bubblegum glam of "Little Willy" by Sweet, and his heart swelled when he saw that it was still there, at J9, where it had been all those years ago. The first time he saw the Seeburg in Greg's shop, Mike dropped in a quarter and played it, conjuring the aroma of green peppers and parmesan cheese in the process. Mike recalled that Anthony had reserved J5 for the Jackson 5, and Greg did the same. "I Want You Back" sat there, sounding as immediate and perfect as it ever had. The more quarters Mike dropped in the slot, and the more he examined the titles, the more he began to notice about Greg's approach to stocking the jukebox. The thing held just fifty singles, A and B sides, accounting for one-hundred songs. Mike had not previously given much thought to the process, but upon considering it, he understood that Greg, limited to fifty records, would be sure to make each one count. And he did. It was a stellar collection. It was also a word game that went way beyond Anthony's dedicated spot for Michael, Jermaine, Tito, Marlon and Jackie. Each side of each single was denoted by one letter (A through K, omitting I) and a number from 1 through 10 (the ten was actually a zero, but they always called it ten). The first one that caught Mike's eye was B1 - "You Dropped A Bomb On Me" by the Gap Band. "The B-1 bomber," Mike whispered to himself. Then he noticed George Clinton's "Atomic Dog" at K9, and at K2 a song by Mountain ("The Laird," B-side of "Mississippi Queen," which sat at K1). Though most were relatively obvious, he smiled at making the connections, and began to look for more esoteric references. He saw "One Way Ticket Home" by Phil Ochs sitting at C3, and thought it seemed out of place. Greg loved music but had little use for old folkies, so Mike began to turn it over in his mind until he stumbled on the connection – C3 . . . Phil Ochs . . . *Phil* . . . *Ochs* . . . *PO* . . . *C3PO!* Mike immediately jumped to D2, where, in the spot that should have been devoted to a B-side, he found, flipped over, Peter Gabriel's "Red Rain" – *R2D2!* But the discovery that made Mike laugh out loud was "Texas Tornado," a single by The Sir Douglas Band. The stereo mix could be found at

F3, and the mono version, apparently a little more powerful, at F4.

After a few days of study, Mike leaned against the counter and said to Greg "do you really think that Olivia Newton-John is a nine or a ten?"

Greg was momentarily puzzled by the question but then he thought of the record he had stashed at A9/A0, and he broke out into a broad grin. "You cracked my code. You're the first. She's definitely a ten. That's why I flipped the single over and put 'Physical' at A10."

"I'm surprised. She never really did it for me."

"You're crazy, but whatever. Buy your own jukebox and you can make her a one. Though I really need to find a song about steak sauce for that slot since I've never been able to snag a copy of 'A1 on the Jukebox' by Dave Edmunds."

"Wouldn't a Lawrence Welk record be great at *A1 and A2*?"

Greg seemed stunned, as if he had been caught by a jab. "Oh my god, that's great. I never thought of that. Now I have to find a Lawrence Welk record."

"I found B1, K9, C3PO, R2D2," Mike said. "How many are there?"

"Not a lot. It was fun for a while, but it got too damn hard. Finding that Sir Douglas record was a complete fluke."

"Am I missing any?" Mike asked.

"It's no fun if I tell you," Greg said, "but I always did find 'Philadelphia Freedom' to be pretty *benign*."

NINE

At the dawn of the first week of the rest of his life, Mike sat sipping coffee in the Mellow Submarine office as Greg explained some of the finer details of the sorry-ass business that he now owned half of.

"You never told me that you had a partner," Mike said.

"Mostly a silent investor. We get together once a month to talk over the business. We're going to meet here in a little while."

"I can leave."

"No, stay. Please."

"How was your Sunday?" Mike asked. "I think it was the first day in two weeks that I didn't see you."

"I crashed like the stock market on Black Tuesday. I don't know how you handle this shit."

"I got an offer to write a book," Mike said. "It happened Saturday. I also got a couple of cable news offers. One is to be a financial analyst on the third-rated business channel, and the other is to go on Lacy Nantz's show for four straight nights to tell my side of the story. And a guy from *Esquire* floated the idea of doing a long profile, which would include photos of me wearing the next season's fashions, or something like that."

"What are you going to do?"

"I said no to everything but the book, and I only said maybe to it."

"I wasn't sure I wanted to mention this," Greg said, "because I feel pretty weird about it, but I got an offer, too. I got a call last night about a commercial for an energy drink. They want to show me huffing and puffing as I ride my bike up a hill. Then I stop and have the drink, and I shoot up the hill like a rocket, with smoke and sound effects, kind of like the Road Runner, they said."

"You should do it."

Greg scrunched up his face. "I don't want to exploit you and your situation, at least not more than I already have." He pinched his eyes closed and then opened one to see what Mike was thinking.

"I'm not going to be in the commercial, and my name's not going to be in the commercial, right?"

"Of course not."

"Then all you're exploiting is your inability to get your fat ass up a hill."

"Your words are hurtful, sir," Greg said in mock offense.

"Are you in a position to turn down free money?"

"I would check with my accountant, but my alcoholic father handles my books, and he likes to tell me that I'm a failure and my shop is a failure and that I'll never be able to repay him the money I borrowed to start the place, so, no, I suppose I am not in such a position."

"Then take the offer. Wait. Don't take the offer. First, tell them you want twenty percent more than they're offering, and then take whatever they offer after that."

Just then, the outside door to the office flew open and a little girl bounded in. "Hello, Geggy!" she said, and jumped into his arms.

"My business partner is here," Greg said to Mike.

"This is your business partner?"

"No, this is my partner's daughter, Liv. *That's* my partner," Greg said as he nodded toward the doorway.

Mike saw the woman backlit by the morning sun and felt the latest in a string of serial shocks. He stood up like a punch-drunk boxer.

"Dr. Emory," Greg said, "you remember Mike McAfee."

She smiled, said "I do," and wrapped her arms around him. "It's so good to see you," she said.

"Jill," he whispered, and then breathed in a scent that awakened long-dormant places in his memory.

"I have to take Liv to school, but I told her that we could stop by the shop and get a blackberry muffin. Could I drop her off and then come back?"

"Sure," Greg said.

"I was talking to him," Jill replied, glancing at the other guy in the room.

"That would be great," Mike said.

Jill had been pretty in high school, but not like this. Mike had long admired the way that some women's beauty deepened over time. But if Jill kept going at this rate, he thought, hers would rip a hole in the time-space continuum about the time she hit sixty.

Jenna notwithstanding, Mike preferred women his own age. Younger women weren't better looking, just unmarked. No lines around the eyes, no spots on the skin, just helium-filled breasts and a thin layer of baby fat that made them smooth, soft and undefined. All of Jill's baby fat and baby weight was gone. She had been chiseled into something lean and pure, her truest self uncovered by time.

She looked fucking great.

She also looked tired, her eyes dark at the surface, as if she had receded into herself just a fraction of an inch.

As they sat and shared a pot of coffee, Jill gave Mike the thumbnail sketch of her life. She met Dan Emory in medical school. They got married during their residencies, and Jill later joined her dad's pediatric practice in Cameron while Dan went to work with an orthopedic surgery group in Champaign, sometimes commuting and sometimes staying in an apartment he kept there. "I was so stupid," she said, "letting him have his own place in a town full of college girls. Surgeons are as narcissistic as bodybuilders. And they're conquerors. He made conquests." On Liv's fourth birthday Dan surprised her with a backyard playhouse modeled after Sleeping Beauty's castle. The next day he surprised Jill by asking for a divorce. He had met someone. He knew he couldn't be happy without her and he knew Jill couldn't be happy with a man who was in love with another woman, so this was the best thing for everyone. Demanding a divorce was practically altruistic he reasoned without saying it in quite those terms. *You should meet her.* That's what he said. *You should meet the woman who fulfills me more than you ever could, and then you'd understand, and you'd be happy for us.* That's what Jill heard in a haze of pure heartbreak. Her name was Christina, he said, a former member of the Illini dance squad, an aspiring "fitness model" (air quotes supplied by Jill), and a new Chicago Bears cheerleader. She was twenty-four.

"That was three years ago," Jill said. "She's twenty-seven now, getting up there in years, but the boobs Dan bought her are only two years old, so she should do for a while."

"I'm so sorry," Mike said.

"Don't be. I'm better off without him, but it wasn't a mistake. I got Liv out of the deal. She's the best thing that's ever happened."

"She seems pretty awesome."

"She is." Jill paused and then muttered "Dan never offered me new boobs," like some private thought that slipped out.

Mike pondered a response – "Your boobs look perfect the way they are" was the first to come to mind – but he thought better of it.

"I suppose I would have been offended if he had," Jill said. "I'm not a blow-up sex doll, and my boobs don't need upgrading."

Again, Mike opted for silence, but he was glad to know that they were on the same page.

"I'm sorry," Jill said. "It's been twenty years. You're probably not all that comfortable talking about my breasts. Or interested."

Comfortable? No. Interested? He tried to shake the thoughts out of his head. After recent events, considering a woman sexually felt like contemplating the oysters that caused your food poisoning.

Mike looked down, opened his mouth to speak and hesitated, aware of the awkwardness of the transition. "How did you wind up being partners with Greg?"

"I hadn't really kept up with him," Jill said. "When I moved back home after med school, I would see him around sometimes, and his son was one of our patients. The day he died, I just sobbed. It's still so awful to think about. And I never knew Kim very well, but they always felt like an odd match. She seemed so joyless, even before they lost Luke. After it happened, I started to come around the shop every once in a while, really just to check in on Greg. And then I started to come around more often and Greg and I reconnected a little. I really liked the shop. It was nice that he could maintain some of the spirit of Gould Records. And the sandwiches are amazing."

"You became partners because you liked the shop?"

"No, sorry, I forgot where I was going. When Greg and Kim were getting divorced, this place was one of the only assets they had. And even though it really wasn't worth much, her half was still worth more than Greg could afford to pay. So they were stuck with either operating the place together after the divorce, which wasn't going to work, or with shutting it down. And not to be too dramatic about it, but the shop was all he had left and I hated the thought of him losing it. So I wrote Kim a check for $5,000, she moved to Iowa, and now I'm half-owner of Mellow Submarine."

"That was really kind to do."

"It wasn't much of an investment. During my divorce, Dan looked at the line item on our list of assets, laughed a little and said 'keep it.'"

"I don't know," Mike said, "I think the place has potential."

"Maybe," Jill replied, "but it has the wrong owners. Greg is great at making sandwiches but not so good at running a business, and I'm trying to maintain my practice while being a single mom. I just don't have the energy or the interest to devote to the shop. I can barely handle the other things in my life, let alone this place. Thankfully, my parents are around to help. They're great with Liv."

"How are Dr. Murdock and her husband, Dr. Murdock?"

"Awesome. Mom is still teaching history at Central, and dad is mostly retired. He sees patients one day a week. He plays at lot of tennis. Do you still play? We could set up a match."

"That might be nice. After everything that has happened lately, getting my ass kicked on the court by a seventy-year-old man wouldn't seem so bad by comparison."

"What about you?" Jill asked. "Every five years we have a reunion, and each time I hope that you'll walk through the door but you never do."

"I had some scheduling conflicts. I was in London for one of them."

That's the truth, Mike thought, but hardly the whole truth. He had skipped the five-year with no excuse better than that he didn't want to go, that he wasn't ready to see Jill and Greg, that it all seemed a little too fresh. It wasn't that the past ate at him or that he pined for Jill. In fact, he had a lovely girlfriend at the time and was as happy as he had been in his brief adult life. In grad school at NYU. Loving his time in the city. Living beyond his means, but just a little, like a runner moving fast, leaning at the tape, feeling like he was flying for an instant. He saw no reason to come back to Cameron where he would be fumbling between handshakes and hugs with his former friends when instead he could hang out in the East Village and ignore that anything was happening back home.

And while it was true that he was in London
for the ten-year gathering, it was also true that he
had scheduled the trip so that he would be out of
the country at that precise time. His mom had tried
to talk him into attending. "You don't ever have to
live here again," she said, "but it's nice to have a
hometown that you can come back to." Mike didn't
see the need. He had found a home in Denver
where he had become a rising star at EDK, raking
in cash in those heady years before the economy
plunged into the toilet and the toilet crashed
through the rotted floor and the rotted floor was
swallowed by a hungry sinkhole. As the reunion
approached, he also stood in the receding tide of
his breakup with Sarah, who had left Denver for a
swank job in San Francisco, taking a sizeable chunk
of Mike's heart with her. Alone in bed at night, he
found himself drifting back a decade, feeling Jill's
skin against his, remembering the curve of her hip,
the base of her neck. He didn't want to carry those
feelings back to an event where he might see her
(and perhaps her husband, if she had one, though
no newspaper clipping from his mother had ever
confirmed it). And because Mike didn't want to
confess or confront those feelings, he flew across
the Atlantic for a business trip that could have
been scheduled for any time in a four-week span.

As for the fifteen-year reunion, he couldn't
muster up a reason to care. He had been gone almost half his life. The people he remembered all
seemed like ghosts. His scheduling conflict that

night was nothing more than a low-key dinner party he attended with Courtney, his last girlfriend before Jenna.

"Our twentieth is coming up soon," Jill said. "You have to come."

"If I'm still here," Mike said, "I will."

If I'm still here. Mike had spent six days pondering where his life should go next, but he still couldn't envision his future. He felt no real urgency. He had money to live on and he could buy even more time by selling his place in Denver if need be. It was hard to imagine going back. Jenna, Edward, EDK, Maggie, the whispers, the pointing. He had friends there, but not roots, or even a job, no matter what Edward said. He felt too old to start again in New York, even though that's where the best work was for someone like him. Maybe Charlotte, North Carolina. Nice place. Plenty of financial jobs. Chicago seemed like the most obvious destination. The Board of Trade was there. And he could zip down to see Greg anytime.

"Well I hope that you are," Jill said. "Still here, that is."

TEN

The man sat in a chair in the middle of his living room as others buzzed about, setting up lights, cameras and microphones. A few days' growth on his face was neatly sculpted, and his closely-cropped hair tapered to just the hint of a fin. He wore a denim shirt with a vest over top, his sleeves turned up to offer glimpses of tattoos on the inside of each forearm. The tip of a dagger peeked out from one sleeve and an ornately-scripted J-E-N disappeared beneath the cuff of the other without revealing any more letters. Wrapped around his ankle, but tucked beneath his pant leg, was an electronic monitoring bracelet.

A long-haired guy in a black t-shirt clipped a small microphone to the vest and said "Can I get you to count to ten so we can get a level?" The man in the chair said "absolutely, bro," and then counted up to ten and back down again for good measure.

"Hey, bro," the man in the chair said, "what's this chick gonna be like?"

"Lacy?" the guy in the black t-shirt said. "She's a pussycat. She plays a hard-ass on camera but if you give her a good show she'll love you. She'll bring you back again and again. She can't get enough of this story. But don't be offended if she doesn't talk to you before the interview. It goes back to her days as a prosecutor. She wants the audience to see you as a hostile witness, not as a friend."

The crew continued to scamper around, setting out water for the interviewer and her subject, and putting the finishing touches on staging. A fake rhododendron in a basket was deemed to be the thing that made the backdrop perfect.

Moments later a short woman in tall heels walked in and sat down across from the man in the chair. Though her spiky hair and crimson lips seemed more severe in person, somehow she seemed prettier than on television, nearly human.

The woman flipped through her notes as the guy in the black t-shirt clipped a microphone to her jacket. "Check, check, check, check," she said, and minutes later a voice from some place beyond the lights said "Lacy, we're ready to go in three, two . . ."

The woman looked into the lens and said "Good evening, America, I'm Lacy Nantz, coming to you tonight from Reno, Nevada, at the home of Craig Doolittle, who represents one corner of a love triangle that has captivated the nation. We are at Mr. Doolittle's home because he is confined here as he awaits trial on federal drug-trafficking charges. I assure you that no stipulations have been put on this interview, and Mr. Doolittle is not being paid. This will be a no-holds-barred conversation."

She moved her eyes from the camera to her subject. "Mr. Doolittle, gutless defense lawyers normally prevent interviews like this from happening. Why did you agree to talk to me?"

Doolittle flashed a wide grin. "Well, Lacy," he said, "I'm currently in-between lawyers, so no one gets to tell me what to do, and even if someone had tried to stop me, I would have done it anyway. I'm a big fan of you and your show and I have nothing to hide."

Lacy tried to suppress a smile but the flattery overpowered her. "Did you kidnap Jenna Kaye?" she asked.

"No, Lacy, I did not."

"Then why did she leave her luxurious life in Denver to come live with you here?"

"Because we're in love."

"You say that in the present tense. Are you still together?"

"To the best of my knowledge. She's never told me that we're through and I've sure never told her that."

"Have you heard from her since you were arrested?"

"No, but I understand. She needs to lay low for a while."

"So you think there's a future for the two of you?"

"Absolutely."

"But you're going to prison. You're a drug dealer."

"Lacy, I'm a card dealer, not a drug dealer. I'm also a musician. People can check out my EDM at www dot –"

"You were arrested by federal agents. They seized evidence from this very house."

"Just because I was arrested doesn't mean I'm guilty."

"I was a prosecutor for ten years, Mr. Doolittle. I never saw a single innocent person charged with a crime."

"I'm sure you ran a tip-top operation but these folks made a mistake. It happens. It'll all work out in the end."

"You're facing some very serious charges. You don't seem concerned about this at all."

"I'm not. The truth shall set me free."

"But what about all of the communications with China that have come out in the press?"

"My music is huge there. It's all a misunderstanding."

"Do you know Mike McAfee?"

"Never met him. Never even knew his name until I saw it on the news."

"Jenna Kaye never mentioned his name?"

"I knew that she had been seeing someone in Denver but she didn't make it seem like a big deal."

"But they were engaged to be married."

"Were they? Really? I think that was just a show she put on to please her dad."

"They had a date set."

"I could set a date to fly to Jupiter. Doesn't mean I'm leaving the earth. And that wedding didn't happen, either, did it?"

"We've invited Mike McAfee on our show repeatedly and as recently as a few days ago, and he has turned us down every time. What do you think he's hiding?"

"Dude's probably embarrassed. I took his girl and the whole world knows it. That's gotta be, you know, a little humiliating."

"So you don't think he had anything to do with Jenna leaving Denver?"

"What happened here is that Jenna wanted to be with me, so she came to Reno. Ever hear of Occam's razor? The simplest explanation is usually right. And the simple explanation is that Jenna was in love with me and not him. So here we are."

"In the months since you reconnected with Jenna –"

"Months? You think it has been months?"

"All the information we've learned says the two of you got together last summer at your high school reunion."

"We were both at the reunion, that's true. But we've been getting together as often as we can for years."

Edward Kaye watched the spectacle, alone, in the study inside his home. After Doolittle explained that Jenna had long manufactured reasons to go west for EDK business – San Francisco, Boise, Salt Lake City, Las Vegas – in order to spend days and nights with him in luxury hotels, Edward bolted out the door and sprinted fifty yards across his property to the guest house where Jenna had been staying since she returned from Nevada. As he ran, a light in the living room went out, leaving the house in darkness. Edward skidded to a stop at the front door and began to pound on it.

"Jenna, open the door!" After a few seconds of silence, he pounded again. "Jenna! Open! The! God! *Damn*! DOOR!"

Moments later, Jenna opened the goddamn door.

"Daddy, did you listen to him? He's insane."

"Is it true?" Edward asked.

"He thinks we're still together. He thinks we have a future."

"*Is it true?*"

When Greg noticed customers watching Mike watching Craig Doolittle, he said "enough of this bullshit," grabbed the remote and flipped to a baseball game.

Mike put his hands over his face and said "I'm so stupid."

"No, buddy, you're not," Greg said.

"Jesus, Greg, weren't you watching? Jenna was sleeping with that asshole the entire time we were together and I didn't have a clue."

Greg glanced over his shoulder and saw that people were still watching.

"You think this is some fucking freak show?" he shouted. "Take your sandwiches and get the fuck out. We're closed."

No one moved. They just stared.

"Get out!" Greg shouted.

Six frightened customers scurried out the door.

Greg locked the door, flipped the sign to say "We're Not Sorry, But We're Still Closed," and turned off the front bank of lights. He grabbed a bottle of whiskey from behind the counter, picked up two cups from the stack by the soda fountain, and filled a bowl with ice. He sat down at the back table with Mike. Arizona led Chicago by four runs as they headed to the ninth inning.

"You know it could be worse," Greg said.

"How is that?"

"You could play for the Cubs."

"That actually might be worse."

"Do you still love them like I do?" Greg asked.

"Yeah. I tried to adopt the Rockies when I moved out there but you can't tell your heart what to do."

"Why do we let them do this to us year after year?"

"Because they're all we know," Mike said, "and because it's going to be so sweet when they finally win it all."

"A lot of people have lived their whole lives saying that and a lot of them are dead."

"But we're not dead."

"By god, we're not," Greg said and filled both cups. "And anyway, *Back to the Future II* said they're going to win it all in 2015."

"When has *Back to the Future II* ever let us down?"

"Not a single goddamn time as far as I can recall."

"Here's to Ernie Banks," Mike said, raising his drink.

"And Ryne Sandberg," Greg replied.

"To Lee Smith."

"And Bruce Sutter."

"And Greg Maddux," Mike said.

"Fuck Maddux. He left us. He's the Jenna Kaye of Chicago Cubs."

"OK, then," Mike said, "here's to Fergie Jenkins."

"That's right. To Ferguson Goddamn Jenkins. And to Ron Santo."

"To Ron Santo," Mike said. The friends clinked their cups and drank.

"You need to write that book," Greg said.

"I don't want to keep reliving this. I don't want it to be my whole life."

"You need to do it so you can get on with your life. If you don't tell your own story, your life is going to be defined by what Craig Doolittle and Maggie Kleinsasser say. How's that sound?"

"Not great, I guess."

They sat quietly for a moment until someone knocked on the door.

"We're closed!" Greg shouted without turning to look.

Mike saw the face in the window and gestured at his friend to get up.

Greg walked to the door and let Jill in.

Mike grabbed another cup and filled it with ice. "Come sit with us," he said.

"Thanks," she said quietly, looking past him.

"The aura of pity that surrounds you suggests that you've been watching Lacy Nantz's show," Mike said.

"It's not pity, Mike. It's recognition."

"So you've suffered a national humiliation?"

Jill's back stiffened. "Just because my humiliation wasn't seen by the whole country doesn't mean it wasn't painful."

Mike reached across the table and took Jill's hand. "You're right. I'm sorry." Then he stood up, leaned across the table and kissed her on the forehead. "I'm really glad you're here," he said.

Greg poured three fingers of whiskey into Jill's cup and she took a sip. "Some truly excellent barware, gentlemen," she said. "Shall I get lids and straws?"

ELEVEN

Mike sat behind the desk in Greg's office and unpacked supplies. A stack of legal pads, some pens, mechanical pencils, highlighters, a composition book, Post-It notes, a digital voice recorder, AAA batteries, paperclips, a stapler, extra staples, a dictionary, a thesaurus, Strunk & White, Garner's *Modern American Usage*, a thermal mug and a case of Altoids. He didn't know exactly what he would need, so he got everything. He turned on his laptop, opened Word, pulled up a blank page. He stared at it for several minutes and then stepped into the shop for another cup of coffee.

It wasn't yet nine a.m. Greg stood over a pile of dough, kneading and twisting. Everyone loved everything about his sandwiches, but many agreed that they loved the bread the most. He prepared four different kinds each morning, and by lunchtime he had the savory, chewy, soft and crispy foundations for his creations. Mike thought if Greg could pipe the aroma into the street, business would triple.

"Can I pour you one?" Mike asked, waving a coffee cup.

"Sure," Greg said. "How's the writing coming?"

"I've laid my pencils out if that counts for anything."

"Pencils? Are you writing a letter to Santa?"

"Are you sure it's OK for me to work in the office? I feel too isolated at the house. I could go to the library instead."

"No, please, work here. It will be the first good use ever made of that office."

Mike walked back to the desk and sat down with his cup of dark roast. He had negotiated his own deal with the publisher. A handsome advance allowed him to feel like he was doing real work and not wasting time, and his rejection of the offer of a ghost writer meant that his time would be fully occupied for the four months until the first draft was due. He asked his editor, a kind woman named Elaine, how to get started. She said there is no right or wrong way. Some writers start at the beginning and go, some make meticulous outlines, some write scenes in any sequence that comes naturally and then reorder them along the way. The most important thing, she said, was to never let any idea go unwritten. When the thought comes, put it down on paper or it's gone.

Mike took a gulp of coffee, looked at the blank screen, and let his fingers go.

How did you feel?
That's the question everyone asks.
But it's really a series of questions.
How did you feel when Jenna disap-

peared? How did you feel when Maggie sold her story? How did you feel when you were alone in an interview room with two detectives? How did you feel when Jenna turned up alive? How did you feel when you learned that she ran off with her boyfriend? How did you feel when he made a fool of you on national television?

How did I feel?

In order: terrified, mortified, petrified, exhilarated, humiliated and emasculated.

In other words, I had two minutes of all-consuming, bewildering, incomprehensible, heart-stopping joy between the time I learned that Jenna was alive and the time I learned that I was a dupe. The days on either side of those minutes were pure, unadulterated shit.

But "How did you feel?" is the wrong question. It reveals nothing of any value. It's just voyeuristic. But let's be honest. If you're the kind of pathetic peeping tom who would shell out your hard-earned cash for a book like this, the voyeuristic questions are the ones you want answered. Well, fuck you. I threw you a bone and answered that one. From here on out, I'll ask the questions that I want answers to, like, *how did you get yourself into this mess?*

I met Jenna when she was seventeen. I was twenty-six. I know how that sounds. But that's not how it was. I had just arrived in Denver. She was my new boss's daughter. We met in passing two or three times before she went off to college. I would like to tell you that I barely noticed her but that would be a lie. One of the times we met was when I dropped her dad off at their house on the way home from the airport. Jenna was an athlete, a cross country runner, and as I was leaving she came sprinting up the drive, the final kick in a six-mile workout through the hills around the Kaye estate. I had just gotten into my car. Edward was inside the house. It was the kind of spectacular Colorado dusk that makes you never want to leave. I had just put the top down on the two-seat roadster I bought with the bonus I got for signing on with EDK. Jenna glided to a stop by the driver's-side door. She was five-feet-eight, maybe 115 pounds. She wore shorts cut high at the hips and a sports bra, hair back in a ponytail. Her skin glistened. Her abs rippled. She put her hands on the side of the car and leaned over to catch her breath. She smiled at me and said "you're Mike, right?" and I agreed that I was. "Nice car," she said. And that was it. She walked to the house. I may have glanced at her in the mirror. She may have glanced back at me.

I saw Jenna just a time or two in the next few years. She went to an Ivy League school. She worked on Wall Street. And then she came back to Denver to claim her birthright. From its beginning, EDK has been closely-held, owned entirely by the Kaye family. And it had long been assumed that one day it would belong to Jenna. Marlene Kaye, Edward's wife and Jenna's mother, had died years earlier in a car accident that also claimed Edward's brother, with whom she had been having an affair. People who knew Edward back then say that he was devastated, but that Jenna, just eight years old at the time, took it with a peculiar calm. Perhaps she was too young to fully comprehend it.

Edward, to his credit, wanted to ensure that Jenna had the skills to run the company well, so he demanded that she get a high-level education and top-flight experience in New York.

Jenna was in her mid-twenties when she came to EDK. I was in my mid-thirties. I was Edward's chief operating officer, having advanced a long way since the day Jenna came running up the drive.

Though Jenna and I both traveled a lot in those days, we saw each other in the office frequently. Our relationship was cordial and professional and, I'll confess, a little flirtatious. We might have a drink after work, but only in a group with other colleagues, including Maggie Kleinsasser. And while the young EDK employees maintained a strong camaraderie, Jenna and Maggie never shared any warmth. I think Maggie knew how I felt about Jenna before I did, and I don't think she liked it. Jenna just thought Maggie was loud.

Jenna had been with EDK for a couple of years when we traveled to New York to visit a new media company that we were considering buying. After dinner with the company's founder we went back to our hotel to discuss whether we could be the ones to find a way to turn a profit in the new information economy. We sat in her room, across a table from each other, unable to make the numbers work. We had been at it for an hour or so when Jenna said "Do you remember that time when I was about seventeen? I had been out for a run and I was coming up the drive just as you were leaving."

I said I remembered.

"I was walking away, and I looked back at you and saw you looking at me in your mirror. Do you remember that?"

I said I did.

"I think about that all the time," she said.

You want to know what happened next, don't you? Well, it's none of your goddamn business, but you can probably guess. Let your imagination run wild. And then go back to my original question: *how did you get yourself into this mess?*

How did you let yourself sleep with your boss's daughter?

How did you rationalize sharing a bed with an employee who, while the heir to the throne, was still technically a subordinate?

And what did you answer when the morning light crept in and she laid her head on your chest and asked "what are we going to tell my dad?"

Mike leaned back in his chair and read the words that he had just written. He clicked on *File* and then *Close*. A box popped up and asked if he wanted to save the document he had just created. He clicked *No* and then went for another cup of coffee.

TWELVE

Mike found his routine. Up at five-thirty, out the door fifteen minutes later, four quick miles through the streets while the town pried open its eyes and yawned. At that hour, even as summer approached, the air possessed a chill that jumpstarted his thinking. Alone with the sound of his footsteps, the images came to him. Then came the words. Most days he had several paragraphs sketched out in his head before he hit the shower. Five days a week, he sat in Greg's office by seven-thirty, stacking up words while his friend made sandwiches.

Mike struggled with his own history. This was a memoir more or less, not an autobiography. How much personal backstory should he include? As little as possible he decided. He would offer just enough to let people know who he was before. He wrote about how he ended up at EDK, about how he met Jenna and how he slept with Maggie. He focused on what Greg said about not letting Maggie and Doolittle define him. He went on the record with his side of any story that they told.

A couple of weeks in, Mike found his rhythm. He could see pages piling up behind him like sidewalk sections on his morning runs, and he felt good about making some observable progress.

Once he began to feel comfortable with his ability to finish this thing, he turned to the hardest parts of the story.

He determined to devote a day to knocking out a chapter about his unpleasant interactions with Colorado authorities. After a hard run through a cold rain Mike sat down at Greg's desk even earlier than usual and mapped out five quick breaks in his day, two to refill his coffee cup, two to empty his bladder, and one to grab a sandwich to take back to the desk. He shifted in his chair every half-hour or so to prevent the writer's equivalent of bed sores.

Mike pecked out his memory of the moment he came to understand that it was all about him. He had gone to the station at the request of Detective Jim Russo, a friendly sort who asked him to set aside a few hours so that they could capture the most complete picture possible of Jenna's life in the months leading to her disappearance, in hopes that some detail that seemed unimportant to Mike might spark ideas to pursue. Mike arrived at the station early in the morning and Russo led him to an interview room. It wasn't some austere space with a metal table like he had seen on TV. It was more like a conference room you might find in a lawyer's office.

"Do you drink coffee?" Russo asked. "The stuff we brew here is terrible, so I went across to Starbucks. We have milk and sugar if you'd like."

"Black is fine, thanks," Mike said.

They were joined moments later by another detective, David Hale, a younger guy, trim like a fighter, with a scruffy beard and tired eyes. Despite the seriousness of the task, Mike let his mind wander. "Russo and Hale" sounded like a cop show on TNT. Or maybe "Hale and Russo." He wondered who determined which name came first and how they decided. Some might think that the order shouldn't matter, but Mike couldn't help thinking that "Oates and Hall" and "Costello and Abbott" never would have gotten off the ground.

Russo asked most of the questions. They talked about what Jenna did at EDK, where she had traveled on business, who she spent time with outside of the office, her favorite restaurants, the routes she took on her frequent runs, whether she hung out at any bars or clubs. Could she have gone away on her own for a weekend? If she did, where might she go? Did she ever have a stalker? Any trouble with old boyfriends? As they talked, Russo put pins in a map and made notes on a laptop.

About an hour in, Hale leaned forward. "The two of you ever fight?"

"No, not really."

"Is that so?" Hale asked. "You must be the only couple in the world."

"Well," Mike said, "of course we disagreed sometimes."

"That's a fine distinction," Hale said.

"Is it really?" Mike asked. "I don't know why a disagreement has to be a fight."

"So you never got physical?"

"God no."

"Never even yelled?"

"Not that I recall."

"So when the two of you got pissed, you'd just sort of whisper at one another?"

"What are you suggesting?" Mike asked.

"Nothing," Hale said. "It's just unusual. Everybody fights. Most people admit it."

"I don't have anything to admit," Mike said. He knew he sounded defensive.

"What if I told you that we have a witness who says that you and Jenna were arguing on the last day that she was seen?"

"I'd say that's a lie."

"Are you calling me a liar, Mr. McAfee?" Hale grinned. He was having fun.

"No, I'm saying the information you claim to have received is untrue."

"Claim to?" Hale said. "That sounds like you're calling me a liar. But, hey, that's OK. Nobody cares whether I'm telling the truth. But they're damn sure gonna care whether you are."

"Do I need to get a lawyer?" Mike asked. It sounded like an admission to him. He could only imagine what it sounded like to Russo and Hale. Or Hale and Russo.

"I don't know," Hale said. "Do you?"

It got no better from there.

Mike emerged from Greg's office just after four o'clock, eyes on the beer tap. The only souls in the shop were the regulars and a part-time kid behind the register. "Nine hours of this shit is exhausting," Mike said.

"Poor thing," Greg said. "Are your fingers tired?"

"This one still has something left," Mike said as he extended the middle digit of his right hand.

Jenks sat at the table closest to the counter, drinking a beer. Jacob sat two tables over, enjoying a meatball sandwich with peppers.

Greg motioned toward the kid. "Jacob brought in one of his dad's records today," he said. "I think you'll dig it."

Greg dropped the needle, and an acoustic guitar was joined by a violin and then that unmistakable voice singing about the middleweight champ stuck with a bogus murder charge. Mike felt a glint of recognition that had not previously occurred to him.

"Robert Zimmerman," Jenks said loudly enough for everyone to hear.

It was Bob Dylan doing "Hurricane." The album was *Desire*, one of Mike's favorites.

"You ever hear this one, Jacob?" Mike asked.

"No, and I wish I wasn't hearing it now. You old dudes listen to some horrendous shit."

"There was a time when I would have fought you for saying that," Mike said. "What do you like?"

"Kanye, Kendrick," Jacob said.

"I'm down with Kanye and Kendrick. Hang with us a while and you'll be down with Dylan."

Jacob shook his head. "It's embarrassing when people from your generation talk that way."

As Mike and Jacob talked, Greg looked up and saw the old man come through the door, unsteady on his feet.

"Afternoon, dad," Greg said. Mike, Jacob and Jenks turned around.

Mike stepped toward the old man. "Hi, Mr. Allen, I'm Mike McAfee. Remember me?"

Jerry Allen ignored the question and looked at his son. "Give me a beer," he said.

"Dad, you're drunk."

"You don't know that."

"I have a pretty good idea."

"You're so fucking smart, aren't you?"

"Hey," Greg said. "Cut it out. Not here."

"Then give me a beer."

"It's not even five o'clock," Greg said.

"What difference does that make? It's probably midnight in London. Those cocksuckers are falling off their barstools. Use your imagination. Let's get in a time machine, go to England."

"I don't care what time it is or what country we're in. You're drunk and I'm not serving you. For one thing, it's against the law."

"You a big rule-follower, are you?"

Greg looked at his father and said "Don't make me throw you out of my shop."

"So you're a tough guy now?"

"Tough enough."

"Ungrateful little shit," Jerry Allen said. Then he turned and walked out of Mellow Submarine.

"Sorry," Greg said to no one in particular.

Jacob and Jenks pretended they hadn't seen anything.

"How often does that happen?" Mike asked Greg.

"Depends on what you mean by *that*," Greg said. "If you mean stumbling around drunk and getting his ass thrown out of here, not very. If you mean stumbling around drunk, pretty much every day."

The two stood silently for a moment.

"I don't know what you're thinking right now," Greg said, "but I get the feeling that everybody looks at me and thinks *Why don't you do something about him?* Like maybe I should have a talk with him, reason it out. Or dump out all of his liquor. Or take him to rehab. Like I haven't done all those things."

"Nobody's thinking that."

"*Everybody's* thinking that."

"I'm not thinking that."

"You're a good guy. It's hard to believe you murdered your girlfriend."

Mike smiled. "It was actually my fiancée."

Greg began to smile and then stopped. Joking about killing someone you loved really wasn't that funny, he thought, no matter how alive they actually were.

THIRTEEN

When summer came everything slowed down in Cameron and at Mellow Submarine. From June through August, the university's students scattered to their homes or far-flung internships, cutting the town's population in half.

Those months weren't profitable for Greg but they were peaceful. One of his failures as a businessman was that he preferred the shop when it was empty save for a few friends. Since Dan left, Jill had been bringing Liv in for lunch on Saturdays, and since Mike arrived, he had been joining them. Greg didn't bother to call anyone else in to work on most summer Saturdays. More often than not, the four of them had the place to themselves. When the odd customer walked in, Greg excused himself for a couple of minutes and then came back.

Being a favored customer, Liv was allowed to order off-menu. She said that Greg's peanut butter and jelly was her favorite. The other three ate whatever was left of the week's specials as Greg tried to clean out the fridge before Monday came and the menu changed.

They sat in the shop on a flawless June day, the summer's blanket of heat yet to fully descend on

Cameron. They listened to XTC's *English Settlement*, which Jacob had traded for half of an Italian beef and a shrimp po'boy. The sleeve still had the plastic around it, slit carefully at the opening. An old Gould Records price tag showed that the album retailed for $7.99.

"It's weird," Greg said, "but I feel like I'm getting to know Jacob's dad through these records."

"I know," Mike said. "The guy had great taste. This is a good album, but not one I would have expected him to have."

"That's MTV creeping in," Greg said. "Remember when we were little kids and Mark and his friends would hang out at our house and watch it all day long? Like in 1982? That's when new wave came to Cameron. Before that it was just Boston and Foreigner."

"Martha Quinn gave me feelings that I didn't quite understand," Mike said.

"I don't understand those feelings yet," Greg replied.

Jill's phone rang and she got up to answer it. Two minutes later she came back to the table. "I have to go to the hospital. We admitted a kiddo with pneumonia and things aren't going very well. Come on, Liv, we need to go to grandma's."

"But I want to stay here."

Mike looked at Jill. "She can stay with me if it's all right with you. There's nowhere I need to be."

"Are you sure?"

"Of course."

"Liv, do you want to stay here with Mr. Mike and Greg?"

"Uh-huh."

"OK, then. I should be back in an hour or so. Be good, babe. Thanks a bunch, guys."

A few seconds after Jill left, Liv said to Greg "can I have a torta with extra hallapeenos?"

"You like jalapeno peppers?" Mike asked.

"Liv's mother, um, is *unaware* that Liv has sampled certain foodstuffs while in my care."

"Hallapeenos are awesome," Liv said.

"Then why didn't you just order the sandwich you wanted?" Mike asked.

"I tried to once," Liv said.

"Yes, Liv once came in and asked for a torta, but her mom said that she wouldn't like it. And as Liv was about to say that she'd had one before, I gave her the universal *ix-nay on the alk-tay* hand sign, just to – "

"To cover your own," Mike looked at Liv and paused, "behind."

"Yes, I engaged in a little behind-covering. It's not like I gave her meth. So now the torta with extra jalapenos is just sort of our thing."

"What's meth?" Liv asked.

Mike looked at Greg, eyebrows arched. "Yes, Greg, what *is* meth?"

"It's a topic for another day, that's what it is," Greg said and then hopped up to make the little girl her super-spicy sandwich.

When he came back a couple of minutes later, Liv consumed the torta with a ravenous glee. "I love this so much," she said to no one in particular.

A group of customers came through the door, so Greg got back to work.

"Do you like ice cream?" Mike asked Liv.

"Yep."

"Want to get some?"

"Yep."

"We could go to that place just down the street."

"Lulu's," Liv said.

"Do you like Lulu's?"

"Yep."

Mike and Liv gave Greg a wave as he tended to business and they walked a block over to Harrison Street and stood in front of a tiny hut that sported a retro neon sign that read *Lulu's Frozen Custard*.

"This wasn't an ice cream place when I was a kid," Mike said.

"What was it?" Liv asked.

"It was a photo booth."

"What's a photo boof?"

"It's where you got your pictures developed."

Liv looked at him as if he had said "it's where you bought your unicorns."

"Back then," Mike said, "when you wanted to take pictures, you used a camera. But you couldn't see the pictures right way. There was something inside the camera called film, and you gave the film to the person who sat here behind the window, and you came back a day later and they gave you your pictures."

"Why didn't you just take pictures on your phone and post them on Instagram?"

Mike tried to imagine where the conversation was headed and he determined that they were at least nine questions away from a resolution.

"What kind of ice cream do you like?" he asked.

"I like the vanilla with peanut butter and marshmallow."

"How does that work?"

"It's called a concrete. They mix it all up like magic."

"Cup or cone."

"Cup."

Mike stepped to the window and ordered one peanut butter and marshmallow concrete and one with bananas and caramel.

"You like Morgan Park?" he asked Liv.

"Yep."

"Want to take our ice cream there?"

"Yep."

When Mike first got back to town he asked Greg when Cameron got so small. "It didn't," Greg said, "you got big." But Mike still seemed surprised some days when it felt like you were never more than four or five blocks from where you wanted to be. Less than two minutes from picking up their treats at the window, Mike and Liv were sitting side by side in swings.

"How's your ice cream?" he asked.

"Good. Wanna try?"

Mike took his spoon and scraped a taste off the top. "Wow," he said. "That's delicious."

"I know."

They made quick work of their frozen delicacies and Mike threw the cups and spoons away. He sat back in his swing. "What kinds of things do you like?" he asked. "Ponies? "Princesses?"

"I like bugs," Liv said.

"Like insects?"

"Insects and arachnids. Also little arthropods like centipedes. And worms."

"What's a person who studies insects called?" Mike asked rhetorically. "I want to say philatelist, but that's not right."

"Philatelists collect stamps," Liv said, "which seems pretty *booooo*ring. An entomologist studies insects."

"Jeez, you're smart."

"I know."

Liv then jumped from her swing, lunged ten feet forward, fell to the sandy dirt on her knees and said "oh my gosh!" She put her face close to the ground and hovered over two ladybugs sitting side by side. She took her finger and began to draw large shapes around them.

"It's a mommy and a little girl ladybug," she said, "and they're inside their house."

Mike walked over and crouched down beside Liv. He saw a big house with lots of rooms and a vaulted ceiling, all created by Liv's finger as if she were the benevolent god of the insect world. The ladybugs had plenty of space. Mike imagined the little ladybug, in her teenage years, shutting herself away in her little ladybug bedroom.

Liv bounced up and plopped down a few feet away and began drawing in the dirt again. Mike followed her to find a new house populated by two spiders.

"That's the little girl ladybug's daddy and his girlfriend," Liv said. "The little ladybug has to go there on weekends."

Mike watched as Liv continued to draw. She landscaped the houses with bushes and trees. She created a sky with clouds and a sun, beams of light falling on the ladybug house. There were streets with stick-figure pedestrians and bicyclists, stop signs and traffic lights. Whenever the ladybugs or spiders tried to exit their homes, she gently nudged them back inside and warned them that it looked like rain. She drew lightning bolts in the distance to emphasize the point.

"Wow," Mike said, "you're really good at drawing."

"I know."

"What's a person who's good at drawing called?"

"An artist. Everybody knows that."

"So you're an artist and an entomologist?"

"Yep."

"But not a philatelist?"

"Nope, 'cause they're *booo*ring!" she said, giggling to reveal her toothless smile.

She kept drawing. She made another small house for two pill bugs.

"What's that?" Mike asked.

"That's Geggy's house, where you and Geggy live."

"But I don't live with Greg."

"You should," Liv said. "He needs somebody."

Liv continued to draw, making a street that ran from Greg's driveway to a big boxy structure with a sign that said *Mellow Submarine*.

She stood up and admired what she had created.

"You're like God on the eighth day," Mike said.

"What?" Liv wrinkled up her face.

"Never mind," he said. "We should probably get back to the shop and get you cleaned up before your mom gets back.

As they walked, Liv asked "do you like my mom?"

"Of course," Mike said, "your mom is very nice."

"But do you *like*-like her? Like boy-girl like her?"

Mike felt like he was entering a minefield, every word a potentially fatal step.

"I used to," he said, "a long time ago, before she met your dad."

"My daddy doesn't boy-girl like my mom anymore."

Ka-boom! Mike felt like the first of his limbs had been blown off.

"Well, Liv, I don't know much about that sort of thing. I've never been married or had a little girl. All I know is that your mom loves you very, very much."

They turned the corner. They could see Mellow Sub. It looked like sanctuary to Mike.

"How about now? Do you boy-girl like my mom now?"

"That's a good question."

"Are you going to answer it?"

As Liv got to the end of her question, they reached the front door. Mike opened it to find Jill waiting, hands on hips, with a smile on her face.

"You are filthy, Olivia Jane Emory," she said.

"I've been drawing a bug town with Mr. Mike."

"It was amazing," Mike said. "There was artwork and a narrative. It was like a Disney movie playing out in real life."

"I also asked him some questions," Liv said.

"What kinds of questions?" Jill asked.

"Boy-girl questions."

"And did he answer your boy-girl questions?" Jill looked at Mike, not Liv.

"No," Mike said, "because I don't have a clue about that sort of thing."

FOURTEEN

Mike hovered over the Seeburg. He hadn't told Greg yet, but he had just won an auction on eBay for a Lawrence Welk single, "Moritat" and "Lisbon Antigua" on the A side and "Chain Gang" and "Rock and Roll Waltz" on the flip. Four songs on one 45 rpm record! Mike tried to imagine Greg's face when he saw it for the first time. Mike had long been impressed by how much emotion Greg's expression could convey, even through the beard. There would be shock and then elation and then wonder and then gratitude. Mike was already planning to deposit a full roll of quarters in the slot and play "Chain Gang" and "Rock and Roll Waltz" on repeat for hours. He was feeling as proud of himself as he had in years when the phone in his pocket rang.

On the other end a man named Roger said that he worked for a TV production company in Los Angeles that was developing a new reality show called *Star Crossed* which would reunite couples who "and I apologize for putting it this way, once had a relationship that could be described as scandalous, tawdry or otherwise noteworthy for not necessarily the right reasons, and pit them in competitions against other similar couples, like *Couples Therapy* meets *The Amazing Race*. I'm calling because

Jenna Kaye is already signed on. But that, of course, is contingent on you joining the show as well. What do you say?"

Mike said nothing. He thought about nothing beyond whether there was any meaningful distinction between being mortified, terrified or horrified. He just knew that whatever the worst was, he was that.

"You there, Mike?" Roger asked.

"Not really," Mike replied. "I'm sorry, why would I want to do this?"

"Because it's going to be a huge hit!" Roger exclaimed with either genuine enthusiasm or convincing fake enthusiasm. Mike assumed it had to be the latter.

"We're going to have couples like Bill and Monica –"

"Wait, they're going to do this?"

"No, we couldn't possibly get the kinds of security clearances to put an ex-president on a show like this," Roger said, as if the former commander-in-chief would be all over the idea but for the Secret Service's objections. "But couples *like* them."

Mike laughed at the thought that he and Jenna were somehow like Bill and Monica.

"I'm sorry," Mike said, "but Bill was a President of the United States who got a blowjob from an intern. I'm just a guy who was sitting around minding his own business when his fiancée ran away from home."

"And America loves you for it!" Roger said.
"You went from being the country's biggest villain
to its most sympathetic figure overnight. When
you said you didn't know what happened to Jenna,
it turned out you really didn't know what happened
to Jenna! The audience isn't used to that kind of
honesty."

Mike never thought of the millions who had
rooted for a lethal injection as "the audience."

"Mike, when I talk to people in the middle of
the country they all think that we're made-up characters out here. 'Hey, it's Roger from La-La land,'
they think, and they picture me as Roger Rabbit
instead of Roger Ramsey." Only then did Mike envision the voice on the other end as possessing
long white ears and bright red overalls. "But we're
real people," Roger said, "and we can empathize
with you. You got fucked over big-time, dumped,
accused, ridiculed, pitied. People relate to that."

How could they possibly? Mike thought.

"These people, they want good things for you.
And I can provide those things. It's time for you to
cash in on your misery."

"Cash in?"

"We'll give you $15,000 just to sign on to the
project and $50,000 for the season once it's picked
up by a cable or broadcast network. Then the winning couple splits $250,000. *Two-hundred-fifty-
thousand dollars,* Mike. And it's only a few weeks'
worth of work. After that, there are all kinds of
possibilities. We could do a development deal with

you, help you create a show of your own, work on getting you on other shows. You'll do a book, go on talk shows, whatever. It beats working, and you get to be famous."

"I'm already kind of famous," Mike said with a powerful sense of regret.

"We'll make you a better kind of famous."

"You say America will love me because I'm a sympathetic figure. What about Jenna?"

"She's a villain," Roger said. "They'll love her more!"

Mike paused for a moment to consider whether this was all in Jenna's plan the day she decided to go to Reno.

"So, what do you say, Mike? Are you in?"

"I'm sorry, Roger. No."

"No is just a speed bump on the way to Yes," Roger said. "You're going to think it over and you're going to come around. Everybody does. I'll call you back in a few days."

Three days later when the woman on the other end of the line introduced herself as Tessa Goldstein from Paragon Entertainment in Hollywood, Mike asked if she worked with Roger.

"Roger who?" she asked.

"Rabbit?" Mike replied. He knew that wasn't right.

"The cartoon character?" Tessa had not expected their conversation to start this way.

"It's not Rabbit," Mike said. "It's something that sounds like that." *Was it Robins?* He couldn't remember. "Never mind."

"I want to talk to you about a reality show we have in development," she said.

"Yeah, the one that Roger called about."

"Roger Rabbit?"

"Sure, that'll do for now," Mike said. "But I haven't changed my mind."

Tessa paused and Mike could see her screw up her face through the phone connection.

"I don't think we're on the same page, Mr. McAfee. I don't work with a Roger and no one else from my office would have contacted you about this."

"OK, I'm sorry, go ahead," Mike said, as if pitches for reality shows had become a common thing.

"We're developing a show that reunites couples from notorious relationships," Tessa said.

"Yeah, this is the show that Roger called about."

"I don't mean to be argumentative, Mike, but there is no Roger. Are you OK?"

"I sure thought I was until about thirty seconds ago."

"Anyway, Maggie Kleinsasser has already signed on, so now, of course, we need to talk to you."

"Wait," Mike said. "*Maggie?* You mean Jenna, right?"

"No," Tessa said, "and I'd like to keep this between us if we could. We reached out to Jenna first before getting a call from one of her father's lawyers who pretty forcefully told us to go to hell. So then we approached Maggie and she was all over it. Luckily you have two different women who would make for ideal partners on our show."

Goddamn, that is lucky, Mike thought.

"The project doesn't have a real name yet," Tessa said. "We're calling it *Celebrity Couples* as a placeholder until we come up with something snazzier."

Out of politeness, incredulity or both, Mike let Tessa finish her pitch, which included timetables, other potential cast members and dollar-figures that blew Roger Rabbit's proposal out of the water. He didn't have it in his nature to tell her to go to hell, at least not forcefully.

"Tessa, is it?" Mike said. "Tessa, it was nice of you to think of me, and honestly, the offer sounds like a crazy amount of money for something like this. I guess I don't know what the going rate is, though I'm starting to accumulate some comps. But this is just something that I could never do. I'm afraid the answer is no."

"No is just a speed bump on the way to Yes," Tessa said. "Give it some thought. I'll call you back. I'd really like to work with you on this."

"Are you sure you don't know Roger?" Mike asked.

"No Rogers, no rabbits," Tessa said. "Goodbye for now, Mike."

FIFTEEN

Greg hated to think of it as an anniversary. It fell on a Sunday this time, which provided him the smallest sense of comfort. He thought of it as a holy day, but of the most terrible variety, his own personal Good Friday in desperate need of an Easter that never came. And this time, for the first time, he decided to begin his remembrance in church. Unlike some who suffered similar grief, Greg had never hated church or raged against God. Growing up, he enjoyed church. He and his friends would finish Sunday school at St. Mark's, grab a donut and run outside to play touch football while their parents lingered over coffee. His mom never complained about the grass stains on his good pants. She considered it cheap tuition for a quality religious education.

For the first thirty years of his life, St. Mark's Lutheran Church had been Greg's spiritual home, though he wandered away and back and away again in the later years. He had performed in eleven Christmas pageants there, had been baptized and confirmed there, had watched his sister get married there, had attended his mother's funeral there. He also stood by his son's coffin there. He had not stepped through the door since.

Greg snuck into the last pew just as the service started. He wore a gray suit that wouldn't close in the middle, a white shirt that wouldn't button on top, and a black tie that wouldn't reach his belt. He followed along in the hymnal, but he remembered the liturgy by heart. The *kyrie*, the *sanctus*, the *nunc dimittis*. These things stuck with Greg. If he had recited algebra problems and chemical equations once a week for his whole life he never would have flunked out of college. Pastor Carver, who had been there for ten years or so but who was no older than forty, stood at the front of the church in his traditional robe. The last few times Greg had seen him he had been dressed more casually. For the first couple of years after Luke died, Alex Carver would stop by Mellow Sub from time to time, dressed in blue jeans, fitting in with the college crowd more comfortably than any man of the cloth that Greg had known. He was there to check on Greg, and Greg knew it, but he didn't know why he resented it. On these visits, the reverend insisted that Greg call him by his first name, but it felt too awkward, so Greg didn't call him anything at all. Greg wasn't rude but he wasn't welcoming and Alex Carver wasn't dumb. As he left the shop for the last time, Alex handed Greg a business card. "I think my visits here bring up bad memories. If you ever want to talk, if you ever need anything, give me a call or come to my office."

Greg thought of that small kindness as Pastor Carver delivered a lovely sermon on the power of grace and forgiveness. As he spoke, he asked the ushers to pass baskets down each row. Inside the baskets were keys that had been painted a vibrant blue. He then asked each person in attendance to take a key, put it on a ring, and use it as a reminder to exhibit more grace and to be more forgiving every day.

During the recessional hymn, Pastor Carver walked down the center aisle to the back of the church. He made eye contact with Greg as he walked past, and he smiled. As Greg got up to leave, Pastor Carver was waiting for him. Instead of standing in the entry and shaking hands with the exiting congregation, he put his hand on Greg's back and gently directed him into a far corner.

"It's really good to see you," Pastor Carver said. "It's been a while."

"It has," Greg said.

"Would you be up for getting coffee some time?"

"Stop by the shop any morning after nine and knock on the door. I always have a pot going by then."

"I'll do that. How have you been?"

"That's a hard question. Not as good today as other days. It happened six years ago. Six years ago today."

"I spend a lot of time with people who are grieving. I know how hard these days can be."

"I'm going to go and visit him."

"Would you like me to come with you?"

"That's very kind but I need to go alone. But could you do me a favor?"

"Sure, anything."

"Could you visit him some other time, maybe some day this week? Sometimes I worry that I'm the only one who remembers."

"Of course I will."

Alex Carver gave Greg a warm embrace and watched him walk away.

When he arrived at the cemetery, Greg parked, opened his trunk and pulled out a weed trimmer. The last time he visited, the grass was longer than it should have been, not to the point of neglect but not far either. Greg found the big oak tree that leaned south and seemed to point to the right spot. He walked straight there and stood over the little stone engraved *Allen* with a small angel etched just above. He started the trimmer and cleared a circle in the grass, six feet in each direction. When he finished, he noticed a bunch of freshly-cut yellow tulips, still wet, the kind that Jill grew in her garden.

Greg laid a teddy bear on the gravestone and remembered the worst moment of his life. "I'm so sorry," he said. "Oh, Luke, I'm so sorry." When the body-wracking sobs began, he fell into the fresh clippings, digging his knees into the grass. "I'm so sorry," he said over and over, "I'm so sorry," and he reached into his pocket and squeezed the blue key of forgiveness as tightly as he could until it gashed his palm and blood trickled down his fingers. After

a few minutes, he stood up and kissed the gravestone. Then he returned to his car, trimmer in
hand.

At home, Greg closed the blinds, turning a
sunny day to dusk. Usually, the first thing he did
when he came through the door was to turn on
music. But this day he chose silence, just him and
his thoughts at the kitchen table, with a bag of
Doritos and a bottle of whiskey watching him from
the counter. Years before, when Greg finally understood what his dad was, when he hated him for
it most, and when he feared he shared the same
fate, he made a list of barriers not to cross and then
he proceeded to fly past them like a champion hur-
dler: Don't drink every day; don't have multiple
drinks every day; don't lose your car; don't be
hungover; don't walk into walls. The last line he
drew was day-drinking, surmising that he didn't
have a problem if he only drank at night. But when
he looked at that bottle of Wild Turkey, it called to
him with a mammalian warmth, like a baby drawn
to a breast. He didn't move toward it, but it kept
getting closer. He remembered a trip to Kansas
City with a friend, one induced by the promise of a
plate full of life-changing barbecue. When Greg
stepped through the door of Arthur Bryant's, the
scent was unmistakably pre-coital, a rush of flesh
and pheromone. When the weathered old man behind the counter handed him his plate, and when
Greg covered it in the sweet and spicy musk of the

house sauce, he didn't eat so much as he went down on his lunch.

He felt about this bottle the way he felt about those burnt ends. He didn't want to drink it. He wanted to ravage it, to consume it in a flash of pseudo-sexual rage. He wanted to wrap his body around it until he collapsed and then drifted off to sleep. He wanted some respite from consciousness. He wanted all feeling to vacate his body.

He looked at the time. 1:42 p.m. "It's 5:42 somewhere," he said to himself.

The Monday morning sun oozed through the blinds like lava, viscous and white-hot. The rays strafed Greg's skin and kick-started the cacophony in his head. He thought that people who drank and forgot were lucky. He never forgot. Sometimes he threw up and sometimes he passed out and sometimes he woke up with a mule kicking inside his skull but he always remembered how and why he got there. Liquor didn't ease the pain. It only deferred it and then paid it back with usurious interest.

A half pot of coffee, three fried eggs and a shower did him some good. He came out of the bathroom wrapped in a towel and saw that he had missed a call. It was the energy drink people. Greg had done as Mike said. He asked for twenty percent more and they didn't blink. Pennies from heaven. He sopped up the residue of the eggs with a piece of toast and then called back. They put him on speaker as three voices pelted him with information. They had scripts and a shooting schedule and an idea that went beyond the commercials, with compensation that went beyond the agreement. Greg wouldn't just act in a spot; he would become the company mascot. He had the charisma to pull it off. There would be a series of commercials and appearances and interviews. He would do events at football games, on college campuses, at Hollywood parties. He would get out of Cameron and finally live the high life for real.

Greg asked what they expected from him at the appearances and interviews. Just talk about the product, they said, maybe put on a bit of a show like he had the day the satellite trucks came to town. But what if they asked about other things, he wondered, like his life and his background? Answer them honestly, they said. You're famous now. People want to know you. Be an open book.

SIXTEEN

Wednesdays were the worst. Greg never understood why, but no one came in on Wednesday afternoons in the summer, at least not anyone he wanted to see. Sure, Jenks was there sipping a beer and working on a journal article, and Jacob stopped by just long enough to trade a Dire Straits record for a chicken parmigiana, but that was it. When school started in the fall a few students would camp out at tables and study, spending just enough to justify keeping the place open, but Wednesdays in June sucked the remaining tiny remnants of hope out of the remaining tiny remnants of Greg.

Alyssa stood at the prep table in the kitchen and sliced onions on the off-chance that some modest dinner business might materialize. Greg popped his head in and said "think you can handle this rush alone? I need to head out for a couple of hours." She said "sure" and Greg walked into the office where Mike sat in front of a closed laptop reading a book called *A Supposedly Fun Thing I'll Never Do Again*. "Recharging," Mike said.

"Let's recharge at the legendary lounge."

Ten minutes later, they were standing at the door of Cameron's oldest bar beneath the vertical neon sign that flashed *Max's*. "When we were kids,"

Mike said as they moved inside, "I thought that sign was the most glamorous thing in town. I wish I could have been here in the Sixties. I bet it was like *Mad Men*."

Greg laughed. "Only sad men have come here since the day it opened."

They sat at their booth and Greg ordered a basket of wings and a club soda with lime. "I'm taking a break," he said.

Mike nursed a gin and tonic and asked about the commercial for the energy drink.

"That fell through," Greg said.

"What happened?"

"They, I guess, decided to go in another direction. I think they're having some financial issues. It's a pretty crowded market right now, you know. They might be pulling back some on advertising."

"That's too bad. I know some people who know some people. I could make a couple of calls and we could find you an agent if you want to try something else."

"That's OK. I'm good. I never felt right about it anyway. I'm going to focus on keeping the shop afloat."

"What can I do to help you with that?"

"You could buy a million sandwiches. I'm also open to other ideas."

"I don't want to stick my nose where it doesn't belong, but if you'd like, I could study the shop, make some notes, give you some ideas on how to make things more profitable." Mike neglected to mention that a legal pad full of such notes already resided in his bag.

"Knock yourself out. And speaking of sticking noses where they don't belong, what are you waiting for with Jill?"

"I don't know. Everything is complicated."

"What's complicated about it?"

"There's you and Jill, for starters."

Greg snorted. "We dated for fifteen minutes twenty years ago, and we've lived in the same small town ever since. I'm the incompetent younger brother she cares for. Trust me. I am no impediment to your romantic ambitions. Do you want my blessing? Here it is." Greg made the sign of a cross over Mike. "Go forth and fornicate."

"It's more than that. I'm probably not going to be around much longer. I'm not sure it would be a good idea to start something and then leave."

"She's a big girl. She can handle herself."

"Maybe," Mike said, "but there's not much reason to think that I can handle myself."

Mike's phone rang. A southern California area code.

"Hello."

"I know about Roger," the woman on the other end said.

"Roger Rabbit?"

"It's Roger *Ramsey*, Mike. From Ardent Productions. Why didn't you tell me about him?"

"I tried to, really hard. This is Tessa, right?"

"Yes, it's Tessa. Tessa Goldstein at Paragon Entertainment. You tell Ramsey who he's messing with. Are you really trying to leverage a better deal with me by flirting with him?"

"Not that I'm aware of."

"Listen, Mike, I have eyes and ears all over this town. I know all about *Star Crossed*. It's got a good name but it's going to be a shit show. It's all low-level disgraced politicians and heroin-addicted ex-rock stars and their skanky supermodel girlfriends. You're too good for that show."

"That's nice to hear."

"Plus, they want to pair you with Jenna Kaye, who, as you may know, is a total lunatic. She turned your life upside down. You don't want to do a show with her when you could do one with Maggie instead."

"Wait, you wanted Jenna first, and Maggie didn't exactly do me any favors, either."

"You're good at this, Mike, the way you pretend that you're not interested."

"I'm not pretending."

"This is television. Everyone is interested. Tell me what Ramsey is offering you. We'll beat it by fifty percent."

"There isn't enough money, Tessa."

"There's always enough money, Mike. Give me a number. Go ahead. Try me."

"Okay. Five hundred trillion dollars. That's trillion with a T."

"All right, I like it. Now we're negotiating."

"I'm pretty sure we're not."

"I'm going to work up some numbers and get back to you."

"Please, Tessa, don't."

"Remember what I said about No being a speed bump on the way to Yes? That's all this is."

"This isn't a speed bump. It's a brick wall with barbed wire and snipers in a watchtower. This is East Germany in the Soviet era."

"We all know how that turned out. That wall came down. I'm going to tear down the wall that's keeping you from working with me. We're going to do a great show together, Mike. Be well."

"But –" Mike realized that Tessa was gone. "No one in Hollywood says 'goodbye,'" he said to Greg.

The two friends sat for a while longer talking about Jill and Liv and old records and the high school reunion that was just a few days away. They talked about commercials and reality shows and all of the money they were leaving on the table.

"Speaking of leaving money on the table," Mike said as he put down twenty dollars to cover their bill. Before they could get up, the front door opened and sent a beam of scalding light through Max's wood-paneled darkness, like someone had blown a hole in a cave. A silhouette shuffled through, and when the door closed behind it, Greg could see that it was his father. The old man seemed somewhat more lucid than the last time he stumbled into Mellow Sub. Jerry spotted his son and lumbered toward him.

"Looky here," he said and pointed toward Greg's glass. "Why don't you buy me one of those?"

Greg stood up and waved at the bartender. "Club soda with lime for my friend here." Greg dropped five dollars on the bar as he and Mike moved toward the light.

SEVENTEEN

S o, you'll pick me up at six tomorrow night," Jill said.

"I thought it started at seven-thirty," Mike said.

"It does, but I have to get there early to make sure everything is set up right."

"I thought you were setting everything up tomorrow morning."

"We are, but I have to meet the DJ. And then I have to check over everything we did earlier in the day. The other girls will be helping. I love them all but I don't trust them to get it right. If there's anything left that needs to be done, you can help me. So, six, OK?"

"Sure. Is this, you know, a date?" Mike asked.

"Do you want it to be a date?"

"I guess I wouldn't mind if it were a date."

"You guess you wouldn't mind? I'm flattered."

"I mean, of course I want it to be a date, but I want to make sure that you want it to be a date. Do you want it to be a date?"

"Well, I mean, I guess I wouldn't mind if it were a date."

"So," Mike said, "it's a date."

"It's a date." Jill leaned in close and spoke softly into Mike's ear. "Liv is with Dan this weekend. I can stay out as late as I want." She kissed him on the cheek and then turned to leave.

Mike watched Jill walk out of Mellow Sub like she had just dropped a microphone.

Jill headed over to what everyone called the Old Gym, which is what it was. Cameron's original high school had been turned into an administrative building, but the gym was left intact. The Old Gym was used for large events, both public and private, and through some special dispensation alcohol could be served there with the proper permits, which made it the venue of choice for all Cameron High School reunions.

Because she was highly competent and perpetually local, Jill had become entrenched as chair of the reunion committee. She thought of it like the Haitian presidency without the graft or occasional military coup, a title for life that she hoped never to pass to Liv. Though the event lasted just five hours, the planning went on for a year, starting with Facebook posts, emails to classmates, reserving the room, checking the balance in the reunion account, and refilling it from her own pocket when it was depleted. There was a DJ to hire, food to order, bartenders to secure, insurance riders to renew, programs to print, memorials to write. This was the third straight time they would observe a moment of silence for a classmate who failed to survive the five intervening years. It was also the third time that Jill had organized the event, having previously led the effort at ten and fifteen years.

She had been unavailable to organize the five-year reunion, having just begun her second year in medical school, but five-year reunions don't require much planning anyway, just a couple bottles of tequila and a cooler full of Bud Light. That was the last reunion where no one needed a program. Everyone looked like they did as kids, not yet old or bald or gray or heavier or dead or faded from memory. Jill attended with her new boyfriend, the handsome fellow med student with the swimmer's shoulders and toothpaste-commercial smile. Dan turned heads and shook hands all night. He could have dispossessed most any guy of his date, but engaged only in the most harmless flirting with the ladies while partaking in more serious drinking with the gents, talking big league baseball and high school football, integrating easily among the natives, flashing dominance without encroaching on territory. Five years later, at the ten-year affair, Jill and Dan were newly married, and the same guys lingered at the bar, like they had been waiting for him that whole time. He had traded favors to get a night off from his surgical residency, and the guys were grateful to see him, to hear his stories about reconstructing the knees of football players (might be collegians, might be pros, patient confidentiality and all). When some wiseass asked why Dan hadn't picked gynecology, another said that Dr. Dan probably saw plenty of pussy recreationally and didn't need to turn it into a job, as if the man's wife, their lifelong friend, weren't just a few steps away sipping chardonnay with all of the other women. Dan just gave a muted smile, perhaps politely, perhaps knowingly, and changed the subject to pitchers and their fragile elbows. He seemed a little distant, they all thought, probably just tired. Imagine being that awesome twenty-four hours a day and then adding a residency on top. A lesser man would have dropped from exhaustion, and as lesser men, they knew it.

By the fifteen-year reunion, the boys at the bar showed various signs of expanding and receding, not yet middle-aged, but weighed down, burdened with kids and wives, houses and mortgages, dead-end jobs and dying dreams. Dan remained a hand-some slab of granite, but dulled at the surface, maybe not as happy to see them as he had been before. A father now but less of a husband, he glad-ly flashed photos of little Liv but rarely glanced at his wife, the local pediatrician who insisted on planning a party for these yokels once every five years. Jill didn't know it was over yet but she knew it was different. Maybe it was just because they had a child and each had a practice, making them busi-ness owners in addition to physicians, another lay-er of complexity to sap another bit of energy. Maybe adding more layers to their lives required another level of conditioning, like moving from recreational running to marathons. Or maybe it was that other thing that Jill was ashamed to think about so often because she had no evidence to support her suspicion, and no real basis to accuse Dan of doing *that*.

At the Old Gym, back in the present, Jill's heels clicked on the hardwood of the basketball court and echoed off the limestone walls. The dying light of a long summer day seeped through windows that sat just below the ceiling. She walked the floor, inspecting and counting supplies that had been delivered earlier in the day – a palette of tables, dozens of chairs, tablecloths and streamers, soft drinks and water. Some of her old girlfriends would meet her there the next morning to set up and decorate before heading to lunch to catch up. She thought she could handle the reunion, where the dance-floor hits of their high school days would drown out conversation, and where much of the talk figured to focus on the town's prodigal son and his tabloid-tawdry recent history. It was the lunch she feared, just six or seven girls sitting, sharing, sipping a drink or two. They had all been friends since elementary school, had been each other's bridesmaids in cap sleeves and taffeta, and though separated by time and distance, they shared a well-earned intimacy that revived itself whenever they got together. It was difficult enough to keep small secrets from one another. It was impossible to avoid hard facts recorded in courthouse documents and newspaper clippings.

Jill imagined her end of the conversations. *Yes, I'm doing fine. Liv, she's doing great. It's true, he is getting married again soon. Oh, you saw her on Facebook?*

You're still friends with Dan? Of course, that's OK, I still am, too, but we share a daughter and we have to play nicely. Yes, that's right, her name is Christina. She IS hot, no doubt about that. So good of you to notice! Yes, he was TOTALLY fucking her while we were married. What? You didn't ask that? Sorry, I suppose I'm oversharing. But you were thinking it, weren't you? OFF-WHITE, yes! Ha! That's what she'll wear. No, I haven't had sex with anyone since we broke up. Oops, oversharing again. "Broke up" sounds so juvenile. Since we DIVORCED. But it really goes back further than the decree, because once he told me that he was in love with another woman's perky tits and hairless vagina, my labia clamped shut like a Venus fly-trap. Not that he came around trying to get in there after that, but – BELIEVE YOU ME – he wouldn't have had any luck. No, I'm fine, just three or four cosmopolitans so far. It's not that I necessarily wanted three years of celiba-cy, you know, things just happened that way. And have you seen the men in this town? No offense to our former classmates, but, seriously. Do you think that I don't go to bed at night and fantasize about a man's weight on top of me, the prickle of his stubble on my face, or, better yet, my thighs? Do you think I don't crave it like heroin?

Jill didn't care that they knew about the divorce. Everyone knew about the divorce, and she wasn't even the only one of the girls to endure a split since the last reunion (poor Kayla; that asshole Phil made Dan seem monastic by comparison). Jill didn't even mind that they knew about the upcom-ing wedding. People move on. Dan was moving on.

She thought it might be nice for her to move on one day, too.

What Jill didn't want to talk about, think about or even recognize as a fact is that Liv would be getting a new mother. Sure, Christina would be a *step-*mother, but the idea that any other woman – especially this woman – would be any kind of mother to Liv filled Jill with a mix of dread and panic so powerful that she sometimes had to sit down and let the feeling roll through her before regaining her legs. Now the thought of having to discuss it with the girls felt like scissors in her ribs. And so Jill dropped to the floor of the Old Gym, cross-legged and right on top of the scripted "C" that marked the center of the court. Her mind went to weird places when she felt this way. Just after Liv was born, Jill had imagined herself dying and had hoped that a woman would come along to care for her baby. Dan didn't even have to marry this woman, but she didn't object to the idea. Jill just hoped for someone kind, gentle, warm and loving to come along and give Liv the kinds of things that Dan, even at his best, could not. Someone who could braid hair, explain boys, and teach from experience about having a period. Hadn't Julia Roberts been in a movie where she played a good stepmother? Jill thought she had but she couldn't place it. Still, if Jill died, she imagined Julia Roberts stepping into her place and being the mother that Liv deserved.

In those days after her baby was born, Jill never thought about divorce and never considered that someone like Christina might ever be any kind of mom to Liv. And on the eve of her twenty-year high school reunion she could still hardly fathom it, this woman with her ripped abs and D-cups swooping into Jill's life, stealing all of her husband and part of her daughter and getting rewarded with a diamond ring and fairytale wedding. Jill should have hated Dan. He broke the vow. But she rationalized that she shouldn't hate the father of her child, that it was unfair to Liv, and so she hated Christina by proxy. When Jill and Dan got married, they were young and broke and exhausted from the demands of their careers. She remembered making love on their wedding night, feeling fatigue along with her joy, and thinking that they were earning a life together. And now she couldn't stop thinking about Christina and her wedding day and how she had done nothing to deserve it. Jill imagined Christina, manicured and waxed, floating down the aisle on rock-hard legs that she would wrap around Dan later that night like some ravenous spider preying on Jill's life.

A text message popped up. A picture of a smiling, pajama-clad Liv from Dan's phone. "Good night, mommy, I love you!" it said. Reflected in the window behind Liv, Jill could see Christina taking the photo.

Jill sat alone in the center of the basketball court and sobbed, wracked by an anguish that dwarfed the moment she first learned that her marriage was over.

EIGHTEEN

Mike woke up on Saturday morning thinking about the kiss he could still feel on his cheek. He should have gone for a run but Jill said she could stay out late, and on days he ran he always felt dead-tired by ten p.m. So instead he hopped out of bed and into the shower, got dressed, opened his laptop, and began to write about what it was like to feel something good for a change. When the doorbell rang, he hoped it was Jill with coffee and bagels and bad intentions. It was not.

"Weird shit happens when I open this door," Mike said upon seeing the woman standing on the other side.

"Well, hello to you, too," Jenna Kaye replied.

He studied her for a moment, unsure of what to say. Her hair had grown out some since the pictures from Reno. It looked like her natural color but with red highlights. Nearly a year had passed since Mike had seen Jenna in the flesh, and he felt like he had never laid eyes on this woman before. He used to love someone who looked like her, but he couldn't muster any feeling, good or bad, for the person standing in front of him.

"I'm sorry," he said. "I wasn't expecting you."

"I wanted to surprise you," she said with a smile too familiar for the circumstances. Mike rolled through his mental thesaurus until he got to *surprise* and saw its synonyms: *shock, stun, ambush, astonish, daze.*

"You never fail."

"Can I come in?"

"Let's go out," Mike said, wanting there to be witnesses. "Do you drink coffee?"

"You've seen me drink coffee a million times."

"I thought so," he said, "but I don't always know what to believe anymore."

Jenna's rental blocked Mike's car in the garage. "Toss me the keys and get in," he said.

Inside the car, Jenna said "there's something I want to talk to you about."

"Let's save it for coffee."

"I just –"

"Let's save it."

It wasn't that Mike didn't want to hear what Jenna had to say. It was that he was not prepared to hear it. Her voice was familiar yet strange, and the sound of it overwhelmed his ability to understand anything she said. He just needed a couple of minutes to get used to the idea that Jenna Kaye and Cameron, Illinois, previously distinct and separate elements of his life, were occupying the same space and time. As they rode in silence, Mike's mind buzzed with the possibilities but he was relieved by the knowledge that whatever she had to say, it couldn't be that bad. Jenna's presence meant that she was verifiably alive, which meant that he verifiably had not killed her, a significant improvement on the previous predicament. She couldn't be pregnant, at least not by him, and he could find no reason that he should care about her carrying another man's child, especially not Craig Doolittle's. Mike considered the idea for a second, and the thought that Jenna might be gestating Doolittle's baby filled him with a fleeting and perverse pleasure. Maybe she would tell him she still loved him, maybe she would tell him she never did. He could see no meaningful distinction between the two.

He parked in front of the Charles Towne Inn, a town-square coffee shop that the locals had called Charlie's since it opened in the Sixties. Inside, next to a sign that said *please seat yourself*, a magazine rack displayed a copy of the *Inquisitor*. Unflattering photos of former lovers sat beneath a headline that shouted "Jenna, Mike and Craig: Shocking New Details!" Mike and his ex slid into a booth where they were greeted by a smoke-hardened waitress with *Stacy* stitched on her shirt. Stacy looked at the *Inquisitor* and then at her customers and then back at the *Inquisitor* as if identifying fugitives from a post-office photo. Stacy knew that Mike was a local boy but had never seen him in person. Still, she had been on his side from the get-go and, like most folks in Cameron, Stacy felt vindicated when that skank turned up alive. Seeing them together, Stacy feared that Mike had taken Jenna back. But she had worked in the hospitality business long enough to be fluent in body language, and she could tell that theirs was all fucked up.

"What can I get you?" Stacy asked.

"Can I have a half-caff vanilla latte with just a touch of cinnamon?" Jenna asked.

"You can have coffee," Stacy replied.

"Two of those, please," Mike said.

Mike and Jenna sat quietly for a minute, like this was normal, the two of them relaxing in a small-town coffee shop on a Saturday morning. Jenna seemed to be waiting for Mike to say something, as if his previous demand for silence was part of a game and he had not yet uttered *Simon says speak.*

"OK, I'll bite," Mike said. "What's on your mind?"

"I want to talk about the reality show."

"I don't."

"Oh, Mike, don't be that way. This is our chance to keep being famous."

"We're not famous, Jenna, we're infamous."

"Oh, baby, there's no difference anymore."

Mike sat quietly and looked down at his hands resting on the table. He noticed that his right index finger was picking at the skin around his thumbnail, something he did when he was uptight, an action no more conscious than breathing. He could see the raw layer of pink skin that he had unearthed. Mike grabbed the offending finger with his left hand before it drew blood. Such a weird habit. A sort of self-flagellation, he supposed.

"Aren't you going to say anything?" Jenna asked.

"I'm sorry, but you disappeared nearly a year ago, and I haven't heard from you since. But I did hear your boyfriend tell the entire country that the two of you were having an affair the whole time that we were together. I feel like there's some protocol we should follow before you try to, you know, further exploit me."

"How would you like this to go?"

"Most people would start with an apology."

"For god's sake, Mike, we have an opportunity here. Do we have to hash out the past?"

"Everyone thought you were *dead*," Mike whisper-shouted as a fleck of spittle escaped through his teeth, "and most thought that I killed you. I could've gone to prison, or worse. Didn't you have a TV? Didn't you know what was happening to me?"

"Oh, Mike, don't be so dramatic. They were never going to convict you without my body. And anyway, you hurt me, too."

"How did I hurt you?"

"You fucked that cow Maggie Kleinsasser."

"You had broken up with me. I didn't have any duty to be faithful."

"I wasn't hurt by the infidelity. I was hurt that people would think that pig and I were somehow equivalent."

"Jesus, Jenna, she's not a farm animal. And I don't know what you're talking about."

"Sure you do. People mate at their own level. Rock stars fuck supermodels. Cab drivers fuck Maggie Kleinsasser. And if you're going to sleep with me and with her, that makes me the same as her. I was all set to leave Reno and come home, and then that story came out and I was so humiliated that I stayed. I couldn't face anyone."

Mike stared at Jenna blankly. He had come within inches of pledging his life to a woman who had seemed smart and kind and beautiful. But at some point when he wasn't looking, a rapacious creature had burst through the desiccated husk of Jenna's body. He was just glad that the metamorphosis hadn't happened during sex, lest he be crushed by her inhuman thighs and shredded by her alien teeth.

"Here's your coffee," Stacy said, interrupting Mike's reverie of terror. "Sugar and creamer is on the table."

Mike said "thank you," but Jenna didn't look up.

"Anything else I can get you?" Stacy asked.

"I think we're good," Mike said, and Stacy backed away slowly, eyes on the interloper.

"Listen," Jenna said. "I'm sure you're sorry about Maggie. I won't press you for an apology. Back to the show. If you don't care about the fame, you must at least care about the money. You're living in your mom's house here in Hooterville. That can't be very satisfying."

"It's fine for now," he said, "and it's not about money. There isn't enough money. And it isn't that much money, anyway. Nobody retires on what they're offering."

"But it's just the beginning," Jenna said. "My agent says that with the right plan, you should never have to work a real job the rest of your life. You can go from one reality show to another. If you're good, you can host your own show about food or home renovations or tattoo shops. Whatever. You get appearance fees to show up at boat shows and mall openings. You can do celebrity boxing. This is such a great opportunity. You really should be grateful."

Mike imagined himself between the ropes, getting ass-whupped by Coolio.

"Why don't you do it with Craig Doolittle?" Mike asked.

"Craig is going to be unavailable for the next six to eleven years."

"But he told Lacy Nantz that it was all a misunderstanding."

"Craig is . . . irrationally optimistic."

"And I'm just the opposite, I suppose."

Jenna paused for a moment, then her chin began to quiver.

"Mike," she said, "I don't know what else to do. My dad is letting me live in the guest house, and someone from his staff stocks the pantry. But that's it. Food and shelter. The production company paid for my trip out here. Dad won't take me back at EDK. He says no one wants me anywhere near their money, which means I can't use the one professional skill I have. I'm unemployable. All I can do is trade on my notoriety, even if it's humiliating."

"Well, you're going to have to find a way to do it without me."

"I know what I did to you. I know it was wrong. I know you must think that I'm an impulsive self-centered bitch. But I just lost control of myself. I panicked. I'm sorry. I really am."

"Okay."

"And I know that I owe you an explanation but I don't really have one that makes any sense. For better or worse, I've been in love or something like it with Craig forever. We have a weird magnetism. He fucks like a volcano and he treats me like a queen."

"Hard to compete with a volcano."

"It was never a competition. It was like parallel universes, with my heart in one and my head in the other. My dad always hated Craig, and I understand why. Dad is a very persuasive man. For most of my life, the thing I most wanted was to not disappoint him. He insisted that I break it off with Craig before I went to college, so I did. But it was like insisting that I break it off with crystal meth. I didn't have the willpower. And then I met you. You're smart and funny, good-looking, successful, my dad loves you. You're exactly the guy I should be with. My head knows this. And if I'd never been with Craig, my heart might understand, too. But I was living these two lives and I just couldn't sustain it. Eventually the heart universe started to consume the head universe. What I wanted might not have been rational but it's what I wanted. And I could never think my way out of it. The closer we got to our wedding, the more I understood it, and I just ran as fast as I could."

"What about your dad?"

"Do you remember what I said about not wanting to disappoint him?"

"You'd rather him think that you're dead than tell him the truth about Craig?"

"I never said it was sensible."

For the first time since he learned that she was alive, Mike felt something like a pang of sympathy for Jenna. "Something will work out," he said.

"You think?"

"Something always does."

Stacy approached the table, coffee pot in hand. "Anything else I can get you?" she asked as she warmed their cups.

"Just the check, thanks," Mike said.

She handed him a bill for four dollars and he handed her back a twenty. "Keep it," he said. Stacy gave him a wink and sashayed away. Mike had insured that he would always get the best service at Charlie's.

"Thanks for the coffee," Jenna said.

"My pleasure."

Jenna looked down at the table and broke out into a broad smile.

"What?" Mike asked.

"Nothing."

"No, what?"

"I just flashed on a funny memory. Do you remember the first time we slept together, in that hotel in New York?"

"Sure."

"I remember that there was wine, and then sex, and then more wine, and more sex, and by the middle of the night we were pretty drunk and happy. Do you remember that?"

Mike said he did.

"Somewhere in there I said that one day I would own the company and this would either be a moment we regretted or the start of an empire. And you jumped up on the bed, fully erect, and in your best Shakespearean accent said 'If we muh-duhr your fah-thur, we can have it all right now!' Do you remember that part?"

"I had recently seen a production of *Macbeth*, I believe." Mike stood up. "You can finish the story on the way out."

As they walked past the magazine rack that held the *Inquisitor*, Jenna said "and I picked up this hat that I'd been wearing and tossed it just right and shouted 'ringer!' "

They laughed as they stepped through the door and onto the sidewalk, where they stopped right in front of Jill, who was carrying two big bags emblazoned with the Party City logo. Mike and Jill saw each other and Jill flinched and Mike saw her flinch and he knew that it looked wrong and he flinched and felt the terror ripple through his body.

"Jill," Mike said, unsure of what words would come next, "this is, um, Jenna. Jenna Kaye. This is Jenna Kaye. My ex-fiancée. Former fiancée. We were going to get married, but we didn't. We used to work together. In Denver."

"Nice to meet you," Jill said, nodding at the bags she was grasping as explanation for why she failed to extend her hand.

Jenna watched Mike watch Jill. "Well, aren't you pretty?" Jenna said to Jill. "A definite step up from Maggie."

"Jill is, um, a good friend," Mike said. "We go way back."

"Just a friend," Jill said, eyes dropping to the ground.

"I don't know if I believe that," Jenna said. "There's a definite chemistry between you. But that's OK. You two can have your thing, and Mike, you and I can still do our thing. It'll work out for everyone."

"I really have to go," Jill said and began to walk away.

"I'll see you later," Mike said.

Jill said nothing. Mike watched her walk to the corner, turn right, and then disappear.

"Are we finished?" Mike said to Jenna.

"I want you to think about the show. You can do it and still have your townie girlfriend. And if it doesn't work out with her, maybe you and I could try again."

Mike looked at Jenna and tried to lash out with a violent torrent of words, but his tongue went numb, disconnected from his brain. Instead, he dropped her car keys on the sidewalk and set out for home on foot.

NINETEEN

The moment he got home, Mike texted Jill. "I know that was weird. I can explain. Can we talk?"

When he got no answer, Mike optimistically chalked it up to Jill being with the girls, having lunch, having fun, catching up, having drinks, lacking cares.

Two hours later, after he called and got no answer, he settled on Jill being busy, setting up, feeling stress, lacking time.

When he texted at four o'clock with "Pick you up at six, right?" and got no response, he was down to hoping that Jill had dropped her phone in the toilet.

Mike showered, shaved, dried his hair, applied the right product to achieve a soft, carefree hold, and spritzed himself with just enough Bleu de Chanel to make it seem that he had returned to Cameron with the exotic scent of the world about him.

He stood in front of his closet, in his underwear, and contemplated the clothes and the evening that lay before him. People would look. They probably would not point but they certainly would talk. Mike felt that he shouldn't care about what they said or thought, but found that he did. He had grown accustomed to judgments from strangers. They didn't really know him and clearly didn't care about him, and because of that they didn't matter. But these people were different. Though twenty years had passed since he last saw most of them, Mike found that they mattered very much. Since the day he stepped into Mellow Sub, since the moment Jill and Liv walked through the back door, Mike understood that life in Cameron had mattered in a way that life elsewhere didn't. Ninety-nine-point-nine percent of the people in the world who knew his name learned it only after Jenna disappeared. One-hundred percent of the people attending the reunion knew it long before.

Mike ran the numbers in his head. Depending on who showed, there could be two guys who he had fought on the playground, three girls whose breasts he had touched, twenty-two classmates who signed a card when he had his appendix out in fourth grade, close to thirty who had been baseball teammates for a season or more, probably fifty who had seen him in the locker room during the pubescent spring when the crotch hair began to take root, and more than two-hundred who had held hands and cried together just before senior year when Toby Blevins closed the garage door and started his car after word spread that he had been arrested in Decatur for fellating a boy his own age in the back seat of a Honda Civic.

The only conclusion Mike drew as he stood there was that he should wear dark jeans, brown brogues, a blue and white gingham shirt, and a tan linen jacket.

Once dressed, Mike got into the car he had vacuumed, deodorized, washed and waxed after Jill left the shop the night before. He considered music, searching for something that seemed offhand yet just right, familiar yet mysterious, accessible yet refined. He found Van Morrison's *Veedon Fleece* in the glove box. The first track, "Fair Play," soothed his nerves on the way to Jill's place. By the time he pulled into her driveway, it had given way to "Linden Arden Stole the Highlights." He imagined starting the car again. "Is this Van?" Jill would ask. "It is," he would reply. "I don't know this one," she would say. "It's one of my favorites," he would offer. "It's lovely," she would remark, and he would say "so are you," and she would give her embarrassed little smile and look away.

After he rang her doorbell and found no one home, Mike got back into his car and turned the music off.

He tried another text. "At your house. No one here."

To his relief, one came right back. "At the OG. Came early. DJ problems."

Mike stepped into the Old Gym ten minutes later, more than an hour before the shindig was set to begin, and found the place teeming with last-minute preparations. Jill's army ants scurried, moving chairs, setting out centerpieces and alphabetizing name tags while their dates, mostly husbands at this point, gathered at the bar and inspected the liquor. In the far corner, Jill's arms flailed as she scolded a man Mike figured must be DJ SethSation based on the banner draped over the table that supported his gear.

Mike had stepped fewer than five feet into the room when he was intercepted by the former Shelly Abel ("if only she were willing," the boys used to say) whom he first met in kindergarten but had not seen since graduation. A good volleyball player, Mike recalled, who morphed from tall and gawky to long and graceful over the summer when she was sixteen. She had barely changed.

"Mike!" she gushed and gave him a hug.

"Shelly," he replied, "it's so good to see you. Is it still Abel?"

"Stafford," she said. "My husband Doug is over there at the bar. We met in college." Shelly and Mike gave Doug a wave and Doug gave one back.

"You look great," he said.

"Lots of Pilates and yoga," she said, "and the occasional triathlon. I'm a personal trainer at a club in Champaign." Then she lowered her voice. "I used to work out with Jill's ex-husband's fiancée. Total bitch, but with that ass she can get away with it."

Mike scanned the room and saw at least thirty people. "Can you help me with some names?" he asked. "It's been a long time and people have changed."

"You'll definitely be at a disadvantage tonight," Shelly said. "Everyone knows what you look like."

Shelly gave him the full rundown. Carol Barnes, emptying bottles into the punch bowl, was now Carol Warren. Lived in Terre Haute. Two kids. Sold jewelry out of her home on the side, just for a little fun money, and her husband taught at Indiana State. The former Tina Potter, now Tina Thornton, who was hanging the *Welcome Class of 1993* sign, lived in Northbrook, suburban Chicago. She sold life insurance for one of the big companies, and she and her husband played a lot of golf. No kids, fertility issues, thinking about adopting from China. Molly Keen got married but kept her name. Lived in Santa Fe. Owned a little art studio and painted. Her husband made sculptures that moved in the wind and they had either three or five children. Shelly remembered that it was an odd number and that it was more than one and less than seven but she had never seen pictures. She went on at length while Mike occasionally peered over her shoulder to try to catch Jill's eye. Shelly must have given him the skinny on two dozen classmates but when she finished talking all Mike remembered was that Molly Keen lived in New Mexico.

He thanked Shelly, said he hoped to catch up with her later and he looked around the room again for Jill. He spotted her in the far corner. She looked in his direction but she wasn't wearing her glasses and he wasn't sure that she saw him. Mike had already been in the Old Gym for fifteen minutes but never near her. Maybe she hadn't noticed him or maybe she didn't care. He knew for sure that she had not come looking for him, which suggested at the very least that she was in no mood to find him.

Mike wanted to get to Jill, to stand in front of her, grab her gently by the shoulders so their bodies could square up and they could look each other in the eye. And just as he took a step in her direction, a big hand slapped him on the back and a booming voice rang out "Mike McAfee! God-DAMN, it is good to see you! In person that is. I feel like I've seen your ugly mug on TV every day for the past year."

Mike turned to find Andy Barry, a good-natured, moon-faced guy who lasted a season and a half in the minor leagues before coming home to work in his dad's insurance agency and serve as a part-time assistant for the Cameron High School baseball team. Andy married their classmate Julie Nash when they were twenty-one. Mike went to the wedding, home that summer from college, but he had not seen Andy since.

"Hey, Andy," Mike said, and then did the awkward half-handshake, half-hug common to men unsure of whether they are lifelong friends or distant memories. "Why are you here so early?"

"Julie is helping set up and I came to test the beer. I've had three and I'm almost ready to declare it fit to drink. I may have another just to be sure. Can I get you one?"

"Maybe later, thanks. Still selling insurance here in town?"

"You bet. My dad retired a couple of years ago. He sold me the agency for a buck. It's worth at least twice that." Andy slapped Mike on the shoulder and laughed at a joke he had told and laughed at a thousand times before. "Life, home, auto. What do you need? I can package 'em all together and save you a bundle."

"My life is kind of in flux right now but when I figure it out maybe I'll give you a call."

Andy took a business card out of his pocket and wrote on it. "You do that. I wrote my home number on the back. I don't do that for everyone. Call me anytime, day or night."

"How about three a.m.?"

"Perfect. That's when I sneak out of bed to watch porn." Andy's laugh echoed through the gym. Mike suspected that he was only half-kidding.

"Last I knew, I think you and Julie had two kids. Is that right?"

"Three. Chip is going to be a junior this year. Good ballplayer. Better than me. I think he's got a chance to be a pro. Kelsey is a year younger. Badass basketball player. She's at an AAU tournament in Milwaukee right now. And Lila is in middle school. She's smarter than the rest of us put together. She's in a club that builds robots. She's a good kid, which is great, because if I ever had to ground her, I'm afraid that she'd have one of those things murder me in my sleep." Andy stopped abruptly. "Sorry to joke about, you know, murder."

It took Mike a second to get Andy's meaning. "I never actually murdered anyone, so, you know, don't sweat it."

"You don't have any kids, do you?"

"Nope."

"At least none that you know of, right? Ha-ha! I've seen the news. You are a champion womanizer, my friend. That Jenna – she's hotter than a habanero. Not so sure about that other one – Margie is it? But still, good work. I'm totally faithful, but your set-up sounds like fun."

"Probably not as much fun as you think." Mike noticed people filing in. No one was going to be fashionably late. When grownups in Cameron got a chance to party, they packed in all the fun they could.

"How about you? Why are you here so early?" Andy asked.

"I came to help Jill."

"So, the two of you. Are you –?"

"Jill and me? No. No. We've just been, you know, hanging out a little since I got back to town."

"OK, because I heard you were back together with that Jenna woman."

"Where did you hear *that*?" Mike asked, his pulse quickening.

"I heard it three or four times today. They said the two of you were walking around downtown today, holding hands, shopping. Hey, I'm not judging. Every couple has its problems. It's great if you can work them out."

"We haven't worked anything out," Mike said. He knew it was a small town but sometimes he forgot how small.

"Well, it's good that you're trying."

"We're not trying."

"Ah, just the sex then. Even better! Damn, I envy you."

"No! *No sex!*" Mike said loudly enough to make heads turn in their direction. "I'm not having sex with her," he said in an urgent whisper. "I'm not working things out with her. I'm not doing anything with her."

"So you weren't with her today?"

"I was, but not like that. We went to Charlie's and had a cup of coffee." Mike stopped. He knew that no explanation could help.

Andy put his hand up. "Whoa, dude, I'm sorry. It's none of my business."

Mike stepped past Andy, saw Jill across the room, and started to move toward her before Greg stepped in front of him.

"There he is!" Greg said, and gave his friend a bear hug. "You didn't come into the shop today. I haven't seen you in twenty-four hours. I was getting separation anxiety."

"I had a weird day," Mike said.

"That's what I gather. You and Jenna Kaye kissing in broad daylight? In Cameron? I never saw that coming."

"You didn't see it coming because *it didn't happen.*"

"But people saw you!"

"Who?"

"I don't know, *people.*"

"I had coffee with her. That was it."

"If you say so, but the people seemed pretty reliable."

"*Godammit.* This has to stop. *Right now.*"

"Hey, hey. What's going on?"

"Nothing. Nothing is going on. But apparently the whole town thinks I'm back with Jenna. As far as I know the only people who saw us were the waitress at Charlie's and –"

Mike hit the end of the thought like the side of a mountain.

"Shit," he said.

"What?"

"Jill."

"What about her?"

"Is she telling everyone?"

"I don't know."

"Have you talked to her today?"

"Just for a couple of minutes. She stopped by the shop with the girls. They grabbed some sandwiches and left. Sounds like they had a liquid lunch at Max's. They all seemed pretty tipsy except Molly Keen. Designated driver."

"Did she say anything?"

"She said that she saw you and Jenna. She asked what I knew. I told her I didn't know anything. She called me a liar and left."

"I've got to talk to her."

"Not now. I know that tonight is like high school, but don't make it *that much* like high school, all right? You think it was bad that somebody saw you with Jenna? Wait until everyone sees you argue with Jill. You need to do your business in private. Take it from someone who has mated in this town."

"We're not mating."

"I've seen bare-assed orangutans at the zoo preen more subtly than the two of you. Listen. I'm going to help you. Remember how I bailed you out when the reporters were at your door?"

"You led a nationally-televised parade of satellite trucks through town."

"*Exactly.* I'm going to do that again."

"You're going to lead a parade of satellite trucks through town?"

"No. I'm going to extricate you from an unpredictable and unpleasant situation."

Greg took Mike to a table in the farthest corner of the gym and told him to sit. They were going to do this *Godfather*-style, Greg explained, with Mike holding court and Greg acting as gatekeeper. It only made sense, Greg said. Everyone was going to want to talk to Mike, to reminisce, and maybe to feel the glow of celebrity by association. This would allow for the easy flow of traffic. And it would prevent Mike from bumping into Jill.

Just as Greg finished explaining the details, the room echoed with the hum of the PA system warming up, followed by a "check one-two, check one-two."

"Hey, hey!" the voice said in a high nasal whine, "I'm DJ SethSation, Cameron's number one portable party! Get up on your feet! Let's party like it's 1993!"

A familiar tune began to pulse at extreme volume, bouncing off the gym's old stone walls. "Let's get jiggy!" DJ SethSation shouted.

Mike paid no attention to the song. He just knew that every beat smacked his temples like a rubber mallet.

"This is from 1998," Greg shouted over the din.

"What?"

"This song – 'Gettin Jiggy Wit It.' This guy says we should party like it's 1993, and then he plays a song from 1998, like we had limited time-travel capabilities twenty years ago. Imagine that you're the first person to successfully pilot a time machine. You open the door to the future hoping to find insatiable sex robots but you get this shitty song instead."

"Did you think we were just five years away from sex robots in 1993?"

"Being five years away from sex robots is the hope that keeps me going," Greg said. "Sit here. Let me get you a drink. What do you want?"

"Ginger ale with an orange twist. I'd like to sit and watch other people embarrass themselves in public for a change."

As people continued to stream in, Greg came back with Mike's drink and began shepherding classmates to and from the table. He did it deftly, like a *maître d'*, a job he occasionally covered in his old restaurant days. There was Tyler Lakin and his wife Nicole, then Courtney (Carter) Davis and her husband Tom, and Tara Waller and her wife Lori Higgins, who had just gotten married in upstate New York. Dozens of old friends stopped by, but DJ SethSation's volume remained at peak level, so Mike barely understood a word anyone said. Someone had some job and someone had some kids and someone had been on some vacation.

The music kept pumping and Greg pointed out that SethSation's sense of history improved as the evening progressed. He rolled through the big hits of their high school years: "I'm Too Sexy," "Baby Got Back," "Rump Shaker."

Noticing a theme in the songs, Mike said "I don't remember butts being so big in '93."

Greg looked around the room and said "I think they're bigger now."

Greg continued to shuttle friends to and from the table for the next hour until the room fell silent for a slideshow tribute to the four classmates who had been lost – Toby Blevins, who didn't make it to graduation; Cory Burton, who laid down his Harley on a rural highway; Jennifer Barnes, who succumbed to breast cancer; and Jeff Byron, who took a blast in the face from a careless duck hunter. Greg thought that having a name that started with B might be fatal, and he felt nervous for that poor son of a bitch Andy Barry. And then he thought of the Seeburg and wondered if there were any killer B's that he could incorporate.

The images played over "Tears in Heaven," which had been a big hit during junior year. Mike usually found the song maudlin but it felt right for the moment. He hadn't been close to Cory or Jeff but he had known them for most of his life and always thought they were good guys. The pictures of Toby stung. He had been a sweet kid and Mike had never been cruel to him. But Mike held on to a lingering feeling that he should have been kinder. If everyone had been more sensitive to Toby's experience, maybe only three people would be in the slideshow. Still, even worse than the shots of Toby were the ones of Jennifer. Mike and Jen had been neighbors and he always had fond, if not romantic, feelings for her. Strung together, the photos played like the slow-motion dissolution of a life. There was her senior picture, and then shots from her wedding, and, finally, one of her lying in bed, completely bald, cuddled up with two little girls. Shitty day or not, Mike felt grateful to be alive.

When the slideshow ended, Jill stood under a spotlight on the stage at the far end of the gym and tapped on a microphone.

"Is this thing on? Can you hear me?" She held the mic in one hand and a glass in the other, and wine sloshed onto the stage as she gestured.

"Good evening, Cameron Cougars! And hello to the men, too!" The room erupted in laughter. "I'm Jill Emory. I used to be Jill Murdock but I've known most of you since we kept clean underpants in a cubby in our kindergarten class, so I guess you know that. Given the number of drinks I've had tonight, I kind of wish I had a clean pair here somewhere."

Her former classmates hooted and egged her on.

"Before anyone else asks, yes I'm keeping the name. Probably. And for all of the guys at the bar who are missing Dan tonight because he was such a good dude," Jill said and then shifted into a whisper, "he was only pretending."

The hooting was replaced by muted nervous laughter.

"I'm sorry. Where was I? Yes, welcome to the Cameron High School class of 1993's twenty-year reunion. I used to always say that I hoped to see more of you, but now I *really do* see more of you." Jill paused but no one laughed. "Because we all got older and gained a few pounds. So there's *more* of us to see, get it? Just a little joke. Everybody looks great. And speaking of elephants in the room – ha, ha! – since we last did this, one of us got famous. Like really famous. Like really, *really* famous. He even put Cameron on the map for a day or two just a couple of months ago. And he's attending his first reunion *ever* tonight. Ladies and gentlemen, please welcome Mike McAfee."

The crowd gave Mike a polite round of applause.

"Mike, of course, became famous for not killing his girlfriend. Everybody in the world didn't kill her, but he's the only one who got famous for it. How fair is that? Anyway, it's good he didn't kill her, because I met her today. Lovely woman. *Lovely*. Is she here tonight? Is Mike here? Where's Mike?" Jill shaded her eyes with her hand and looked around the room.

A few dozen fingers awkwardly pointed towards Mike, who pressed his lips together tightly. He waited until heads turned back to Jill and then began walking toward the stage.

"She's not here? Oh, OK. That's too bad. Anyway, thanks to everyone for coming tonight." Mike skipped up the steps to the back of the stage as Jill kept talking, and he slipped up behind her. "OK, we've got the place until one a.m., so I hope you all got babysitters who can stay late. So everyone, please party up and remember –"

Mike snatched the microphone from Jill's hand.

"Don't worry. I'm not going to kill her, either," Mike said and smiled and the room laughed in a moment of comic relief. "I know I speak for everyone when I say thanks to Jill and all of our classmates who put in the hard work to make tonight happen. How about a big round of applause?"

Two-hundred sets of hands clapped enthusiastically.

"To Toby, Cory, Jeff and Jen," Mike said, raising his glass high, "we're thankful for the time we had with you, though it was far too short."

"Hear, hear!" Greg shouted, followed by dozens echoing him.

"And, finally, everyone has troubles in their lives. Some troubles are painfully public, some are quiet and private. It's good to have so many friends to be able to lean on. Our good friend Greg Allen turns thirty-eight on Monday, so when you see him tonight wish him a happy birthday. Anyway, it's great to see all of you. Let's keep on having a great night. Who's up for singing the Cameron High School fight song?"

As a cheer rose in the room and voices began to belt out *Hail! Hail! Cameron Cougars!*, Mike put his hand on the small of Jill's back, whispered "come with me," and led her off the side of the stage and through an exterior door into the humid Illinois night.

Jill looked up at the stars and said "where did the reunion go?"

"Into the annals of history, I'm pretty sure."

"I need to go back in there," Jill said.

"You really don't. I'm going to drive you home. I'll come back and clean up."

"But my car."

"Greg and I will get it for you."

"But my purse."

Mike called Greg and asked him to bring Jill's purse outside. Two minutes later, Greg popped through the door, handed over the bag and slid back inside.

"Come on, let's get you home," Mike said. They walked quietly to his car and then rode silently to Jill's house. The day was ending much as it had begun.

Mike pulled up to Jill's curb and stopped. They both got out of the car, but Jill said "thanks for the ride. I'm fine. You can go."

Mike walked around the car to Jill's front step. "I know you're angry with me. Can I please explain?"

"You don't have to explain. I might have been a little angry before, but I don't have any right to be. You and I aren't some exclusive item. We haven't even had a real date, for god's sake. You don't owe me anything. And it's not just about you. I'm just feeling sort of alone right now. Liv is off with Dan and her soon-to-be stepmother, and I . . . ." Jill's lip began to quiver and she bit it as tears welled in her eyes.

Mike tried to put his arm around her but Jill bristled.

"There's nothing for you here," she said. "There are no jobs for someone like you here. This town is just a pothole on the road between St. Louis and Indianapolis. You probably think those places are just potholes between New York and L.A., and you might be right. I saw you and Jenna. You two should be together. Really. You can go back to your old life. It will be so much easier than you think."

"Listen to me," Mike said. "I know what you think you saw, but you are wrong. Do you understand? Jenna showed up at my house this morning. I wouldn't let her in. I didn't want to be alone with her. We went to Charlie's for coffee so that she could say whatever she came all this way to say. And that's it. And it's over."

"But why were the two of you laughing?"

"Because she once threw a hat on my penis."

"What?" Jill squinted her eyes and tilted her head.

"It doesn't matter."

"But –"

"She came here to try to talk me into doing some stupid reality TV show. A television show. Can you believe it? I told her no. And it doesn't matter how many times she shows up at my door or how much money they offer me. The answer will always be no. No. *No.* I'm not interested in that. I'm not interested in her. I'm not interested in her bullshit or her dad's money or Craig Doolittle. I'm not interested in a single goddamn thing in my entire life except you."

Jill smiled and flicked her eyes toward the ground.

"When I saw you again for the first time," Mike said, "and I heard that you had another man's name, I felt this terrible ache because there you were, more beautiful than I even remembered, and

I felt like I had lost you all over again and that I was just going to spend my life losing women that I loved. Then you said you were divorced, and I shouldn't take pleasure in something like that, but it was pretty exciting news to me. And meeting Liv made it even better. She was like some proof of every good thing I ever felt about you. I've been trying to put my life back together but I still felt empty. Then I saw you and I didn't feel that way anymore."

Jill leaned close and put her forehead on Mike's chest.

"I'm sorry," Mike whispered. "I said too much."

"No," Jill replied, "you said just the right amount." She leaned back against her front door. "We're both kind of fragile right now and I'm pretty drunk, and it's all I can do to keep my panties on. So I'm just going to kiss you now and go inside. But maybe someday soon we'll both be stronger and I'll be sober, and then . . . ."

Jill leaned in and kissed Mike, this time on the mouth, sweet and wet as twenty years ago but somehow better. "Goodnight," she said. She let go of his fingers as she slid through the door and closed it behind her.

Mike turned to walk back to his car but imagined himself floating high into the clear, black night, looking down on his hometown from above, the flickering campus lights softly illuminating birds that flew below him. The view was magnificent.

TWENTY

It's so beautiful," Greg said as vintage punk rock roared from behind the counter.

"It really is," Mike replied.

"No, I mean a different kind of beautiful."

"I'm with you."

"Do you understand what I'm saying?"

"I do."

"I mean, I want to have sex with it."

"Well, then, maybe I don't."

"Metaphorical sex, of course."

"OK, I understand then."

"I'm not used to playing new records," Greg said.

"They're new old records."

"And did you see the book?"

"I did."

"It's so beautiful."

"It really is."

"Thank you so much."

"Glad I could do it. Happy birthday."

Greg leaned forward and kissed the box that contained his freshly-pressed collection of the Beatles' entire catalog on pristine 180-gram vinyl. He went through phases – a punk phase, a soul phase, a country phase, a month of nothing but jazz from the Impulse! label. But the Beatles were the home to which he always returned. Greg cradled the accompanying coffee-table book and flipped through the pages until he found the essay on *Revolver*, which remained his very favorite album. He slid the book back into the box and pulled out the first record, *Please Please Me*. He removed the wrapper and headed to the turntable, where he lifted the needle from side two of *Never Mind the Bollocks, Here's the Sex Pistols*. "Thank god for that," Jenks said. "I like the guitar sound, but John Lydon's voice gives me a headache." Greg heard Jenks but declined to acknowledge him.

Greg slid the Pistols record back in the sleeve and undressed the Beatles LP, removing her clothes and then her panties, his middle finger resting in the hole in the middle, while the black body shimmered around it. Sure, the ritual was sexual, but it was also spiritual, a communion of souls. Greg stopped to admire the label, an authentic reproduction of the original English pressing, emblazoned with the stately Parlophone logo. He had never seen one of these. All of the old Beatles vinyl he had acquired had been American editions on Capitol. This was like holding a copy of the Bible in the original Greek or Hebrew or whatever language the prophets spoke or wrote. Aramaic maybe. He laid the record on the turntable, dropped the needle and listened as Paul counted "one-two-three-*four!*" with the hard emphasis on *four*. Most people would hear it as a simple count-off, but it struck Greg as a declaration – we four, forever – as if they all knew then what everyone would learn soon thereafter. The band catapulted into "I Saw Her Standing There." Greg cranked the volume and danced around the shop like a madman, oblivious to customers who assuredly were not oblivious to him. When the song ended he wrapped both arms around Mike and kissed him on the cheek.

The second song, "Misery," filled the room and Greg resumed dancing. "I always thought those guys were overrated," Jenks said, interrupting Greg's reverie like a head-on crash of freight trains. "Richard Starkey wasn't much of a drummer."

Greg tried his hardest to summon lasers from his eyes, hoping to blast off the top of Jenks's head. When he failed, he opened the accompanying book again and drank in the images, photos as smooth and glossy as mercury. At the beginning were sparkling eyes, four boys unaware that they were about to remake the world. At the end were deadened stares, four men ready to be done with it.

Jacob came through the front door in his usual uniform augmented by a Misfits t-shirt that might have looked menacing on a different person. Draped over Jacob's concave chest and pipe-cleaner arms, though, it had the opposite effect. It made Greg want to hug the poor fatherless urchin.

"Got something for you," Jacob said, and he reached into his bag and pulled out a vintage copy of the White Album.

"That's quite the cosmic coincidence," Greg said.

"What is?"

"Do you hear that?" Greg asked. "Misery" had given way to "Anna." "Do you know who that is?"

"No."

"It's the Beatles. Mike just gave me new pressings of all of the Beatles records."

"So what's the coincidence?"

"This record. That you have. *In your hands*. It's the Beatles."

Jacob seemed unimpressed with the information. "How many sandwiches is it worth?"

Greg took the album from Jacob, pulled out the first inner sleeve and removed the record. The sight hit him like the first sip of a rare and precious bourbon. White vinyl. Purple label. Mint condition.

"Jesus," he said. He could feel his eyes begin to mist.

"What?" Jacob asked.

Greg said nothing. He looked at the second record. It was as immaculate as the first. "Mike!" he shouted. "White Album. Reissued on white vinyl with a purple label, on Capitol. What is that? 1978?"

"That sounds about right, but you'd know better than me."

"What do you think it's worth?"

"Depends on the condition, I guess."

"How about mint?"

"Do you have one?" Mike asked.

"Yes."

Mike walked over and had a look. "She's a beauty," he said, holding the first one up to the light. "Like two perfect little identical twins. Does it have a poster?"

Greg tilted the jacket and out slid four photographs, one of each member of the band, and a folded poster with paper as crisp and smooth as a freshly-printed hundred-dollar bill. Greg unfolded the poster carefully to reveal images of the band on one side and lyrics on the other. "This may be the first time it has been opened up," he said.

"A little bit of treasure right here in Cameron," Mike said.

"So what do you think?" Jacob asked.

"I really don't know, buddy. I need to do some research. But in the interim, you don't sell it, you don't trade it for sandwiches, you don't play Frisbee with it. Understand?"

"OK."

"And we're doing this all wrong. It's obvious that your dad had a good collection. I don't know how much there is but he took great care of it and he had great taste. You and your mom don't have any idea what it's worth, and I can't tell either if you just bring me one piece at a time. How about I come by some time and catalog it? I can see what you have and I can evaluate the condition of all of it. And then we can talk about what you should do with it. That would be so much better than taking one piece at a time and trading it to me."

"I don't know," Jacob said. "My mom said I could have the records but I don't think she'd like a stranger coming in and going through dad's things. She's still pretty sad and stuff."

"You talk to her about it," Greg said. "In the meantime, I'll make you a deal. Let me keep the album here for now. I'll give you a sandwich a week until we can figure out what to do with it. I'll play the album just once, just so I can hear it, and then I'll put it back in the office so I can stare at it. You can have it back any time you want. How does that sound?"

"Does that start right away?"

"Sure."

"Then I'll have the chicken Philly, extra peppers."

While Greg and Jacob were negotiating terms, Mike answered a call from a news organization, his sixth of the day. Word had spread of Jenna's appearance in Cameron, and the nation's curiosity proved durable. Mike did his best to dispel the story with a mix of honesty and reticence. Yes, he had met with Jenna, but only briefly. It was just former lovers tying up loose ends. There were no plans to reconcile or even to talk again. As for the specifics of their conversation, that was personal and private. The people from the big news agencies seemed satisfied. They could tell when a story had burned itself out, and there was no value in reporting on the last embers of a wildfire. But just after he ended the call, two men came through the front door.

One had a camera and the other held a microphone. They ran toward Mike, said they were from TMZ and asked about his meeting with Jenna. Mike just shrugged his shoulders and went back to the office and closed the door. The TMZ guys looked at each other, unsure of what to do. People rarely turned down the chance to be on television.

Greg told them to get lost. After they left, he edged into the office where Mike was sitting at his computer, pecking at the keys. "I thought it would be different here," Mike said, "but I don't think it's different anywhere. It just takes the reporters a little longer to arrive."

TWENTY-ONE

Mike woke up the next morning and checked every news and gossip site he knew. He found his name nowhere. He had never been so happy to be insignificant. When he hit the pavement for his run, he felt light and fast, invigorated by a new sense of liberation.

After a shower, he headed to the shop to write. When he arrived, he slipped into the kitchen to help himself to breakfast. He combed the pantry and shouted out front to Greg. "These bagels are moldy."

"That's not mold. They're blueberry."

"Blueberry onion?" Mike asked.

Greg walked back into the kitchen and looked and sniffed. "I'll make you an omelet and bring it into the office."

Mike ate and worked. He had been writing for nearly three hours when he stepped out of Greg's office to refill his coffee cup. It was a few minutes after eleven o'clock, just before what qualified as the lunch rush during the summer. But Alyssa was the only person stirring. She moved trays of fresh-baked bread from the kitchen to a rack behind the counter and dumped bins of newly-chopped lettuce, tomatoes and onions into bowls. Greg, usually a workhorse this time of day, sat at a table, sipping coffee and laughing with a woman Mike had never seen in the shop.

She took off her glasses and twirled them in her hand, eyes fixed on Greg, smiling as he talked. Mike remembered Greg as a kid, trying to impress girls by making his personality even bigger, but in a self-deprecating way that proved surprisingly effective. Approaching forty, he still deployed the same moves, gesturing wildly with his hands, contorting his broad, bearded face, pointing his finger at his head like a gun to punctuate the only words Mike could catch, "boy was I stupid!"

Mike approached the table at an angle, getting a three-quarter view of the woman. The back of her head and side of her face were framed by crimson hair.

Greg spotted him coming. "Mike," he said, "meet my new friend, Margaret."

Mike smiled and shook his head. "It's Maggie, Greg," he said. "She goes by Maggie."

Greg scrunched his eyebrows, not understanding.

"Your friend's name is Maggie. Maggie Kleinsasser," Mike said. "Maggie and I worked together in Denver. You may have read about that in the papers."

"I've been trying 'Margaret' on for size," Maggie said. "I thought a little change would do me good, but I don't think it's going to stick."

Greg looked at Maggie, then at Mike, then back at Maggie. "But you look so –"

"Hot?" Maggie said.

"I was going to go with *different*," Greg said, "but I think that *hot* is more on-point, frankly. Mike, your friend – *our* friend – is hot, don't you think?"

"You're looking well, Maggie," Mike said.

Maggie stood up and faced Mike. "Would it be weird if I gave you a hug?" she asked.

"Probably," Mike replied, "but why not?"

They shared an embrace that was cordial if not warm.

"Sit with us. Please," Maggie said.

Mike pulled over a chair from the next table, flipped it backwards, straddled it and rested his arms across the top. "Did you come to talk about the reality show?" Mike asked. "Because I'm not going to do that?"

"No," Maggie said. "Well, sorta. If you wanted to do it, I'd do it. Of course I would. But you shouldn't want to do it and I'm not going to try to talk you into it. In fact, I'd probably try to talk you out of it. You're the one person in this mess who has made some effort at preserving dignity."

"Then what brings you here? The sandwiches?"

Maggie's face turned serious. "I'll try the sand-wiches, but I really came to apologize."

Mike looked at Greg in a way that meant "can you give us a minute?" and Greg nodded back in a way that said "sure," and then he stepped behind the counter to help Alyssa brace for the hungering masses.

If Maggie had planned what to say, it didn't show. After fumbling for a place to begin, she said "first, the apology. I am sorry. Unconditionally. I did a terrible thing and I'm sure it hurt you and I regret it. I don't know how I could ever make it right. I could try to explain, I guess, but it would only cheapen the apology."

"Apology accepted," Mike said. He flipped his chair around, reached across the table, and squeezed Maggie's hand.

"Thank you. That means a lot." Maggie exhaled and smiled.

"It's OK if you want to explain," he said. "It won't cheapen anything."

"I'll try." Maggie paused. "I had a thing for you for a long time. Everybody knew that. And that night we spent together was a big deal for me. If my story had ended right there, it would have been perfect, you know. *Two sad drunks fuck each other's brains out.* That would've been my happily-ever-after. I'm not one of those girls who had the Cinderella fantasy."

"I suppose not."

"I mean, I would've blown the prince right there in the carriage."

Mike laughed. "Yes you probably would have."

"I completely took advantage of you that night," Maggie said. "You were drunk and devastated. That wasn't fair."

"We took advantage of each other. I was more at fault than you were."

184

"Anyway, I don't know if I expected it to last forever, or if it would even happen again. But when you went back to Jenna the next day, I was just so hurt. Always losing to the pretty girl."

"I should apologize to you, too, Maggie. I should have apologized then, but I decided to pretend that it never happened. I'm sorry. I treated you terribly."

"Thanks, but we're way past that now. Anyway, I was angry and I held on to that anger for way too long. Then, when Jenna went missing I had this fantasy that you would come back to me for comfort. God, it's so embarrassing to say out loud."

"You don't need to be embarrassed."

"Then when all the focus turned to you, I thought, no, there's no way you could have killed her. You just don't have it in you. And then I realized that's what everyone always says whenever there's a story like this. 'We couldn't believe it. We didn't think he had it in him. He seemed like such a good guy.' And then it turns out that it's the husband or the boyfriend. It's always the husband or the boyfriend. So I started to think that maybe you did do it. And then I somehow convinced myself that you did. I thought 'I fucked a murderer,' which was kind of sexy in a weird way, you know? And so when all the tabloid people came poking around, I thought 'what the hell?' Where's the harm in humiliating a murderer? I thought of it as some weird sex-vigilante justice. And so I thought it seemed like a pretty good deal. Make some cash, get famous. I didn't consider that I might get fired and destroy my career. I exhibited some lack of fore-sight there. Does any of this help?"

"I don't know. It doesn't hurt."

"For what it's worth, I'm sorry that I thought that you might have done such a terrible thing. I should have known better."

"You were hardly alone. So how do you feel about all the attention?"

"It's the worst. It might be different if I were famous for something good. But I just made myself a target for ridicule. I try to make the most of it by taking on the trolls on Twitter and by doing the media stuff and trying not to come off like a com-plete wacko. That's why I did the Lacy Nantz thing at first, but after the initial rush, I figured out that I was just another freak under glass on that show. I know it was worse for you. How did you handle it?"

"I ran away to Cameron, Illinois to live in my mother's house. Speaks for itself, doesn't it?"

"I'm glad that you're being so decent about this. It's nice to talk to someone who understands what any of this is like."

Mike looked around the shop. "People are go-ing to come in here soon for lunch," he said, "and if they see us here together they're going to point and whisper. Then they're going to take pictures and post them online. We'll be trending in half an hour. Do you want to move this into the office?"

"Sure."

"Greg!" Mike yelled. "We're going to the back. Could we get two of your very best sandwiches delivered there?"

"Anything for our friend Margaret," Greg hollered back.

Back in the office Maggie saw Mike's things scattered around the desk.

"Writing a book?" she asked.

"Maybe. I got an advance. I dumped the money into a separate account so I can just pay it back if I don't produce anything worth reading. What about you? What are you up to?"

"I'm trying to figure that out. I really would like to get back into some sort of financial job. And I'd like it to be in Denver. My parents are there and they've had some health issues. I want to be there for them."

"What do they think about all of this?"

"They were horrified, especially my mom. She's very traditional. Since I've never been married she was holding onto some shred of hope that I might still be a virgin. Oops."

"My mom didn't love learning the specifics of my, um, *technique*, either."

"Sorry. I never stopped to consider that our parents would read it. Again, lack of foresight."

"How did you get to Cameron?"

"It wasn't easy. I flew into St. Louis and got a rental. Dodge Charger. I love those American muscle cars. I hauled ass getting here. Got acquainted with a state trooper who liked my eyes and let me off with a warning. By the way, Illinois is *flat*."

"If the corn weren't so tall you could see forever."

Greg knocked at the door and stepped in holding baskets with sandwiches and chips. "I have one *cemita* and one *porchetta*," he said. "Margaret, you should take whichever one you want, and you want the *cemita*."

"Then that's what I'll do," she said.

"When are you headed back to Denver?" Greg asked.

"Tonight."

"On a Tuesday? That's too bad," Greg replied, as if Tuesday were the one bad day to escape Cameron. "I would have made us all dinner. Mike, we could've gotten Jill to join us."

"Actually, I don't have to leave tonight," Maggie said. "I don't need to be anywhere tomorrow. I could change my flight."

"That would be great!"

"Is that OK?" Maggie asked.

"Of course, it's OK," Greg said. "Isn't it, Mike?"

"Well, Jill and I sort of left things in weird place on Saturday night, so –"

"Great!" Greg said, "It's a date. I'll take the night off and call in the new kid. What's his name? Kyle? Carl?"

"It's Cole, Greg. The new kid is Cole."

"Cole! Like coleslaw! I'll never forget his name again. So you'll call Jill? She can bring Liv. I'll make the mac and cheese she likes."

"I don't know if that's a good idea," Mike said. The memory of introducing Jill to Jenna remained fresh in his mind.

"Of course it's a good idea. But can we do it at your place? Mine is a bit untidy. And I need you to go shopping. I'll make you a list. You take the groceries back to your house and I'll show up at around four to start cooking." Greg winked at Maggie and bounced out of the room.

"Who's Jill?" Maggie asked Mike.

"A friend. From high school."

"A girlfriend?"

"In high school."

"How about now?"

Mike pretended not to hear the question.

Maggie bit into her sandwich and her eyes widened as she tasted the crispy, chewy pork for the first time. "Oh my god," she said. "Oh. My. God. This is the best thing I've ever eaten. Greg makes this? *Here?*"

Mike looked at the list and doubted that these things could be found in Cameron: fennel, arugula, shallots, white asparagus, prosciutto, Pecorino Romano, polenta, kale. He could not testify that a single one of them existed before 1998. But two hours later when he placed sacks full of them on his mother's kitchen counter, he took a moment to appreciate how his hometown had changed. *Pecorino Romano.* Goddamn.

Greg showed up on time with a box under one arm and a cooler in the opposite hand. "Wine," he said, gesturing to the box, "and lamb sausage," he added, lifting the cooler.

"Where did you get lamb sausage?"

"I made it." In fact, Greg had been making sausage for years in small batches: chorizo verde, porcini and thyme, andouille, garlic and rosemary. Ever since his divorce, once every couple of months he drove just over the line into Indiana, to a speck on the map southwest of Crawfordsville, where an old farmer had a butcher shop. Greg once used the word "charcuterie" in the man's presence and prompted howls of good-natured laughter. "Good food doesn't need fancy names," the man said. "That's how people who've never been to a farm trick themselves. We raise hogs, cows and sheep, and then we kill 'em and cut 'em up and put 'em in the case." The man wasn't cavalier, just honest. He was proud of what he did. He didn't want it obscured by squishy names.

Greg bought just a little meat at a time. He wanted his sausage to be fresh. He didn't make it for the shop. He made it for himself. It was a secret, like a journal composed of animal flesh. He would linger at Mellow Sub after it closed, crank a record, crack a beer and retire to the kitchen's far corner. He pushed the meat through a grinder and added spices, herbs, garlic. Sometimes he added onions or apples or cheese. He mixed it and pushed it through casings, tied them and cut them. It was a thing he did to relax but, more than that, it gave him a product to hold and savor. You can't eat a round of golf, he thought.

Greg went to his car and returned with more supplies: pans, knives, oils and a compact disc. "*My Life in the Bush of Ghosts*" he said to Mike as he handed him the disc, an implicit instruction to play it. "Mood music," he said.

"What kind of mood are you going for?"

"Exotic!" Greg's eyes danced. Mike had rarely seen him so happy.

Mike had made a bullet-pointed list of things he wanted to impart to Jill when he called: *Maggie Kleinsasser came to the shop today; I did not know she was coming; she came to apologize; Greg wants us all to have dinner together tonight at my place.* Jill noted that the last piece of information made for a world-class non sequitur, but life in Cameron had gotten pretty non-sequitorial ever since Mike showed up.

"This seems important to him," Mike said.

"OK," Jill said, as if that were all she needed to know.

While Greg cooked and the afro-electric beats throbbed, Mike vacuumed carpets and polished silverware and ironed a tablecloth and checked wine glasses for spots. He scrubbed toilets and refilled toilet paper holders. He deodorized the house with Lysol, and when that made the place smell too medicinal he went over the same areas with pot-pourri air freshener until the house reeked of disinfected flowers. He opened the windows to dissipate the stench and then closed them to retain the glorious aromas drifting from the kitchen.

Greg had tied a bandana around his forehead to keep from seasoning the food with his sweat. He spun gracefully from surface to surface, from counter to island to stove. He grabbed a fennel bulb and a heavy knife and began slicing like a samurai, revealing the edible interior and then dicing it in an instant, the *ratatat* of his blade on the cutting board echoing like machine gun fire. He assembled salads and composed sauces, building flavors one layer at a time, slowly and deliberately because there was no other way. He opened a bottle of wine and poured it into a decanter. "Aeration," he said. He gathered up scraps, scraped surfaces clean and counted sausages for a fourth time. Then he reached into a bag and pulled out a grill pan. He washed it and said to Mike, "this happens last. I'll cook the sausages while we're having salad." Then he went to his car and came back with a garment bag and a Dopp kit. "Hitting the shower," he said.

Thirty minutes later he emerged with his hair tamed and his beard trimmed, trailed by a subtle trace of cologne. He sported a new two-button navy blazer, crisp white shirt and light khaki pants. He closed the top button on his jacket, stood at an angle with one foot pointed forward and his shoulders pulled back. "How do I look?"

"You really like her," Mike said.

"Yes, but how do I look?"

"You look great. Best I've ever seen you. But take it easy. You just met Maggie and, trust me, she has some damage."

"Well," Greg said, "the mint-condition girls never call."

Moments later, Jill and Liv arrived. Greg took Liv into the kitchen so that they could prepare her special macaroni and cheese, which was really cavatappi pasta in a tomato cream sauce with fresh basil. The kid had sophisticated tastes.

In the living room, Jill fidgeted with her rings and looked at the old photos that adorned the walls. Her eyes went everywhere except at Mike.

"Hey," he said, "are you all right? I know this is weird. I know that everything is weird."

"Me? I'm good. Great. How about you?"

"Great. Had a good day writing. Better than yesterday when TMZ showed up at the shop to ask about Jenna being in town."

"Oh. I didn't know. I'm sorry. That was probably my fault. At least indirectly. I guess I let the cat out of the bag. And then I walked around and showed everybody the cat. And then they blabbed about the cat on the internet."

"Don't worry about it. It seems to have blown over."

"That's good. That's great." Jill started to speak again and then stopped.

"What?" Mike asked.

"Nothing."

"Really, it's fine. What?"

Jill hesitated. "The other night, when you took me home, I said something about my" – she shifted to a whisper – "*panties*, didn't I?"

"You indicated that you were having some trouble keeping them on, yes."

"Oh god. I thought so. I'm so embarrassed. I was hoping it was a dream. 'Panties' is a terrible word."

"Is it?"

"It seems unbecoming of a grown woman."

"Are you embarrassed by the choice of words or the gist of the statement?"

"I'm embarrassed about everything, I guess."

A brief silence was interrupted by the rumbling, hemi-powered drone that announced Maggie's approach. Mike looked through the window to see the sparkling, cherry-red Charger pull into the drive. Maggie climbed out in a short skirt, tall heels and a sleeveless top that revealed her chiseled new arms. Mike let her in.

"This is your mom's place?" Maggie asked. "It's lovely." She handed Mike a tasteful arrangement of lilacs in a vase.

"This is Jill," Mike said.

"Good to meet you. I'm Maggie." They shook hands and Jill smiled.

"I've seen your face before," Jill said. "I'm sorry. This whole thing has made me feel awkward. When you watch the news, in some ways those people don't seem real to you. They're more like characters in a TV show until you start meeting all of them in your little hometown."

"Who else have you met?"

Jill looked at Mike, unsure of whether she should say anything more.

"Jenna," Mike said. "She showed up unannounced three days ago."

"You're kidding. Here?"

"On that very doorstep. I didn't let her in the house. We went out for coffee. The whole thing lasted less than an hour."

"What did she want?"

Mike explained about Jenna and the dueling reality shows and her general lack of self-awareness. He said that he was glad that Maggie didn't know that Jenna had been there. It was further evidence that the news didn't spread as far and wide and fast as he had initially feared. He said that he remembered from his college psychology class that most people's conceptions of themselves were greatly exaggerated, and this was largely a defense mechanism because if people truly grasped how insignificant they were in the grand scheme of things, most would want to kill themselves. We are all tiny specks in a cold and limitless universe that cares little for us. Mike used to think that being on television every day had transformed him from a tiny speck to a larger blotch, and so he assumed that the universe, or at least some critical number of the people in it, cared about him, not in a good or bad way, just in a way that confirmed that he was part of the consciousness. Now he was finding, after the initial wave of attention, that blotches shrink back to specks, perhaps not all the way down to original size, but small enough to regain most of their insignificance. It made him appreciate all the work that went into becoming and remaining famous. Actors and musicians pay managers and publicists and stylists to work on their behalf to help put them on the public's radar and then they continue to pay them for years and years, and some of them still manage to fade back into obscurity or worse, to the kind of low-level fame that prompts pity and/or ridicule. Every day, they have to keep pumping hot air into the balloon to stay aloft.

"I'm mixing the shit out of my metaphors," he said.

"You owe me a dollar," Liv said.

"How come?"

"Naughty word. Geggy has to pay me a dollar every time he says one."

"How much has he paid you?" Mike asked.

"College is pretty much covered," Jill said.

Mike reached in his wallet and slipped Liv a five. "Let me pay for a few in advance."

"I'd prefer that you not use them all," Jill said.

"Can I say 'crap'?" Mike asked.

"That's two dollars," Liv replied.

"How about 'bollocks'?"

"I don't even know what that means," Jill said, "so it's allowed. Unless it's really dirty."

Mike was glad for Liv's presence because it meant that conversation would unfold with a certain level of decorum. There would be no talk of Mike's lurid encounter with Maggie or with Maggie's lurid encounters with others or with whether and to what extent Mike might have a lurid encounter with Jill in the future. The conversation would focus mostly on how freaking amazing Greg's food was.

"Three dollars," Liv said.

"I have to pay up for saying 'freaking'?" Mike asked.

"Four dollars."

Greg rolled out the dishes deliberately. He presented his friends with the *crostini*, the salad, the prosciutto-wrapped white asparagus, which had been trimmed and simmered with care and finished with a touch of butter. But the heaviest fawning was reserved for the sausage, his take on a *merguez*, which he paired with a simple, rustic Chianti Classico. A soft porridge of polenta finished the plate.

"I feel embarrassed to admit this," Maggie said, "because I don't want it to sound like I was expecting to find hillbillies here, but I never imagined that I would be eating something like this in Cameron, Illinois."

"Before Greg started cooking," Jill said, "we never imagined it either." She took a bite of the sausage and felt the pleasure flow from her tongue through her brain and then to her extremities. "*Holy shit*, this is fantastic."

Mike looked at Liv. "I'll cover that one for your mom. That's five. Shall I give you another five in advance?"

"Probably a good idea," Liv said.

Mike fished another bill out of his wallet.

"This sausage originated in Morocco," Greg said, "which touches the Mediterranean Sea. I remember looking at a map of the world when I was in cooking school and having this light bulb come on. People think of Europe, Asia and Africa as being separate. I think that comes in part from living here, where we're so isolated from the rest of the world. But look at a globe someday. It all comes together there on the Mediterranean. Italy, Egypt, Turkey, Greece. The cradle of civilization. That's where all the cultures collide. But they don't really collide. They blend and synthesize, get all smashed together. It blurs the lines between all of these different people. It makes borders seem arbitrary, even though those nations have fought for centuries. That's where my very favorite food comes from."

"This is the sweaty guy who rode the bike while the news trucks followed," Mike said to Maggie.

"If we really try," Greg said, "I think we can achieve peace through sausage."

They all lingered for another hour as Greg brought out dessert, again inspired by the Mediterranean. It was a ricotta mousse with balsamic vinegar and cherries. Maggie rolled it over her tongue and closed her eyes. "This is bliss," she said.

"It is," Jill said, "but it's past Liv's bedtime. We're going to need to get going."

"It was so lovely to meet you," Maggie said. "You are a firecracker, Liv."

"She knows," Mike said. Liv smiled her gap-toothed smile.

As Jill and Liv made their way out, Maggie said to Mike "I'll help you clean up."

"No, I'm sure you're exhausted. You must want to get back to the hotel. Greg and I can handle this."

"The hotel?" Greg said. "First let me give you a tour of our happy hamlet – the mostly vacant university, the withering downtown, the streets named for obscure presidents. What could be better? Are you up for it?"

"Sure, that would be great. I can drive. We'll come back for your car later."

"Leave the dishes, Mike," Greg said. "I'll take care of them tomorrow."

Moments later, Mike heard the Charger's engine roar to life and disappear. Then he filled the sink with hot, soapy water and started to scrub.

TWENTY-TWO

Mike tied his running shoes and stepped into the living room, where little evidence of the previous night's events remained. Greg's cooler, pans and knives sat by the front door, washed and dried and ready to go. Every dish, plate, glass and piece of flatware was back in a cabinet. After his guests left, Mike poured the last of the wine, put on a Dexter Gordon album, did the dishes, thought about Jill, and then collapsed into bed warmed and exhausted by the food and the wine and the company.

Mike was still thinking about Jill as he put in his earbuds and pulled up Dylan's *New Morning* on his phone. He stepped out the front door and was surprised to see Greg's car still in the driveway. Mike started down the street through the warm, thick air. Summer days in central Illinois often had the feel of the jungle about them. When Mike was a kid, back before his parents split, his dad reserved air conditioning for special occasions, of which there were few. There were suffocating July afternoons when moisture pooled on the kitchen counter. "Humidity," his mother explained when he was just four or five, and for the next several years Mike thought humidity was a spilled drink. And so when he toppled a carton of milk in the cafeteria in second grade, he looked at the lunch lady and said "humidity," rendering her too confused to reprimand him for his carelessness.

Two blocks into his run, Mike was as wet as the Formica tops of his youth. He wasn't sweating as much as divining moisture from the air. Six blocks later his shirt was soaked through and he peeled it off as he turned the corner toward Greg's house. As he approached, Mike saw a cherry-red Dodge Charger parked in the drive and he smiled. He dropped his shirt in front of Greg's mailbox as he ran past, wondering how much of Cameron Maggie had actually seen. Mike loped through Morgan Park and down past where Papa Anthony's used to be, the spot where Mike first heard Bob Dylan. It was on the old Seeburg, where "Tangled Up in Blue" sat at B7. Mike liked to drop his coins in the slot and play the B-side, "If You See Her, Say Hello," a song that had come to remind him of all the years in between losing Jill and finding her again. Now it seemed that every song reminded him of her somehow.

Mike looped around the university and then past Mellow Submarine on his way back home. A few minutes later, he glided past Greg's place, picked up his shirt and launched into his finishing kick.

Just as Mike moved past the red Charger, Greg opened his eyes and saw the person who had driven it into his life. Twenty-four hours earlier, he could not have imagined that he would be waking up with a woman for the first time in ages. There had been a few since Kim, usually someone he picked up at Max's and then pretended not to know weeks later when they passed on the town square or in the grocery store. Really, though, the pretending was polite. The women didn't want to remember him, either.

As he admired the fiery spirals that spread out across his chest, Greg understood that he wouldn't need to pretend with Maggie. He would never randomly pass her on Tyler, Polk, Fillmore or Pierce. And if he did, he wouldn't let her sneak by like a stranger. He would scoop her up and race her back to his bed and hope against hope that she might stay there forever. But he tried not to think about the future. Instead, he lay there quietly, hoping to freeze time. Her left arm was draped across his body and it gently rocked with his breathing. After they left Mike's house Maggie asked if Greg could show her how he made the *merguez*, and so instead of touring Cameron they went back to Mellow Sub and made a small batch of sausage together. Maggie scrubbed in like a surgeon and plunged elbow-deep into a heap of ground lamb and spices. As they lay in the pale morning light, Greg could smell garlic, paprika and coriander rising from her skin. It was the finest fragrance he could imagine.

After a few minutes, Maggie's hand came up to Greg's face and she lifted her head. "Hello, you," she said, and kissed him. "That was a spectacular night."

"Which part?" Greg asked. He knew that it must have sounded needy.

"All of the parts."

"Are you going back to Denver today?"

"Yeah, I really need to."

"Is there any chance that I'm ever going to see you again? Because I would really like that."

Maggie propped herself up on her elbow and leaned over him. "I would like that, too. I need to go home for a while. Watching you in your kitchen last night, seeing you do what you love, I decided that I need to open my own investment business. It might not sound sexy, but it's what I love to do. And maybe instead of helping one super-rich guy get even richer, I can help some ordinary people get ahead."

"Everything you say sounds sexy," Greg said. "That sounded weird, didn't it? I'm trying too hard."

"Relax. You don't have to win me over. Anyway, I was a little afraid to start my own shop because of how poorly most people perceive me, but in business if five percent of the people love you, you can make a killing. I don't want to exploit what happened with Mike and Jenna and me, but I'm not going to run from my name, either. It's the only one I have. If it brings a few people through the door, I'm going to have to be fine with that."

"That's good. That's what you should do."

"Give me a week or so to get the process start-ed and then, if you want, maybe I can come back for a few days."

"That would be good."

"Then let's plan on it." Maggie leaned in and kissed him again.

Greg paused for a moment. "You know I'm stuck here, right?"

"You're not stuck, you're thriving."

"You haven't seen my books."

"Your books don't tell the whole story. But we can talk about all of that later. I need to leave in about an hour. Let's make the most of the time I have left."

Greg's car was still there when Mike left the house. He made the short drive to Mellow Sub, let himself in and started a pot of coffee. Mike had been work-ing for close to an hour when Greg's car pulled up outside the office. When the door swung open, Mike looked up and said "good morning. You're in a little late."

"I had an eventful evening."

"The location of two cars I saw this morning would seem to confirm that."

"I'm smitten. Sue me."

"No, I think it's great. As long as you think it's great."

"I think it's great."

"Are you going to see her again?"

"I think so. I hope so. But I'm way behind on getting ready for the day. I'll fill in the blanks later."

While Greg worked in the kitchen, Mike pecked away at his keyboard. He had piled up a few hundred words when his phone rang and Jill's name popped up.

"I went out for coffee early this morning," she said, "and I saw you running without a shirt. Are you trying to give the local ladies a thrill?"

"I don't know. Do you know anyone who found it thrilling?"

"Maybe. I'm not seeing patients until the afternoon today. Would you have some time for me if I came by for lunch?"

"I would."

"Good. Can we make it a little early, say eleven-thirty?"

"I'll be here with bells on."

"What about your shirt? Will that be on?"

"Maybe."

"Aren't you a tease? I'll see you then."

Mike tried to write for the next hour but he felt distracted as he worked to come up with what to say to Jill while also coming up with what to say about his life. Neither set of words seemed to come out right, so he picked up a book and read for a while instead. It was his third time through Dylan's *Chronicles*. Mike finally surrendered to the realization that his memoir and Bob's memoir wouldn't be much alike.

Right on time, Jill came through the back door and said "is it OK if we eat in here? What do you want?" She came back a few minutes later with a falafel on pita for Mike and a *caprese* for herself.

As Jill sat down, Mike felt strangely nervous. He leaned forward and said "I've been thinking. There's something I want to talk about."

"OK."

"I'm not attracted to single mothers," he said.

Jill sat straight up and narrowed her eyes. "I'm not sure if that makes you refreshingly honest or a complete asshole, though I suppose those aren't mutually exclusive."

"That came out wrong. Let me try again. I am attracted to you. Definitely. And I'm not *not* attracted to single mothers as a rule. It's just that I don't have a single-mother fetish or anything, if that makes any sense."

"Not a bit."

"Did you ever see that movie with Hugh Grant where he crashes a single-parent support group because he thinks he has a better chance with single moms than with childless women? I wouldn't want you to think I'm like that, because I'm not."

"I haven't seen that movie," Jill replied, "and it never occurred to me that being a mom would make me more attractive to you. It would certainly be a first if it did."

"It doesn't make you more attractive to me. It doesn't make you less, either. I'd like you whether or not you had children."

"Well, I don't have children," Jill replied. "I have a child. Not that it would make any difference. I'd be just as attractive if I had ten kids, got it?"

"Completely. I get it completely. I should probably have asked first whether you had seen that movie, and when you said no I could have moved on to the next thing without, you know, doing what I just did."

"The next thing?"

"Yes, the next thing. I don't think you'll be surprised to know that I, uh, have feelings for you. Liv sniffed that out a while back."

"She's a good sniffer. And, no, I'm not surprised."

"OK, good, no surprise. I feel like I'm coming at this awkwardly because it's kind of complicated. Anyway, I would like it if we – I don't even know how to define it – I would like it if we saw each other. Socially. Romantically. Like boy-girl seeing each other."

"Were you under the impression that we weren't seeing each other like boys and girls do?"

"I was under the impression that it was sort of undefined. We said that the reunion was going to be a date but then it ended up not being one."

"I gave you a pretty spectacular kiss at the end of the night. I don't usually do that when I go out with the girls."

"You were sort of drunk, so I wasn't sure."

"I knew what I was doing."

"So, if I wanted to kiss you again some time – that could happen?"

"I think it could." Jill leaned across the desk, put her lips on Mike's and left them there for a good long while.

"Hey, guys –" Greg stepped through the office door, looked up and left with a single, deft pivot.

"Yeah, well, good. I'm glad it's something that could happen some number of times," Mike said and then paused. "Jill, you know I'm not going to be able to stay here, right?"

"We'll see."

"No, really, I'm going to need to get a job, and I have a very specific set of skills."

"Tell me more, Mr. Bond," Jill said in an upper-crust English accent and then kissed him again.

"I'm serious. What I do isn't done here."

"And I said 'we'll see.' We don't have to decide anything right now. Let's just . . . see."

"OK," Mike said. "We'll see."

"But first," Jill said, "I actually invited myself to lunch because there was something that I wanted to tell you."

TWENTY-THREE

Early Spring, 1993

The clock radio announced the arrival of another day, aided by Snow and his faux-reggae hit "Informer," which sat atop the charts. When the song ended, the disc jockey mentioned "President Clinton," which sounded odd to Jill's ears even two months into his first term. The alarm had surprised her. She didn't realize she had fallen asleep. Sometime after four-thirty a.m. she thought she never would.

What should she do? What could she do? The two questions clashed all night like cymbals, dissonant and deafening even as she buried her head beneath one pillow, and then two.

Jill sat on the edge of her bed and confirmed that she was awake, that the should/could problem was not just a product of her dreams. What should she do? What could she do?

She took the oversized t-shirt from the floor and pulled it over her head. She stood up and began to shuffle toward the door. Even in her despair she took small pleasure in the feel of the carpet against her toes. She wished she could shuffle in circles all day long.

Jill walked downstairs and into the kitchen. When she saw her mother pouring a cup of coffee she began to weep softly. Susan Murdock turned around and saw her daughter with hair in her eyes, shoulders slumped, gently heaving.

"Jill, sweetie, what's wrong?"

"Mom." Jill moved her lips but barely made a sound.

"Jill?"

"Mom," she said again, just above a whisper.

Susan watched with a mother's sympathetic eyes and waited.

"I think I'm pregnant."

TWENTY-FOUR

Mike sat slack-jawed behind the desk while Jill explained.

"I didn't have an abortion. I had a procedure."

The look on Mike's face said that he didn't understand.

"Technically, medically, it was an abortion," Jill said. "But it's not what you think of as an abortion. I didn't have a choice. It was an ectopic pregnancy. The egg was fertilized but it implanted in my fallopian tube, not my uterus."

Mike sat quietly, turning the explanation over in his mind.

"Sometimes I forget that not everyone has been to medical school. Do you understand what I'm talking about?"

"I have a basic understanding of the reproductive process. I think."

"An egg that is lodged in the fallopian tube will never grow into a viable baby. But if it's allowed to progress it can kill the mother."

"So you were pregnant with a baby you could never have?"

"Pretty much."

"Why didn't you tell me?"

Jill paused. "You're not going to give me the 'I had a right to know' speech are you?"

"No," Mike said. "I just . . . I don't know."

"I don't know, either, Mike. I told my mom first."

"Why?"

"Because when I didn't know what to do she was right in front of me. And because I was still a girl and she was my mom and I needed her. If Liv is ever in the same kind of trouble I hope she'll do the same thing."

Mike couldn't muster up any indignation and didn't want to.

"I told my mom first thing in the morning. I saw a doctor before lunch. We knew it was ectopic by the afternoon. I had the procedure the next day. It was all over before I had a chance to tell you. And before I could, mom said that I couldn't see you anymore and that telling you would only make things worse for both of us."

"So that's why you broke up with me?"

"Yes. I wish I had a better explanation, but I was scared and confused. I don't even remember the days after that very clearly. It was all so disorienting."

"But –" Mike stopped himself.

"What?"

"Why did you end up with Greg?"

"I don't know. Maybe because I needed someone and I wanted it to be you, but it couldn't be, and he was the closest thing. Somehow it made sense then. And he had just lost his mom. He needed someone. I wanted so much to be with you but you were about to go to Michigan and I was headed to school in Champaign and this thing happened and I was terrified. If we had stayed together I would have told you. And if I had told you I don't know that we could have stayed together. We were too young. I don't think we were equipped for it."

"I thought we were so careful," Mike said.

Jill chuckled. "Remember how all of our friends were so careful when they were new drivers, and how half of them rolled their cars on country roads? That's the kind of careful we were."

"Why are you telling me now?"

"Because when you were gone for so long, it just seemed like something that happened in the past. But since you've been back it has felt like I was keeping it from you. And if something is going to happen between us – if something might happen – I don't want to keep a secret like that. You should know. I'm sorry it took so long to tell you."

As they talked, Mike's phone buzzed on the desk in front of him, announcing the arrival of a text message. He glanced at it and froze. Jill saw the panic in his eyes.

"Who is it from?"

"Jenna."

"What did she say?"

Mike said nothing.

"Can I read it?"

"Would you think I was hiding something if I said no?"

"I don't know. Are you saying no?"

Without a word, Mike handed the phone over.

Jill looked. *I need you to do this show. If you don't I'm going to tell Lacy that you got me drunk and had sex with me when I was 17.*

Jill recoiled and looked at Mike with mile-wide eyes. "This, this . . . isn't true, is it?"

"No."

"Is any part of it true?"

"No."

"Not even the alcohol?"

"No, Jill. Not the alcohol, not the sex. Jesus. Give me just a tiny benefit of the doubt, here. I never spent a minute alone with her back then, for god's sake."

"I'm sorry. You're right. What are you going to do?"

"Establish a record," he said.

Mike typed back. *You know that's not true.* A few seconds later a message bounced back. *So what? Lacy will love it.*

Mike took a screen capture of the conversation and then showed Jill. "Now I just have to make sure I never lose this phone," he said.

TWENTY-FIVE

Mike was running up Van Buren Avenue's long, steep hill, the one the cross country team had named The Bitch back in high school. He didn't tangle with The Bitch often, just when he was feeling particularly agitated. Jenna had made him agitated. The Bitch turned agitation into lactic acid.

A couple of miles in, he tried to force his mind onto something other than the burning in his legs and chest. Something peaceful. He admired the elms that turned the street into a tunnel. They were immense. When he was a kid, they were just trees to him, but now they were landmarks. Nothing about Cameron seemed majestic until he left, but these trees, they were something else. He tried to guess how old they were. He wondered how old elms could get. He guessed these, with their massive trunks, must have been there for more than one-hundred years. He made a mental note to come back some time in the autumn and run along Van Buren when the leaves turned. He couldn't remember their color in the fall, but he assumed they would be spectacular.

He got to the top of the hill and turned left. From there, it was a long, slow descent home. It was unusually cool for a summer morning and as his heart slowed he could feel the air on his face mixing with beads of sweat. It felt like heaven. His agitation evaporated, if only for an instant.

His phone rang. The 212 number that popped up gave him license to be impolite.

"It's six-thirty in the goddamn morning," he said.

"I'm sorry," the voice on the other end said. "It's seven-thirty here. I thought you were on eastern time. Would it be better if I called back later?"

"No."

"Mike, this is Curt Malone. I'm Lacy Nantz's producer. We've talked before."

"Uh-huh."

"Are you OK? You sound like you're out of breath."

"I'm running."

"Oh, OK. Here's the deal. Jenna Kaye came to us and said that you got her drunk and had sex with her when she was seventeen."

Mike stopped cold. "That's bullshit. Do you understand? Bullshit. She tried to threaten me with that the other day but I have a text message from her where she admits it isn't true. I've been pretty polite with you assholes to this point, but if you –"

"Whoa, hold on. I should have started differently. We know it isn't true. The story seemed odd and so we asked her a lot of questions, and she got herself tied up in knots and then admitted it was a lie. So we know. OK? We are not going to air that claim. We would never do that. What I'm trying to

say is that she came to us with that story and we're
trying to turn her in another direction. And I'm
calling to ask for your help. We think it would be
best for everyone, including you. Just between us,
Mike, I think she has a problem. Maybe she started
taking something to help with the anxiety, maybe
it's something else. I really don't know. But we
want to help her. She's getting bad advice. She's
trying to capitalize on her fame without first reha-
bilitating her image. We told her she needs to forget about reality shows and all of that nonsense.
First, she needs to show everyone that she's real,
not just some tabloid character, but a real person
with real problems and real pain."

"What does this have to do with me?"

"We want to do a series, like a documentary,
that takes our show out of the studio and into Jenna's life. Real in-depth stuff. We want to visit her at
home. We want to do a series of interviews with
her over several weeks. We want to talk to her
friends and loved ones on camera. We want to talk
to you. It will be like Barbara Walters. Soft-focus
stuff. Intimate, not exploitative."

"Jenna wants to do this?"

"Actually, she still wants to do that reality
show. But we're working on her."

"I'm sorry, Curt. I can't. I won't."

"Mike, I understand your hesitation. And I want
you to know that, as a reputable news organization,
our network can't pay for your participation. But I
understand from some of our colleagues who visit-

ed there in Cameron that your friend Greg makes excellent sandwiches. We would like to sit down with you in your home for an interview. If you could stop by the shop beforehand and bring us some sandwiches, we would be prepared to provide you a delivery fee."

"A delivery fee?"

"Yeah, something in the range of $30,000 to spare us the inconvenience of going to the shop ourselves."

"Greg's place is barely a mile from my house."

"Our schedules are very tight."

"How do you people live with yourselves?"

"It's not always easy. Think about it. I'll call you later."

"Curt, don't call. I don't want any part of this."

"Just think about it, Mike. Sorry to call so early."

Curt hung up and Mike sprinted home and straight into the shower.

TWENTY-SIX

Greg and Jill hovered over a table near the record bins on Saturday morning while Liv sat nearby eating a sandwich of eggs, prosciutto and provolone with fresh basil on toasted ciabatta.

"How's your breakfast, kiddo?" Greg asked.

Liv, lost in a savory reverie, said nothing.

"You have to stop that," Jill said.

"What?"

"Making her these sandwiches. She'll never eat a McMuffin again."

"That's a bad thing?"

"When I only have five minutes to spare and there's a drive-thru nearby, yeah."

As they sat and sorted through bills and bank statements, some grim realizations rolled over Jill. "We need the students back in town," she said. "There's just not enough traffic without them. I can help float things through August, but if things don't turn around by the end of September . . . ."

"I know," Greg said.

Jill winced. "I don't mean *that.*"

"Yes you do. And if you don't, you're crazy. I would have shut the doors six months ago if not for you. I can't charge college kids enough to cover what it costs to make these sandwiches."

"You know, you could rein it in a little on the ingredients. Maybe be a little less ambitious about the final product."

"The world doesn't suffer from a lack of Subways," Greg said between sips of his fourth cup of coffee. "And I can't beat them at their game anyway."

The partners contemplated their future for a while longer and then Greg said "excuse me, I have to take a piss."

Jill gave Greg a scolding look and nodded toward Liv.

"I'm sorry, Olivia," he said, "I have to go wee-wee."

"I'm not a baby. You have to go pee!"

While Greg was in the bathroom, the shop's telephone rang. Jill answered it. "Yes . . . No . . . Can I take a message?" She began to write on the back of a carry-out menu. "OK . . . OK . . . I don't know for sure, maybe Monday . . . OK . . . You're welcome. Goodbye."

Jill walked back into the office where Mike pecked away at his computer. "Lacy Nantz's producer just called the shop. I told him you weren't here. I didn't know if you would want to talk to him."

"Jesus," he said. "They want to do some special series that includes me sitting down for an interview with Lacy at my house. I told them no, I told them no again, I told them a third time, and then I stopped answering their calls. I'm going to get a new number on Monday."

"He said to tell you that they could increase the delivery fee, whatever that means."

"I'd like to call him back to tell him to shove that goddamn fee up his nose, but he actually seems like a decent guy. He's just doing what Lacy tells him."

"So I take it you don't want this?" Jill asked as she held up the menu.

"No. I have his number," Mike grumbled. "I can call if I want."

Jill folded the paper in half, put it in her pocket and turned to leave.

"Hey," Mike said, "I'm sorry. I don't want it to sound like I'm angry with you. Can I take you and Liv to dinner tonight? We can stop at Lulu's afterward."

Jill smiled. "Sure, that would be nice. Liv has to try on her dress for the wedding at four o'clock. We should be done by five-thirty or so. Can we come pick you up after that?"

"Sure, but why don't I pick you up?"

"Because you don't have a booster seat in your car. There are so many things you eligible bachelors don't know about."

A few hours later, Liv looked at herself in the dress-shop mirror and scrunched up her nose as her mother stood to the side.

"I look stupid," Liv said.

"Oh, sweetie, you look beautiful."

"I don't wanna look beautiful."

"Flower girls are supposed to look beautiful. And you're always beautiful."

"I just want to be the kind of beautiful I am every day. I don't want to be the flower girl kind of beautiful."

"Well, you're going to have to be this kind of beautiful for one day. When the wedding is over, you can go back to being the other kind of beautiful."

Liv plopped down in a chair, put her elbows on her knees and dropped her chin into her hands.

"It fits perfectly," Jill said. "You can change back into your clothes."

Liv started to remove the dress and then stopped and looked at her mother.

"Mommy, how many times has daddy been married?"

"Just once. To me."

"I think he was married another time."

"No, Liv, just once."

"But after I went to bed the other night I came downstairs for a drink of water and I heard him talking to Christina –"

"Were you listening to someone else's private conversation? You know you're not supposed to do that."

"I'm sorry."

Jill paused. "Well, you should probably tell me what they said so I can tell whether you heard something you shouldn't have."

Liv didn't think that was how it was supposed to work but she gave her mom the benefit of the doubt.

"I heard Christina talk to daddy about when he was married to a schwoo."

"A schwoo?"

"No, a sch-woo."

"A *shrew*?"

"Yes, a schwoo."

"She said daddy was married to a shrew?"

"Uh-huh. Is a schwoo a kind of snow creature?"

"What?"

"Christina said daddy was married to an ice-cold schwoo."

Jill bit her lip and closed her eyes. She shoved her hands in her pockets and felt the takeout menu that she had neglected to throw away.

"Mommy, are you OK?"

"I'm fine, sweetie."

"What's an ice-cold schwoo?"

"I think you're a little too young to understand what a shrew is. And I don't think Christina understands, either. But I'll make sure she finds out."

TWENTY-SEVEN

Maggie stayed away for six days during which she felt a metaphysical tugging between time zones. Her professional aspirations pulled towards Denver while her heart and body craved Cameron. So she hurried and did all she needed on the ground in Colorado, finding office space and furniture and a phone system, and then high-tailed it to Illinois, where she continued her preparations remotely after whisking Greg out of Mellow Sub for an afternoon that turned into night and then morning. When he went back in to the shop the next day, she ordered business cards, talked to a lawyer about filing the necessary paperwork, and called up friendly reporters in Denver to drum up some free publicity for Kleinsasser Capital Management, which was due to open after the long holiday weekend.

Maggie insisted on taking the whole gang to dinner someplace good. Greg told her that she would have to settle for something less, and so the two of them met up that night at Charlie's with Mike, Jill and Liv. When they walked in, Stacy the waitress saw Mike and Maggie together and gave him a look that he recognized as *are you shitting me?* He smiled and gave a slight shrug, and Stacy took them to the closest thing Charlie's had to a best table. Mike's sixteen-dollar tip ten days earlier had not been forgotten.

Everyone ordered a hamburger. Everyone always ordered a hamburger at Charlie's ever since they stopped serving breakfast all day. Greg had been in the kitchen before. It wasn't much, but it had a fabulous flat-top grill perfect for putting crispy edges on skinny burgers. The flat-top also toasted buns, charred onions and seared bacon better than any other surface in town. When it was his turn to order, Greg told Stacy to put all of those things together, to make it a double, and to put cheese on top. Liv said that she would have the same, but make it a triple.

Maggie told Mike about her plans to open her own shop, and he gave her every good idea and contact that he could think of. Jill said that Dan's wedding was coming up on Saturday and that she and Liv wanted Greg and Maggie to come. Greg asked Jill if she was sure. Jill said there would be an open bar and a good one, and that she was looking forward to telling Dan that he would need to wedge in a couple of previously uninvited guests. Greg said that he was happy to help. Liv smiled. Her favorite people were coming to the wedding. Maybe it wouldn't be so bad after all.

The next morning, Greg went to work and Maggie took a break from her business and went shopping. She bought curtains, throw pillows, a new comforter, candles, soaps, towels, three lamps, a beard trimmer, face and body lotion designed for

men, and a coffee table book of vintage jazz photos.
She tidied up Greg's place and gave it a mini-
makeover. She hung a black and white picture of
Miles Davis that she had picked up in Denver.
When Greg opened the door that night, his jaw
dropped and his eyes welled. "I'm not much for
traditional gender roles," Maggie said, "but I
thought the place could use a woman's touch." A
woman's touch was all that Greg had wanted for
the longest time.

They stayed in for dinner. Greg put vintage
rhythm and blues on while he cooked. Maggie
helped a little, but mostly she watched as he metic-
ulously constructed a roux out of butter and flour
and the deft touch of a wooden spoon. He added
garlic, onions, bell peppers and celery, stirring
them gently but diligently until they became soft
and translucent. He added tomatoes, salt, cayenne
pepper, white pepper, oregano and a bay leaf. He
gave it all a stir and then added chicken stock,
brought it to a boil, lowered it to a simmer and put
a lid on it. He started a pot of white rice on the
stove and then went to the refrigerator to retrieve
the shrimp he had just bought, the freshest he
could get a thousand miles from the nearest ocean.
He sharpened a small knife and deveined them, his
thick fingers dancing more gracefully than Maggie
could have imagined. He tossed the shrimp into
the pot and gave it all a thorough stir. He grabbed
two bottles of Abita from the fridge, popped the
tops and handed one to Maggie. They clinked the

bottles together and Greg took a forceful swig. He chopped fresh parsley, tossed it in the pot, put fluffy rice into two large bowls, topped the rice with shrimp étoufée, and took the bowls to the table.

Maggie took a bite and closed her eyes. She tasted the pepper, she tasted the shrimp, she tasted the tomatoes. But mostly she tasted depth. A depth of flavor, a depth of character. She resisted the urge to shovel it into her mouth one forkful after another. She slowed her eating, her breathing, her thinking. She focused on each bite and on the man at the table. When the last bit was gone, she took a piece of bread, wiped the bowl clean and ate it. Then she leaned across the table and kissed Greg hard on the mouth. She stood him up and walked him to the bedroom. She threw the new comforter on the floor. The dishes could wait until morning.

Greg rose early and slipped quietly into the bathroom. He started with scissors then switched to his new electric trimmer and finished with the first new razor he had bought in years. He laughed at those five-blade contraptions in the pharmacy section, seeing them as some sort of commentary on American excess. He imagined a guy rolling down the highway in his Hummer, covered in shaving cream, a half-pound bacon chili cheeseburger in one hand, a five-blade razor in the other. Greg instead opted for just three blades. They did the trick just fine.

He could barely believe how silky and supple his skin felt. It was as smooth as Maggie's ass, but softer, as if years of woolly encasement had tenderized it with some sort of follicular enzymes. He caressed his face with his fingertips and then smeared lotion over the places his beard had been. It felt luxuriant and nearly erotic, as if he were touching someone else.

The mirror brought him less pleasure. He knew what to expect but the reflection still startled him. The old man stared back at him. The only difference was the eyes. Jerry's reflected rage. Greg's only betrayed fear.

He walked into the bedroom. The daybreak sun had just begun to creep over the horizon. It lifted the darkness and cast the space in hues of gray. Maggie laid face-down on the bed, uncovered and still asleep. Greg admired her back. It was toned through the shoulders and it narrowed at the waist. To the outside world Maggie seemed hard and jagged, but in Cameron she was a series of gentle curves and pleasing intersections. He sat down beside her and put his hand on her hair which shone wild and red against the room's colorless terrain.

"Hey, you," she said and smiled before fully opening her eyes. Then she looked at him and put her hand to her mouth. "Oh my god. Wow."

"I wanted you to see who I am," Greg said.

"I know who you are."

"Really, you don't."

"Greg, babe, the beard doesn't make any difference. But you are certainly handsome without it. Let me look at you."

Maggie sat up and grabbed Greg's shirt from the night before. She slid her arms into the sleeves and began to button the front from the bottom up. Greg watched her skin disappear bit by bit. A woman in a man's shirt. That did things to him. He loved a woman who could moonlight as a man, one who could sip whiskey or smoke a cigar. He thought it might be a little homoerotic or narcissistic, some sort of Freudian or Jungian lust for one's own self. Who knows? But that shirt. Jesus. The way it framed her firm and tapered legs. The way it clung to her breast. Pure ecstasy. He stretched out on the bed and ran a fingertip along the outside of her thigh. It had been a long time. He had worried that he would fall in love with the next woman he slept with, afraid that it would be too much, that it would be too good, that he would try to hold on for fear that it might never happen again. Right then, Greg was in love with Maggie Kleinsasser. Maybe it wasn't real love, but it felt more genuine than anything he had experienced before. Greg had wanted to believe that he was in love with Kim but something deep down tugged at him and told him he was not. There was no tugging with Maggie. He wanted to get down on one knee, on both knees, and not just propose, but proclaim his love. He wanted to wrap his arms around her waist and lay his head on her chest and hold her, claim her, keep her. He kissed her knee.

"You're too good for me," he said.

"I'm not nearly good enough." She ran her hand over the smoothness of his face.

Maggie looked at Greg and he looked back. They stared silently for a long while.

"I need to tell you something that no one else knows," Greg said, "but I'm afraid."

"What are you afraid of?"

"I'm afraid that you'll never want to see me again."

"Greg, babe, that could never happen."

"Oh, Maggie, you have no idea."

TWENTY-EIGHT

Early summer, 2007

Greg never enjoyed solitude or silence until he lost control over the people he saw and the sounds he heard. The baby crying, Kim harping, burned-out grad students from the philosophy department asking him to spin old King Crimson records. God, he hated all of that prog-rock bullshit. Greg would have preferred to play field recordings of jackhammers busting up concrete, even if it cleared out the shop. Somedays, especially if it cleared out the shop.

His favorite place lately was the spot he called his den, but it was just a quiet corner of the unfinished basement. He brought recent vinyl acquisitions here. There was never time to sort them and clean them at the shop, so he came down here with his brushes and disc-washing fluid and buffed them until they looked like pools of oil. Sometimes he'd play them quietly to evaluate his work, but mostly he played them to keep the silence from consuming him. Today a near-mint copy of *Al Green's Greatest Hits* did the trick.

The shop had been open for a couple of years, but Greg was still surprised by the inventory he'd amassed and by how terrible most of it was. He had become the patron saint of forlorn records, unwilling to let them be discarded or destroyed, or, god forbid, heated until softened and shaped into craft-project bowls. He once saw a perfectly good copy of *Led Zeppelin* IV that met such a fate, and he knocked it off a thrift-store table and watched it explode into shards, freeing its soul.

Greg had been down in the den for an hour or so on this Saturday afternoon when Tori's number lit up his phone. "I shaved it smooth the way you like," she said. "Come fuck me now."

That kind of talk sent him into ecstasy, as good as the act itself. Kim never talked like that, never even uttered a dirty word in bed. Things got tedious after they had a baby but they weren't all that exciting before. During the eighteen months in which they tried to conceive, Greg came to understand the brutal difference between recreational sex and procreational sex. The latter was a job, much drearier than he had imagined, and it wasn't much different from the post-partum maintenance sex that followed. He had expected that having a child would change some things in some ways, but he came to see it as the meridian between two distinct parts of his life: everything that came before and everything that came after.

Greg bounded up the stairs, unhindered by a full-on erection, and shouted "I have to run over to the shop" as he moved from the kitchen to the garage. He was already in reverse before Kim called out "wait, where's Luke?"

TWENTY-NINE

The telephone conversation unfolded just as unpleasantly as Jill had imagined.

"Why do you want to come to my wedding, anyway?" Dan asked.

"I don't. Neither does your flower girl, not unless I'm there. And she wants Greg to come, too. And really, if I'm going to sit through your wedding, I'd like to be joined by some others who don't want to be there, either, so we can all not want to be there together."

"I can't believe you're springing this on me just a few days before the wedding. Christina isn't going to like it."

Jill wondered if Dan could hear her smile through the telephone.

"Christina isn't going to notice," Jill said. "As hard as this may be to believe, I'm trying to help you here. You want Liv to be there. Liv says she won't go unless we go."

"I'm not sure why Liv gets a choice."

"You're right, Dan. We could force her to go without us. And she can be angry and pouty, a stubborn seven-year-old, and you can spend your time trying to control her so she won't misbehave and ruin Christina's special day. Or you could stick four of us in a corner and let me handle Liv."

"Four of you? You and Greg and who else?"

"Our plus-ones."

"You're going to bring a date to my wedding?"

"You brought a date to our marriage."

Dan said nothing. He had never found a way to trump the infidelity card.

"You're getting married to the woman you left me for. I'm offering to come to the wedding so that you can have a nice ceremony and so that your daughter can be happy on a day that's going to shake up her world. And so when I say that I'd be glad to attend with three others, your response shouldn't be to ask why. It should be to say thank you."

Dan, defeated, said "thank you."

Jill and Liv drove to Champaign on Friday afternoon so that Liv could attend the rehearsal. It was an easy trek up I-57, just over an hour. Liv sat in the back in her booster seat on the passenger side so Jill could see her in the rearview mirror. This was how they talked in the car, Jill flicking her eyes toward the mirror every few seconds to get a glimpse of her girl. But as they began the drive, Jill could only look. She could not talk because she could not shake the sense that she was making a delivery. She was a birth mother shuttling her baby to her new family. She knew it wasn't really true. But she also knew that the floor of the Sears Tower observation deck wouldn't fall beneath her feet when she visited as a child, and that didn't make the experience less frightening.

Still, the drive helped to ease her mind. Jill found the central Illinois landscape to be beautiful in a way that she could never adequately explain to someone who saw only hundreds of miles of sameness – nothing but sparsely-traversed highways cutting across agricultural parcels divided with geometric precision. Each acre of corn and soybeans seemed to the eye not only to be square, but to be impeccably square, the length and width perfectly even, down to the millimeter. And the terrain seemed not only to be flat, but to be impossibly flat, as if a carpenter could drop his level at any spot and always find the bubble perfectly centered. A person raised amidst the flash of Vegas or the majesty of the mountains or the caverns of New York might see only the sameness and the squareness and the flatness, and miss the nuances that Jill had grown to cherish. She thought of the Illinois horizon like a painting in a museum, one that reveals new secrets with each subtle shift of light. It reminded her of a Rembrandt that she saw twice in one week at the Art Institute of Chicago, once in the morning and once at night. The brushstrokes were the same, but different light revealed new movement and changed the story within the frame in a way that might be imperceptible to one whose senses had been dulled by neon signs and honking horns. Jill saw in that painting what she saw in the scenery around her hometown – the way that blades of grass shifted with the wind, the way that the sun turned corn tassels into fountains of gold, the way that shadows of trees in the dwindling daylight projected a perspective that was absent at high noon.

Her appreciation of the landscape extended even beneath her feet. Growing up, Jill thought that dirt was just dirt, but as she got older and traveled a bit, she came to understand that Illinois dirt was *soil*, as dark as coffee grounds and rich with nutrients that made it the finest farmland known to man. California had its gold and Texas had its oil, but central Illinois had the best goddamn dirt in the world, and what could be more important than that? If another economic depression ever hit, people might sell their cars and jewelry to buy food, but never the other way around. There was no glamor to it, but the Illinois dirt made her proud.

In the space between Cameron and Champaign, she began to see her hometown as an island and the vast prairie as an ocean of paved roads and corn stalks and black soil. You could go miles without seeing land in any direction, but then you might spot a grain elevator or a church spire in the distance and know that you could swim to shore if necessary. The tractor-trailers whizzing by on the left were massive cargo ships, and the Amish man and his horse-drawn buggy tooling along to the right were what passed for aquatic life.

Jill's grandmother had once showed her an old overlay that her family used in the Fifties to give some color to their black and white television. It was blue on top, green on the bottom and transparent in the middle, and Jill wondered if it made Lucy and Ricky appear to live outdoors. A sunny central Illinois day reminded her of that overlay – blue on top, clear in the middle and green at the bottom. But the green of an Illinois summer was its own peculiar hue, not like the brilliant jade or emerald that television manufacturers boasted to entice customers. Instead, it was something more sun-washed and diffused, like the fading colors in an old photo album. Jill loved few things more than the hazy, dissipating green of an Illinois summer day.

To break the silence in the car, she started a game of radio roulette with Liv. Liv loved pop music. Jill thought that was one of the reasons that Liv shared a bond with Greg. Liv believed the Seeburg to be the most precious historical relic she had ever seen. Before she first encountered it, she thought that music happened magically. You pressed a button and there it was. But when Greg showed her the insides of the Seeburg and explained how the needle rode the grooves and released the sound, Liv saw music as a machine. It was a series of moving parts that produced a product. She saw the Seeburg as an antique music factory. To perceive it through Liv's eyes made Jill flash on the old-time drawings of flying machines she remembered as a kid, those enchanting reminders of a time when soaring through the sky was a barely-realized dream made true by human ingenuity and hard work. The Seeburg made Liv see music as a tangible thing made by human hands, something a worker could hold up at the end of the day and be proud of.

Jill bounced back and forth between stations that played tunes scientifically formulated to lodge in the frontal lobes of small children. She hopped from Katy to Bruno to Pink to Rihanna. Liv could not be stumped. She belted every word to every song like some private backseat audition for *American Idol*, lisping along loudly through the space where permanent teeth would soon descend. Watching Liv sing was one of Jill's greatest joys, but her mind still wandered to weird places. She wanted Liv to be happy when she visited her dad and his new wife, but she desperately hoped that Christina wouldn't turn on the radio. Feed her, bathe her, brush her hair, but please, please, please, do not sing with her.

As they neared Champaign, Liv said she was tired of the radio game, so Jill turned the music down and explained to Liv the details for the weekend. They would check in at the hotel and then Jill would take Liv to Grandma and Grandpa Emory, who were staying in a room two floors below. Whatever bitterness Jill felt toward Dan never carried over to his parents. They had always been generous, gracious and loving to both Jill and Liv, and had privately expressed their dismay over their son's choices. Liv's grandparents would take her to

242

the wedding rehearsal and the rehearsal dinner and then deliver her back to Jill sometime after ten p.m. The next morning, Jill and Liv would sleep late and then swim at the hotel pool. After lunch, Jill would take Liv to the church, get her dressed and then turn her over to her grandmother. Jill reassured Liv that she would be nearby, that she could be there in just a few seconds if Liv needed her, but that she probably shouldn't be backstage as Christina prepared for her wedding. Liv didn't understand all of the grown-up dynamics swirling around her, but she intuitively grasped why her mom wouldn't be helping her soon-to-be stepmother with her garters. Jill said that she would be at the wedding and the reception and that Liv shouldn't worry about anything. And then, at the end of the day, as a special treat, Liv would spend the night with her grandparents, whom she loved very much, and the next morning they would take her to brunch with the bride and groom before the couple departed for their honeymoon.

"Will I ever be a flower girl again?" Liv asked.

"I don't know. I can't think of anyone we know who might get married while you're still young enough."

"What about you?"

"What about me?"

"You could get married. To Mr. Mike."

"Sweetie, I don't know. I don't think so. You shouldn't plan on that."

"But it could happen. You really should marry Mr. Mike. I like him."

"I like him, too. But things are kind of complicated. And I don't even know if I would want to marry him. I don't know if he would want to marry me."

"He does. You do, too."

Jill smiled. "How do you know?"

"Just do."

"That's called a tautology. That's a fancy word you can use on your teachers."

"What's a tallalogy?"

"*Tautology*. It's when you say that something is true because it's true."

"OK, if there's a tautology and you marry Mr. Mike, will I be a flower girl?"

"No."

"Why not?"

"Because you, Miss Olivia, would be my maid of honor."

Later, after she turned Liv over to her grandparents, Jill went out and bought a bottle of wine and a corkscrew. She then retired to her room where she drew a bath, read a book and tried not to think.

Mike, Greg and Maggie arrived at the church twenty minutes before the ceremony began, and they turned heads from the parking lot through the entryway. It took folks some time to recognize Greg without his beard, but once they did, the whispers spread rapidly. People did not gawk but they did watch, subtly, like a teenage boy peering down a blouse.

"People are looking at us," Greg said.

"No, babe, they're looking at *me!*" Maggie said as she tossed her head back and chuckled, leaving no doubt among onlookers that it really was them.

Mike wore a light gray two-button ensemble with a white shirt and a yellow tie. His hair, which he had allowed to grow a little while in Cameron, was casually swept back. He looked like summer in a suit. Greg sported a blue jacket, and the blue checked shirt and red and gold repp tie that Maggie bought him made him look like quite the dandy. She chose the tie, no doubt, to complement the red and gold gown that made clear that a formidable woman lay underneath.

Mike had texted Jill when they arrived, and she met them at the doors. She was trim and pretty in a navy sheath and heels. Her hair was pulled back casually in a way that was neat and effortless. She wore earrings but no necklace, and the lack of decoration highlighted the graceful stem of her neck.

Mike reached his hand to the small of her back and kissed her on the cheek. "You look beautiful," he said.

They stepped toward the sanctuary, where they were greeted by an usher.

"Bride's side or groom's side?" he asked.

"I'm not on either side," Jill said.

"Excuse me?" the usher replied.

"Groom's side," Mike said, "but toward the back. We're the black sheep."

The usher seated them in the last row, which allowed most guests to walk past without noticing them. Over the next several minutes the church filled as a string quartet played quietly. Jill surveyed the room which overflowed with flowers in arrangements that seemed extravagant but not grotesque. A tapestry of white orchids and hydrangea allowed pink roses to pop dramatically. Columns stood wrapped in silver ribbon. The church seemed older than it could possibly be. White marble and grand arches framed elaborate stained glass windows. Hats off to Christina, Jill thought. She got it all.

The quartet began to play the processional as Dan and three groomsmen moved to their places at the front of the church. Black tuxes, black ties, black hearts, Jill thought. Actually, three of the four were decent fellows, and the realization that they were the same guys in the same order from her wedding prompted a smile. Apparently only one thing in Dan's life had changed.

Though she was at the back of the church, Jill could see Dan clearly. He made for one handsome son of a bitch, she confessed to herself. Now that she didn't see him every day, she better noticed how he was changing. His face seemed leaner and harder. Traces of gray flecked his hair. Though a little older, he appeared more muscular and fit.

That was Christina's, influence, no doubt. Probably some boot-camp training and a little co-ed naked wrestling, the kind you could do without a child in the house every night.

As he stood there, Jill felt something for him. She knew it wasn't love. It was more like love's sludgy residue. The sight of him moved her because she had once loved him. But it moved her in a way that made her think less of herself and of him. It made her think less of the idea of love at all, that it could somehow lead to this.

Before Jill could ponder the idea further, Liv began down the aisle, scattering pink petals as she walked. "She's so beautiful!" Maggie gasped. Jill admired her daughter for a moment. With dark hair, dark eyes and pale skin, she radiated in a pearlescent blue dress and floral tiara. Liv looked over and saw her mom. Jill smiled and scrunched her nose, and Liv pursed her lips to suppress a big, nervous smile. Whatever the residue of love made Jill feel, she knew it wasn't hate, because at least Dan had given her this precious little girl.

Behind Liv, three statuesque bridesmaids glided down the aisle in icy blue dresses. Jill tried to recall the names of Barbie's friends. She remembered Christie and Skipper, and thought maybe there was a Taylor, too. Whatever their names, they shared the same proportional dimensions as Christina's attendants. Jill wondered what the groomsmen's wives were feeling at that moment.

When the maid of honor had taken her place, the guests stood and turned to watch as Christina and her father began their walk toward the altar. Christina's chestnut hair was piled high, and her dress's open back and floor-to-hip slit revealed a spectacular terrain of toned, tanned skin.

"*Holy shit*," Greg said, and when several sets of eyes turned in his direction he realized that he had uttered the words out loud and not in his head as intended.

After the ceremony, Liv piled into a limo with other members of the wedding party and headed back to the hotel for the reception. Greg and Maggie followed in Mike's car and Mike rode with Jill.

Inside the car, Jill said "Greg seemed impressed with the bride. What about you?"

"She's a pretty woman."

"You think so?"

"The sky is blue. The sun is hot. Some things are self-evident. But that doesn't make her special. When I lived in New York, I saw ten prettier women on every block, but none who were trying that hard."

"She's going to give Liv a baby sister or brother sometime soon."

"Probably. Are you OK with that?"

"What choice do I have?"

Mike didn't know how to answer, so he didn't say anything.

The hotel ballroom matched the church. White and pink flowers, silver ribbons, grand arches. Some sort of neo-soul-jazz combo played in the corner. The band had a drummer, a bass player, a guy who played piano and electric keyboards, a trumpeter, and a slick, gray-bearded cat who moved effortlessly between alto and tenor sax. They also featured a singer who had been smoothly poured into a black velvet dress with white trim across the bust line. She looked like a pint of Guinness to Greg. The band played "The Girl from Ipanema" as Jill and the other interlopers made way to their assigned table in the far corner.

"A four-top at a wedding," Greg said. "You don't see that very often." He scanned the room and saw that all of the other tables were set for ten guests.

"We're being quarantined," Maggie said.

"I told Dan to stick us in a corner. He seems to have taken me literally," Jill said.

"At least we didn't get stuck with one of those big centerpieces that we would have to look around all night just to talk to each other." Mike was right. There was no centerpiece, just four sets of china, four sets of silver, four water glasses and a basket of bread.

The bar stood on the far side of the room, presumably to funnel guests away from Liv's support group. "Ladies, what can we get you to drink?" Greg asked.

"White wine," Jill said. "Sauvignon blanc if they have it. If not, chardonnay is fine."

"Order for me, babe," Maggie said. "You know how I like that."

As Greg and Mike snaked across the room, the guests became less discreet than before. Heads turned. People looked. Some gently patted them on the back as if trying to politely sneak past them, when they were really trying to touch fame for a moment. Phones came out of pockets. Pictures were snapped. One woman in her twenties said to Mike "I was on your side the whole way." A young guy said to Greg "how's the *au pair* business?" A young woman said "I miss the beard."

When they reached their destination, Greg surveyed the bottles and said to Mike "this is a top-shelf bar." One bartender, an elegant older man who looked like he had been plucked from Toots Shor's in the 1950s, asked Greg how he could help him.

"A sauvignon blanc, a Negroni and a Johnnie Walker Black on the rocks," Greg said. "Mike, what about you?"

"Another Johnnie Walker would be great, thanks."

The bartender produced a generous pour of the wine and filled two squared whisky glasses with ice and Scotch. Then he grabbed an Old Fashioned glass and a jigger and constructed Maggie's drink from memory, one part each of gin, Campari and vermouth over ice. He finished it by skimming a sliver of peel from an orange and expressing the oil over the cocktail before garnishing it with the twisted rind.

"It was a pleasure to watch you work, sir," Greg said as he slid a ten-dollar tip across the bar.

Mike and Greg worked their way back to the corner and set the drinks on the table. Maggie took a sip and said to Greg "*Negroni*. How do you know me so well?"

As the band played, the wait staff brought out salads and then wine and then a main course of petite filet, asparagus and roasted potatoes.

"I've worked in banquet catering," Greg said, "and it's hard to cook well for 400 people. This is excellent."

"I don't even remember the food at my wedding," Jill said. "I was too wound up and Dan was trying to finger-bang me under the table."

"That's why they drape the head table all the way to the floor," Greg said.

Up front the newlyweds looked blissful but mismatched. Christina appeared giddy, almost manic, as she chatted and snapped selfies with her bridesmaids and other friends. Dan seemed pleased but composed. He was a professional. He had been there before.

After the toasts and the cutting of the cake, Dan and Christina danced together for the first time since their vows. The singer in the black velvet dress gave a lovely reading of "The First Time Ever I Saw Your Face."

Jill leaned over and whispered to Mike. "Pretty sure that was at the gym right after the first time ever he ogled her ass."

The band then moved into "Isn't She Lovely," and Dan took Liv by the hand and walked her onto the dance floor as the room let out an "*awww*." The man and his little girl began to dance, and Liv began to smile, and polite applause came up around the room. Then Christina joined them and the new family held hands in a circle and gently swayed.

Jill was glad to be in the corner, removed from sight. She said "excuse me" quietly and to no one in particular, and stood up and left the ballroom through the large double doors at the back. As she hurried down a corridor with no destination in mind, she passed a man in his early thirties who was dressed too casually to be a wedding guest or staff member. As Jill walked away, the man walked toward the ballroom and entered through the same doors. He scanned the room for a moment and then walked toward the table in corner. Mike looked up and made eye contact with him. The man said "Mike McAfee?" and Mike said "yeah," and the man nodded, gave Mike a thumbs-up and walked away and back out the double doors.

Mike said "that was weird."

"What was weird?" Greg asked. He hadn't seen the man.

"That guy. It was probably just a hotel guest who heard that we were here."

As the band kept playing and the wedding party joined in the dancing, the double doors swung open again and the man came back into the ballroom with a professional-grade video camera on his shoulder. Mike thought he was the wedding videographer until he saw Lacy Nantz and Jenna Kaye march in behind him.

The camera's bright light seized the attention of the assembled guests, and a murmur washed across the room as everyone realized who the party crashers were. Mike stood up and grabbed Greg and Maggie by their arms. "You two. Get out of here. *Now!*"

They scurried in separate directions as the eyes in the room followed the light, which moved directly toward Mike. He looked straight at Lacy, who gave him a wink. Jenna stood ramrod-straight, chin aloft.

Most of the guests had risen to their feet, making a crowded room seem full beyond capacity. Mike stood with his back to the corner and realized that he had nowhere to go. He scanned the room for exits. Thirty feet down the wall to his right was a service door. He turned slightly so that the door was behind him.

Mike stood his ground and drew the advancing trio to him. He slid to his left until his shoulder touched the wall. Lacy, Jenna and the cameraman stood just in front of him. The intensity of the light made Mike seem to glow hot and white, and it drove the people behind him out of the glare and toward their tables, opening a path to the service door. Mike glanced over his shoulder and saw two waiters wheel a cart full of champagne bottles through the door and then stop, frozen by the light, blocking the exit.

Lacy stepped in close so the camera could get her in the shot. "Mike McAfee, we heard that you were here and that you might *finally* be willing to talk to us. It's time for you and Jenna to confront your past."

The guests stood stone-still and silent, and the band stopped playing. Mike looked to his right and saw a red-faced Dan Emory walking in his direction.

"You're wrong about me wanting to talk, and you're disrupting this couple's wedding. You should leave."

Greg, who had stepped outside and run all the way around the building, ducked back inside through a door on the far side of the room, just behind the band. He saw dozens of gawkers holding their phones high and pointing them at Mike, who was trapped in the corner.

"Mike, we're trying to tell Jenna Kaye's important and compelling story, and you're not cooperating. People *need to know*."

Across the room, Greg reached into his pocket, whispered in the gray-bearded saxophonist's ear, and slipped him fifty dollars.

Mike looked at the woman he once loved. "Jenna, please. Tell her to stop and let's go outside."

While he waited for Jenna to say something – anything – the band lurched into a funky groove, and Greg snatched the microphone from the Guinness lady.

"Helllllooo, every*body*! Welcome back to Dan and Christina's wedding!" Heads swiveled to see Greg, alone on the dance floor, bouncing to the beat. "Are all you funky mothers having a good time?" When no one reacted, Greg tried again. "I said are all you funky mothers having a good time? If you're having a good time, I want you to say *Yeah!*" About half the room awkwardly replied "yeah." "If you're having a *really* good time, say *Hell Yeah!*" A more enthusiastic "hell yeah" arose, mostly from Christina's younger friends. "Now," Greg said, "everybody clap your hands and sing along with me! You know the words! This one goes out to the bride because everybody knows that she's a *brick . . . house!*"

Phones that had been pointed at Lacy and Mike turned to Greg as dozens spilled onto the dance floor to, as Greg demanded, "get down with funkiest cat in town!"

As the dance party sprang back to life, Mike looked at Lacy. "You want to talk? Follow me, now."

He turned, headed toward the service door, and shoved the champagne cart out of the way. He led Lacy, Jenna and the cameraman through the door, across the liquor pantry, and out an exterior door to the parking lot. He kicked the doorstop down, leaving the door open just enough to allow them to hear Greg implore the guests to shake their bodies down to the ground.

There, in the twilight, on the asphalt, Lacy stood in front of Mike with the camera just behind her, and Jenna behind it.

"Mike, Jenna Kaye has been through a trying ordeal, and so has the nation that has followed her harrowing story. It's important for her to confront her past, and it's also important for us to document it so that Jenna and everyone in the country can move on with their lives. We – *all of us* – need to hear from you."

"Ms. Nantz –"

"Call me Lacy."

"Ms. Nantz, no one needs to hear from me because I have nothing to say. I've already moved on. And I'm pretty sure that the country has moved on, too. The only ones who haven't moved on are you and Jenna." He stopped and looked at his ex-fiancée. "Jenna, please, move on. I don't want any part of this. I don't want to know you anymore. My part of this story is over."

Jenna said nothing. She began to cry and then ran away across the parking lot.

Mike looked at Lacy but said nothing. He just turned, kicked up the doorstop and heard the lock click behind him as he walked back into the hotel.

Inside the ballroom, Greg surrendered the microphone and the woman in black velvet sang "Smooth Operator" as someone hand-delivered Christina a Xanax. While Greg was dancing with the bridesmaids, Maggie was in the restroom where she had retreated after peering through the double doors during Greg's performance. She dried her hands and was touching up her lipstick when the door opened and Jenna Kaye walked in looking for someplace quiet to compose herself. Their eyes locked.

"Just the two of us alone in a bathroom with no TV cameras," Maggie said. "Lacy would try to put this on pay-per-view if she knew."

"I bet you'd like to cash that check. I heard *The Inquisitor* didn't pay much."

Maggie looked Jenna over slowly. "I bet you never had an in-between phase," she said.

"What?"

"You know, some girls are adorable babies and then cute kids, and then puberty comes and their teeth go in crazy directions and their elbows and knees turn bony and gangly and make them look like marionettes. But not human marionettes, more like ostriches, like human-ostrich hybrids bouncing on strings. Then after a little physical development and some orthodontics they go from gawky and awkward to graceful and lovely. One day you look at them and they're swans. I bet that never happened to you. I bet you were born a swan."

"I suppose I was."

"Not me," Maggie said. "I was an ostrich until I was thirty-six years old. And then there was this moment when I was like Godzilla unleashed from the bottom of the ocean. I stuck my head above water, found land and owned it. A million heads turned my way. At first they were terrified and then they couldn't stop looking because I wasn't what they expected. I was fierce and beautiful. I'm the first and last of the fire-breathing, pre-historic swans. I could crush a city in stiletto heels and look fabulous while doing it."

"I should probably find a different restroom. Goodbye, Maggie."

As Jenna turned away, Maggie said "I hope something works out for you, Jenna. Everyone should get a second chance."

Jenna said nothing as she walked out.

When the door closed, a toilet flushed and Jill stepped out of a stall.

"You're something else, Maggie Kleinsasser," she said. "I'm glad that we're friends."

A couple of hours later, Mike and Jill sat alone in a dark corner of the hotel bar dissecting the day's events. He sipped a beer while she drank water with lemon. After Dan's parents and Liv retired to their room for the night, Jill had sought out Dan and Christina to congratulate them. Christina seemed surprisingly tranquil, Jill said, and Dan actually laughed. He thought, at the very least, that they would have a good story to tell. He also said that Greg was still a complete fuckup, but a good-hearted one. His singing had been Liv's favorite part of the day.

"You know the weird thing?" Mike said. "I feel better right now than I have since this whole thing began. I told Jenna and Lacy and, I guess, all of America that it's over. That's the end of the story. I'm going to send my advance back to the publisher. I'm not writing the book. I feel oddly at peace."

"Me, too. I was dreading this day. I thought I was dreading it for Liv but I was probably just dreading it for me. And now that it's over, it seems like no big deal. He's married. So what? It didn't make things any worse. Life goes on."

Mike started to speak, but stopped. He had a confused look about him.

"What?" Jill said.

"There's one thing I still don't understand. How did Lacy and Jenna know I was going to be here?"

"Hmm," Jill said. "Who knows?"

Mike finished his drink and paid the bill. "Walk me up to my room," Jill said.

As they rode the elevator up, Jill put her head on Mike's shoulder. "Thanks for coming," she said. "It meant a lot to me." When the doors opened, they stepped off and walked to Jill's door. "I have half a bottle of wine," Jill said. "Why don't you come inside?"

"I wish I could, but I need to get going."

"No you don't."

"The rest of us didn't make reservations. I need to drive Greg and Maggie back to Cameron."

Jill smiled. "I grabbed your keys out of your jacket pocket and gave them to Greg. They're already gone."

"But –"

"Remember after the reunion, when I said something about us being fragile and me being drunk and having trouble keeping my panties on?"

"Yes."

"Well, I'm glad that we're both feeling stronger now because I'm stone-cold sober and I'm not wearing underwear."

THIRTY

When Greg's eyes popped open from a deep and satisfying sleep on Sunday morning, it took him a moment to process that the previous evening had really happened. He turned his head and saw Maggie sleeping. He touched her to confirm that she was real. Then he grabbed his phone from the night table and began to scroll through Twitter and Facebook and his news and entertainment bookmarks for further confirmation that events had played out as he recalled. Alongside an update on Nelson Mandela's health, one of the network news sites ran the headline "Beardless Glanville 'Greg' Allen Lets It All Hang Out," complete with video shot from various angles by six different wedding guests. There was barely a mention of Mike or Jenna or Lacy.

Greg took the day off. Alyssa wasn't available to work, so he turned the shop over to some new kids whose names he couldn't remember. There was only so much they could screw up on a Sunday in the summer. Maggie had one day before she had to go back to Denver. He wasn't going to waste that day inside Mellow Submarine.

Greg showed Maggie what little of Cameron she had not yet seen. He showed her where Papa Anthony's had been and he told her about his long-term relationship with the Seeburg. He said that putting it inside the old Gould Records space now seemed like some futile effort to save two landmarks of his youth. He took her past the Holiday Inn sign at the city limits and showed her the Wild Prairie Outback. He explained that the little clearing in the woods was where generations of horny kids had climbed into backseats. She suggested that they do the same. He didn't resist. Late that night, they went into the shop, made *merguez* from scratch and grilled it on the spot. Maggie enjoyed the final dinner of her central Illinois summer in the kitchen at Mellow Sub. They went back to Greg's house and enjoyed being together for one last night, at least for a while, and maybe, Greg feared, forever.

Maggie woke up before sunrise. She picked up her phone and went to her Twitter page. She didn't post a message or read any of the replies from her army of trolls. She just calmly deleted her account and then deleted the app. Maggie's flight was due to leave St. Louis just after ten o'clock, so Greg helped her pack up her rental car at six a.m. As they stood by the driver's side door, Greg said "what I told you the other night –"

"It doesn't change anything."

"But –"

"Greg, listen. It doesn't change anything. We'll make this work somehow. I'll be back as soon as I can."

The way she cried when she kissed him one last time made him believe her.

Greg stepped back into the house, where Maggie's absence seemed magnified by the traces she left behind. The drapes, the better grade of toilet paper, the scented candles. A few weeks earlier he didn't know what sandalwood was, but now it resonated more strongly than her perfume on his pillow. The candles didn't just remind him of Maggie being in his bed. They reminded him of Maggie being in his home. Everything in the house shouted that she was gone.

Greg had to get out, so he hopped on the Sting-Ray and headed for the shop. When he arrived at the back of the building he saw his father slumped in front of the office door. Greg jumped off his bike and dropped to his knees in front of Jerry. The stench of alcohol hit Greg like a blast of ammonia.

Greg grabbed the old man by the shoulders. "Dad!" Greg shook him and then leaned in forehead to forehead. "Dad! *Dad!*"

Jerry opened his eyes and looked around. He seemed barely more disoriented than a man waking in his own bed.

"What? Why are you yelling at me?"

"What are you doing here?"

"I need you to take me home, goddammit. I can't find my car."

Greg looked up and saw the Chevy Malibu parked ten feet away. "It's right behind you."

Jerry looked over his shoulder and nodded his head. So it was.

"When did you start drinking?" Greg asked.

"I don't know. Maybe 1965."

"No, I mean this current bender that you're on."

"August 24, 1992." In his mind's eye, Greg saw the date carved on his mother's gravestone.

"Sit here for a minute while I go inside."

"Nah. I found my car. I'm going home."

Greg reached into Jerry's pocket and took his keys. "Stay here. I'll be back in a minute."

Greg went in through the office and came back with a bag of bagels, a few bottles of Gatorade and some bananas. He helped Jerry to his feet, walked him to the passenger side of the car, put him the front seat and buckled him in. Greg handed him one of the Gatorade bottles. "Drink this."

Greg drove to Jerry's house and helped his father inside and into bed. He could tell from Jerry's clothes and breath that he had not thrown up. He put his dad on his side, facing the edge of the bed, and he wedged pillows behind Jerry's back just in case vomiting was still to come. Greg went to the bathroom, emptied the garbage can and put it by the bed, just under Jerry's head.

"You should eat something."

"I'm not hungry."

"OK, try to sleep for a while. I brought some bagels and bananas. They're on your kitchen table, and there's Gatorade in the fridge. Get up in a bit and have some of each. They'll help."

"With what?"

"Your hangover."

"I'm not hungover."

"You will be."

"No I won't."

"Whatever you say, doctor."

"I didn't ask for your help, you little shit, so you can go."

"Actually, you did ask for my help because you couldn't find the car that you were sitting right next to."

"I'm sorry. I forget that you flunked out of school and don't catch on so quick. When I say that you can go, that means that you should fuck off."

Greg stood up and backed away from the bed. "You're welcome, dad. Always a pleasure."

He set out from the house on foot, but instead of going to the shop, he stopped at Charlie's for eggs, bacon, toast and solitude. He drank a full pot of coffee and hid behind the *Chicago Tribune* sports section, savoring every word of the wrap-up of the Cubs' interleague series at Seattle, where they won two of three but still stood ten games below five hundred. He welcomed any small victory that would come his way.

Greg paid his check and headed to Mellow Sub. When he arrived he found Mike at a table having coffee with Alex Carver. It was past ten o'clock.

"Hey, sunshine," Mike said, "did you sleep in?"

"Um, no. Maggie left this morning, so I wanted to see her off." Greg looked at Alex. "Hey, Reverend, glad you could come by."

"I stopped by one morning a few days after I saw you at church, but you weren't here, and then I had some time off and left town for week. I just got back. Sorry it took so long to connect."

"No problem at all. How was the vacation?"

"Good. Went fishing in Canada. My grandparents had a cabin up there. They're gone now but my mom and her brothers and sisters share it. It's peaceful."

"That's great," Greg said. "Let me warm up your cup." He went behind the counter and grabbed the coffee pot.

"I went to visit Luke the day after I saw you. It looks like someone is taking good care of the grounds."

"Thanks for doing that. It means a lot. I see that you've met Mike."

"Yes, he was kind to invite me in."

"I was glad to have the company," Mike said.

"So, Rev, did you get him all sorted out? He has lived a pretty depraved lifestyle. You may have seen it on the news. He's been known to lay with a woman who is not his wife. More than one, actually."

"Jesus, Greg," Mike said and then looked at Alex. "Oops. Sorry."

"I've heard worse," Alex said. "I've even said worse."

"How long have you been here?" Greg asked Alex.

"Not long. Maybe twenty minutes. Mike made coffee and showed me your records and the juke-box. They all seem so exotic to me, like cool historical artifacts. I never owned a record player."

"And there's no reason you ever should," Greg said. "Old records are just a way for guys like me to live in the past."

"The past isn't so bad," Alex said.

"It beats the hell out of the present, that's for sure."

THIRTY-ONE

When Mike was a kid, Cameron had neighborhoods but not subdivisions. There was Lincoln Ridge, as close as the town had to a pocket of affluence, but it was hard for an outsider to tell where it began and where it ended. There were no gates or grand entrances. People just knew that if you were within the square bounded by Sixth Street, Ninth Street, Johnson Drive and Garfield Avenue, you were in Lincoln Ridge, or as those who lived outside its borders called it, Stinkin' Rich. It was distinguished from every other neighborhood in town by its private pool, but it was private only to the extent that no one but Lincoln Ridge homeowners had keys to it. Every kid in town had a friend who lived there and who would open the gate on request. Nobody seemed to mind. Mike, Greg and Jill spent the summer of 1992 floating there on inflatable loungers without ever being invited.

A few years later, a local developer began to buy corn and bean fields on the town's edge from family farmers who finally gave up the fight against the agricultural conglomerates. He built two subdivisions, Prairie Meadows and Illini Creek. He also built Cameron Country Club, which featured an eighteen-hole golf course and a swimming pool. No one opened the gate there.

Jill's parents were the first to buy a lot in Prairie Meadows, and they chose one of the best, a three-acre tract at the far corner of the plat. It featured gently rolling hills and a pond fit for small boats. They designed a house they could grow old in, a sprawling ranch with no stairs but with plenty of room for each of them to have their own space and plenty of space for grandchildren to have their own rooms. The kitchen, which was finished in granite and tile, sat at the back of the house and opened onto a large covered patio made of concrete and stone. They put the tennis court to the side of the property to maintain a clear view of the pond, on which sat a dock with a rack of kayaks and canoes. Liv had no interest in tennis, but she loved to go on the water with her grandfather.

Jill invited Mike to spend Independence Day with her family at the house. He had not seen Lou or Susan Murdock since high school, but he would have recognized them instantly. They had navigated the years between their fifties and their seventies with a rare grace. Lou's hair was grayer and thinner, but playing tennis three or four times a week, year-round (he played at a small indoor club in the winter), rendered his body lean and tough. The only serious maintenance he had needed in the intervening decades was one arthroscopic surgery to clean up some cartilage in his left knee. Susan had changed even less. The lines on her face had deepened a touch. Her hair was shorter and, Mike thought, a bit darker. Jill's genetic advantages were never more apparent to him.

Mike brought wine and flowers and some of Greg's sausage for the grill. Susan Murdock welcomed him with a warm embrace and Lou offered a powerful handshake. Susan protested that Mike had brought too much, but Mike said that he was happy to do it and was grateful for the invitation. He looked around and over at Jill and Liv, and he thought that this would be a lovely family to be a part of.

Jill had warned him that her father would challenge him to play tennis, and so he came equipped with shoes and clothes and a racket that was of little use in a 6-2, 6-1 whitewash. Jill and Susan sat on opposite ends of the court sipping gin and tonics and casually calling lines while Liv chased stray balls.

After a shower, Lou lit the grill and tossed on the sausages, some hamburgers and corn on the cob, while Jill and her mom prepared salads. Mike asked Lou how he could help, and Lou said he could grab a couple of beers from the fridge. Mike brought back two Budweisers and sat and talked with Jill's dad by the grill, mostly about how Lou's Cardinals entered the day seventeen-and-a-half games ahead of Mike's Cubs. Luckily, Mike said, the Cubbies had a full half-season to make it up.

Susan lit citronella candles around the edge of the patio, and they all sat down to dinner. The

Murdocks had plenty of space between neighbors, but they could still hear the pop of firecrackers from three directions. Liv asked why she couldn't set off any fireworks, and Jill replied that pediatricians generally frowned on giving explosives to small children. Liv sighed and dropped her shoulders. This pediatrician business was always keeping her from the chance to stare down danger.

Lou and Susan said they had seen the clips of Greg singing at the reception and they asked for a recap of the wedding. Jill and Mike gave it in a way that disparaged neither Liv's father nor her new stepmother, and Liv said it was awesome when Greg sang his song. Jill pulled up a video from Facebook capturing Liv on the dance floor with Greg, getting down with all her might. Mike and Jill described the chaos of the TV camera and lights entering the room. They detailed the guests' collective shock at seeing Lacy Nantz crash the wedding, and the way that they all nearly got whiplash from spinning their heads to watch Greg fire up the band. Lou and Susan laughed until tears flowed, not out of spite toward Dan and Christina, but just because the whole thing was too damn funny to comprehend.

When dinner was over, Liv asked her grandpa if they could go out on a canoe. Years earlier they discovered that they could sit in the middle of the pond and see the municipal fireworks display as clearly as if the rockets had been launched from a neighbor's back yard. Mike watched as Lou and Liv walked hand-in-hand toward the pond, and Jill stepped into the kitchen to retrieve a bottle of wine. She came back to the table and poured a glass for each of them just as her father and daughter pushed off from the dock.

Mike looked out over the pond and then back at Jill's mother. "This is such a lovely setting. Thanks so much for having me."

"It's our pleasure," Susan said. "Now that Liv is gone, there's something I wanted to talk about."

"What's that?" Mike asked.

"You impregnated my daughter."

Jill twitched but said nothing.

"That has recently come to my attention, yes," Mike said.

"And I read about how you slurped that poor Maggie Kleinsasser."

"Mom!"

"It's OK," Mike said to Jill. "In my defense, Dr. Murdock, I was drunk and distraught when the slurping occurred."

"Which reminds me. I'm concerned about your drinking. And, please, call me Susan."

"I appreciate that, *Susan*, but my drinking problem was largely contained to that one eight-hour period."

"I'm sorry if I seem blunt. I'm trying to be helpful here because I want Jill to be happy. But you don't seem to know much about contraception or how to please a woman or the negative effects that alcohol has on sexual performance."

"*Holy shit*, mom, you have to stop!"

"Jill, it's fine. If Jenna had been this direct with me, it could have saved a lot of heartache." Mike paused to collect his senses, which had been scattered all over the patio and beyond. "Dr. Murdock – Susan – I want you to like me. I want that very much. I like you and your husband, and, obviously, I have a special fondness for your daughter and granddaughter. Did I say 'special fondness?' Good lord. Let me rephrase that. I'm in love with Jill and I completely adore Liv. And given my history, I know why that might concern you. I understand that you wouldn't like the man you think I am. But I'm not that man. I've learned over the past year that when people don't really know a person, he's just a blank canvas onto which they can project their own ideas. I'm thirty-eight years old. What is that, like 12,000 days? I've done a lot of things in that time, most of them good, or at least not bad. But I suspect that you really only know three things about me, and they're probably the three worst things you could know. The first is that I got Jill pregnant twenty years ago. The second is that I had a rather pathetic drunken liaison with a woman who made me a national joke by selling her story to a tabloid. And the third is that I was once suspected of murdering my fiancée. And I know how terrible it sounds when I say all of that together. So I get it. I understand where you're coming from. If I knew only those three things about me, I wouldn't like me, either. But I want you to know how sorry I am about what

happened with Jill. If I had known at the time that
she was pregnant, I would hope that I would have
done the right thing, whatever that was, and I believe in my heart that I would have because I loved
her as much as I knew how at that age. As for
Maggie, yes, I did those things that you read about.
The drinking. The sex. It was the only time in my
life that anything remotely like that happened. But
it did happen, and while I have my excuses, the
fault is mine. Still, I never could have imagined that
a private indiscretion would become so public and
embarrassing. Finally, Jenna. Every day I think
about how everything went wrong, and I wonder
what I could have done differently. But I never
come up with an answer. I fell in love with a woman who didn't love me, who didn't know herself,
and who couldn't be honest. And then it's like I was
walking down the street one day and I got hit by a
meteor. But it's all OK because it led me back here
now, to Jill and Liv and Greg."

"Mike, I do like you. I just want to make sure
that we understand each other. Apparently, Dan
Emory and I didn't understand each other, or I
didn't understand him, and I'd prefer that Jill do
better this time. I don't mean to meddle in your sex
life or Jill's sex life, but she deserves to be fulfilled,
both emotionally and physically. Any parent who
doesn't want her child to have healthy and satisfying sex isn't much of a parent at all. Most people
aren't comfortable talking about these things, but

I'm too old to dance around that stuff. I prefer to get to the point."

"Mom, if I told you that I was being sexually satisfied, could we move on to something else?"

In the five days since the wedding, the tally had been three or four times, depending on how one counted. Mike was glad to hear that he was doing OK.

"It's good that you are," Susan said, "but you don't have to tell me anything. I just wanted to be clear."

"Oh, you've been clear," Jill said. "Perfectly."

Mike looked down at the pond. The light was beginning to fade. "Does Dr. Murdock know about the pregnancy?" he asked. "I mean the other Dr. Murdock."

"Let's call him Lou," Susan said. "And no, he doesn't."

"So he just knows about the slurping and the drinking?"

"Yes. Is that a problem?"

"No, not at all. If I had to pick one thing for him not to know about, that would be the one."

"Good, because I can't think of a single way that things would be better if he knew. It's the only secret I've ever kept from him, and I'm not particularly proud of it, but I thought it was for the best. Being honest with each other is as important as a good and healthy sex life. You two remember that."

"We will," Jill said, "and there's no reason that we ever need to talk about this again, OK? I'm sure that Mike and I will remember this conversation for the rest of our lives."

"Fair enough," Susan Murdock said. "Let's go get in a boat and watch the sky explode."

"Bring the bottle," Jill said to Mike.

THIRTY-TWO

Craig Doolittle heard the thud all the way from his music room, even over the sick beats he was concocting for the dance-floor opus that had been bubbling in his head ever since the feds nabbed him. The working title was "House Arrest" and he was *feeling it* as he put a modern spin on an old-school Atlanta vibe. This was the one. He knew it. He would bring the crunk back to the people, yo, like Lil Jon meets deadmau5. Others might have conceived of it, but no one had executed it, see? It was just too epic a challenge for your garden-variety EDM dabbler. No snot-nosed punk with a rack of computers and a MIDI keyboard could pull this off. No, this was a job for a man of ideas, a true *auteur*. It was a job for a man like Craig Doolittle. Except there were no men *like* Craig Doolittle. There was only Doolittle himself. And the whole vision came with a built-in hook for publicity. Doing a little stint inside the joint would be the best thing for the music. Turn those lemons into lemonade, yo. He had flown ass-over-handlebars into a full-blown marketing plan: *A hard man makes hard beats*. His story alone was going to get this shit *heard*, and once it was heard, who the fuck was going to be able to resist some truly crunk EDM? As Doolittle busied himself with building the rhythm – *boom bah boom bah boom bah boom bah* – the thud hit and knocked the whole thing off its axis. Stupid birds were always crashing into the sliding door that led to the back yard. Usually they stunned themselves and fluttered away. But this one sounded like it might have been fatal, both for the fowl and for the glass. Better scoop it up before it roasts in the sun.

Doolittle walked through the living room where he once chatted with Lacy Nantz and into the kitchen. He looked at the door and saw no cracks or smears of bird remains. Then he looked out to the patio. There was no bird there, either, but there was a padded manila envelope about the size of a Bible. Doolittle thought the Gideons might be getting just a little too aggressive.

He slid the door open and stepped out. He brought the envelope inside and opened it. Three layers of bubble wrap surrounded a small box. Inside the box he found what anyone in his line of work would recognize as a burner phone. Also inside was a small slip of paper with a phone number printed on it, undoubtedly to another burner. He punched the digits. It only took two rings.

"Hey, baby. That didn't take long."

"Where are you?"

"Denver. My dad's guest house. It's my own sort of house arrest."

"Every time I check in with Lacy it seems that you're chasing that douchebag McAfee through the little towns of the prairie."

"That's just business, but he won't play along. I can't believe all the cash he's turning down. He's living in his mom's shitty little house in that shitty little town. He needs a job, but he won't even take free money."

"You sure you aren't secretly into him?"

"Don't be silly, baby. It's always been you."

"I should have killed him when I had the chance. We could have run away right then."

"Don't talk that way. You're not a killer. I should have just kept my cool. Everything would have been easier if I hadn't panicked that night."

"That night" was the evening when Mike's world began to collapse in increments. But he understood little about what actually happened in those few hours. He knew that Jenna didn't answer his calls all day and that when he showed up at her loft she wouldn't let him in. Instead, she pushed him back into the hallway and told him it was over. Mike was too stunned to argue. It was a blow he never saw coming. Jenna gave no reasons beyond "I just can't" and "it's all too much," but the real motivation stood behind the door with a pistol in his hand. Craig Doolittle was no badass, and he had never fired his gun outside the range, but he possessed the fully-flowered paranoia of a small-time drug peddler and so he carried the gun everywhere he went. Never mind that he lacked a permit. Better to ask forgiveness than to ask permission.

They had planned to make a run for it that night. Doolittle sat in Jenna's loft while his car sat around the corner. They were finishing the last of their preparations when Mike showed up. Five minutes later and he would have been on his way up as they were slinking out through the service elevator.

Jenna opened the door only because she knew that Mike had a key and Craig had a gun and the only way to prevent the most awkward of introductions was to keep Mike out. And the only thing she could think to say to make him leave was "it's over," which, though technically true, was not part of the plan.

Minutes later, Mike's broken shell shuffled into the EDK offices to grab some files to take home. When Edward saw him and asked if he was all right, Mike said no, not really, and explained it all before walking out the door and into a bar where he got blind drunk and crashed into Maggie Kleinsasser.

While Mike talked to Edward, Jenna and Craig paused to consider how the confrontation with Mike had affected their plan. Now there was a witness who could place Jenna at her loft at a specific hour. That would help the police narrow the time of her disappearance. The cops could pull surveillance video from the nearby shops and apartment buildings. They would check the license plates that the cameras captured and would find a set of vanity tags from Nevada (DOO RAG) that belonged to a man whose name would jump out at Edward Kaye. While Doolittle paced and cursed, Edward called

Jenna and said that he was coming over. Doolittle
said "fuck this bullshit," hopped into his Camaro
and drove toward the setting sun.

"It's not your fault," Doolittle said back in the
present. "I shouldn't have freaked out and run like
that. I should have come up with a better plan."

"You did come up with a better plan. You came
up with a great plan. And it worked until the cops
showed up at the house. If you had just been working at the casino and making music, it might have
worked forever."

"Babe, I'm working on something right now
that's going to be huge. It's going to set us for life.
My lawyer is working on a deal. I'm going to cop to
dealing in exchange for a reduced sentence. I'll do
three, maybe four years. My music is going to
come out right when I go in. I'm gonna be a super-
star behind bars. When I get out, I'm going to be in
demand, you understand? Clubs, tours, merchan-
dise. And then it can be you and me on our own
terms, forever. You just gotta wait for me. Will you
wait for me?"

"I don't want to wait."

"Jenna, baby, please."

"No, listen. We don't have to wait."

"What are you talking about?"

"Don't worry about it right now. Smash the
phone. I'll get another one to you soon. Everything
is going to be OK."

THIRTY-THREE

It faced east. In Denver there was nothing worse than facing east. Face west and you get the majesty of the Rocky Mountains. Face east and you get the desolate flats that eventually become Kansas.

But the mountains were expensive. Maggie understood that Edward must have paid a fortune for those twenty-ninth floor views of the western horizon but she never appreciated the size of the fortune until she began pricing office space. And EDK was in downtown Denver, not in a cookie-cutter three-story complex in Lakewood. The solution to a lack of windows on the west side was to improvise one by hanging a large panoramic photo of the Rockies on the back wall of her office. It was a sassy little touch, Maggie thought, like carrying a knockoff Fendi bag.

It wasn't much space, but she didn't need much, not yet anyway. Maggie had an office with a desk, a small table and a couple of client chairs. There was a smaller second office that might someday belong to a younger broker, but it would serve as storage until then. In truth, the whole place was in flux. In her mind, Maggie saw a reception area with a desk and two expensive leather chairs designed to make the right first impression. She might not be able to afford EDK's rent but she had learned enough from Edward to know that the inside of the office needed to project success. Sure, her clients would have to come to Lakewood, but once inside the door she wanted the décor to say downtown Denver or New York or London – anyplace the investors' expectations might take them. She envisioned pendant lights with colorful blown-glass hoods hanging above the receptionist's desk. Behind it, in large, sleek script, a sign would read *Kleinsasser Capital Management*. For a moment, Maggie had entertained the idea of truncating her name to make it snappier – *Klein Capital* – but she wasn't going to start running from her identity now.

Maggie knew that she was doing this backwards by opening the office and then finishing the space, but she couldn't wait. She was ready to move from being the punchline of a tawdry joke to a woman with a plan for her life, and she couldn't start the transition quickly enough. If that meant that she had to go and meet her clients where they were for the time being, that was just fine. It played right into her tagline: *full service for the young investor*.

Down the hall was a restroom that she shared with the other tenants – insurance agents, office-supply brokers, a marketing research company. They had whispered when the name went on the directory in the lobby and they had stared briefly when Maggie's high heels and red curls stepped off the elevator, but they had been kind. The woman next door with the solo law practice had delivered a basket with nuts, cheeses, jams and jellies to welcome Maggie to the neighborhood.

The only other room in the office was a small kitchen with a mini-fridge, microwave oven and coffee maker. At seven-fifty a.m., ten minutes before the official start of the first official day, Maggie brewed a pot and took a cup into her private office where she looked at the panorama and admired her imaginary window on the world.

While Maggie gazed at the mountains, Hayley came through the front door. Kleinsasser Capital Management's receptionist and only employee, Hayley sat her things behind a makeshift front desk and then sat in her chair and admired the makeshift lobby. The daughter of Maggie's first cousin, she was a sweet kid, just twenty-one years old and taking community college classes at night. Maggie had known Hayley since she was born. At the start of this new venture, Maggie wanted to be with people who knew her before, who trusted her basic goodness. She wanted to be with people who wanted her to be, and to do, well.

Maggie handed Hayley a cup of coffee and leaned over the reception desk as the clock hit eight a.m.

"This is so exciting," Hayley said. "I wonder what will happen today."

Just then, the phone rang and Hayley looked up at Maggie as if she didn't know what to do. Maggie gave her a reassuring nod and a smile. Hayley answered the call. "Kleinsasser Capital Management," she said. "Yes she is. Please hold and I'll transfer you."

THIRTY-FOUR

After deciding not to finish his book, Mike had no reason but habit to spend his days in Greg's office. He decided to take off the entire week of the Fourth, a kind of vacation from his sabbatical, and he tabled any more thought about the rest of his life until the following Monday. Then, when Monday came, he tabled it further. He slept later than normal and went for his run around ten o'clock, just as the July heat started to rise. He went into the shop for lunch and spent the afternoon in Greg's office catching up on magazines. He discovered that if a man puts his mind to it, he can read the latest issues of *Esquire* and *The Atlantic* cover to cover in just a few hours.

Mike followed the same morning routine on Tuesday and then he sat behind Greg's desk after lunch with no magazines left to read. He pulled out his phone and played poker against the dogs from that painting. He opened his laptop and made a playlist of every Ramones song that included "want" or "wanna" in the title. He sent an email to his publisher explaining his decision to scrap the book, and he put a check in the mail to refund his advance. He thought giving the money back might be a little painful, but he felt a rush of pleasure and relief when he dropped the envelope in the slot. He

trimmed his fingernails and tried to flick the clippings into the trash like folded paper footballs. He
looked at the copy of *Infinite Jest* that sat on the
corner of the desk. For weeks it had failed to entice
him to start reading. It failed once again.

Mike noticed the date on his phone and then
he looked at the calendar. It had been exactly forty-
nine days since Jenna turned up alive. Mike knew
the number lacked real significance, but it felt con-
sequential. Seven weeks of seven days. It felt mysti-
cal, biblical, meaningful. Mike didn't know much
about Judaism but he knew that after a loved one
died the family would sometimes sit *shiva*, a type of
seven-day wake, or so he understood, with *shiva*
being the Hebrew word for *seven*. It had been a shiva's worth of shivas since the world learned the
truth. It seemed like a good time to get on with his
life, to make a plan for whatever came next. But
shiva made him think of *Chivas*, and he envisioned
seven whiskeys lined up on the bar at Max's, so he
slipped out the back door of Greg's office and
headed downtown alone.

Mike regretted that he had grown up in a time
of bias against bars as reputable places to spend
weekday afternoons. He didn't long for the three-
martini lunch but he lamented the loss of the four
o'clock tipple. Now people met in coffee shops, but
those places clouded his thinking. Everyone was
always caffeinated and jittery or isolated and
plugged in to some electronic device. Thoughts
never unfolded at their own pace in a Starbucks.

They were always forced and scheduled, as if a problem could be solved by wedging it into a half-hour window on the calendar with a resolution due at the end. But a dark bar on a quiet day prompted reflection, and reflection promoted wisdom, sometimes straight from the bottom of a rocks glass and never on a strict schedule.

Mike sat alone at the bar with a Chivas on ice and a notepad in front of him. The few other customers sat at tables scattered throughout the place. Johnny Mathis played softly in the background. The music at Max's, like the décor, had not changed in forty years.

In his occasional visits, Mike had come to appreciate Terry, a bartender who was blessed with the gift of discretion. Terry knew who Mike was, but he never asked a question that wasn't invited or offered an opinion that wasn't solicited. He poured drinks and spoke gladly when engaged, but otherwise he tended to his own business and to other customers. Though he had not been part of the bar's ambiance as long as the music or the furniture, Terry seemed of an indefinite age. However long he had been there, he fit the place just right.

Mike sat over his drink for a few minutes and thought about what he wanted to do with his life. He drew two lines down a sheet of paper, dividing it into thirds. The left column was for things he valued, the right was for things he did not, and the center was for things that fell in between. Things he valued, in no particular order, included Jill,

Greg, his mother, having a job that involved incubating interesting ideas, privacy, an urban (or quasi-urban) environment, music, books, Greg's sandwiches, a nice bottle of this or that, and good routes for running. Things he did not value included fame, making money just for the sake of wealth, long-term bachelorhood, any further relationship with Jenna, and, just for the hell of it, yodeling. In the middle was Denver (great city, bad memories) and quinoa (high in fiber, low in flavor).

Mike hoped that if he looked at the list just right, the answer would eventually appear to him like the 3D images in those posters they used to sell at the mall. He had been staring intently for several minutes when a voice snapped him out of his trance.

"Mind if I sit here?"

Mike looked up and saw Alex Carver.

"No, not at all. Please join me. I'm sorry, I'm not sure how to address you. Pastor? Reverend?"

"Alex is good."

"All right, Alex it is. Do you come here often?" Mike smiled as soon as the words left his lips. "I'm sorry, that sounded like I was trying to pick you up. The last time I sat alone at a bar I ended up having a drunken one-night stand that made it to the front pages of the tabloids. Let's agree up front not to do that."

"That's a deal."

"Let me try again. My dad used to come here. I would go past the place when I was a kid and wonder what it was like inside. It was attractive because it was forbidden. The first time I came in here I was disappointed because I expected – well I didn't know what I expected, exactly, but I expected more. But as I've gotten older, I've grown to appreciate how simple and ordinary it is. No music blaring. No wall of televisions. It's just a place without clocks or sunlight. There aren't enough places like that."

"I never thought of it that way, but I guess that's one of the things I like about the place. I come in from time to time because no one looks for me here. It's important for the church for me to be accessible most of the time, but it's important for me not to be so accessible every once in a while. I did a funeral today. A woman who had been a member of the church since before I was born. I had dinner at her house the first night I arrived here. In a weird way, it's a privilege to preside over someone's funeral, but it's never a pleasure."

"Let me get you a drink. What'll you have?"

"Whatever you're having is fine."

Mike waved and got Terry's attention. "Another for me and one for my friend when you have a chance."

"Terry is a member of my church, but he pretends not to notice when I come in. He seems to know exactly what all of his customers want. I usually want solitude in a place where I'm not completely alone."

"Are you married?" Mike asked. "I grew up Catholic, so that's a question I never asked any of my priests."

"Nope. Single. But I'd like to have a family someday. It's tricky for a minister to try to date in a small college town. Most of the single women aren't exactly age-appropriate, and 'hi, I'm a Lutheran pastor' isn't as good a come-on as you might think."

"Try 'no, really, I didn't murder my girlfriend' some time."

Terry sat two fresh drinks in front of them.

"Here's to finding the right kind of woman in the wrong kind of town," Mike said.

"You said you were raised Catholic, which usually means that you aren't anymore. What happened?"

"Nothing specific. I just sort of fell out of the habit once I left home. When I got to college, I discovered that I liked to sleep in on Sundays. I figured that I'd fall back into it once I grew up. Maybe when I grow up I will."

"This is a no-pressure invitation. You are welcome to join us at St. Mark's whenever you'd like. Lutherans are the original Protestants, so in a lot of ways, our traditions are pretty similar to the Catholics. There are many things in our service that will seem familiar to you."

"I appreciate that. Maybe I'll stop in someday soon."

"And if you'd ever want to become a member, we can talk about that, too. We can even talk about that here, but we don't have to talk about it now."

"I like your approach. Go where the sinners are."

"We're everywhere," Alex said.

"I'm not likely to be in town long enough to become a member, but again, I appreciate the invitation."

"Where are you going to be?"

"I don't know. I've been waiting for some bolt out the blue to tell me."

"In my experience, lightning rarely strikes like that. More often, the answer comes from a seed that you didn't even know had been planted."

"Lightning, seeds, whatever it takes," Mike said. "That makes me think of a band called the Lightning Seeds. Ever hear of them?"

"Are you kidding? I used to put the song 'Pure' on my mixtapes when I was in high school."

"You're all right, reverend. Another round?"

"Sure."

Mike waved at Terry and gestured for more Scotch.

"Do you take confession?" Mike asked.

"No, in our church we confess directly to God. We don't go through a third party."

"He already knows, though, right?"

"Sure, but there's value in acknowledging and confronting our missteps."

"I suppose so. I sort of feel like I took confession from Maggie Kleinsasser not long ago."

"The redhead?"

"You know about her."

"It's hard not to. You were quite the sensation."

"Maggie's a good person. She sought out the attention, at least initially, but she didn't deserve all of the blowback that she got."

"What about you?"

"What about me?"

"Do you feel like you deserve what you got?"

"I don't know. Some of it, maybe. Not all of it, for sure."

"Mike, I don't take confession in the Catholic sense but I am happy to let you get stuff off of your chest."

"I appreciate that," Mike said as he looked down at the list of the things he did and didn't value, "but I really only have one thing to confess."

"What's that?"

"I have absolutely no idea what I should do with my life."

THIRTY-FIVE

When Edward Kaye asked for the name of the best hotel in town and was told that it was the Holiday Inn, it took a second for him to understand that Mike wasn't joking. And so the next day he found himself in a room at Cameron's answer to the Ritz-Carlton, waiting for his former chief lieutenant to arrive. Edward didn't mind the place. He wasn't a fussy traveler, and to the extent that he was an extravagant person at all it was only because he could afford to be, not because it fulfilled any deep personal need. Edward was never reckless with his money. He could have owned houses all over the world, but had only his place in Denver and a relatively modest spread in Palm Desert. Likewise, he had two cars, the big Mercedes and a 1967 Corvette convertible that he reserved for sunny Rocky Mountain days. And he didn't actually own a jet, just a share in one, and he left it in Denver on this trip, opting not to announce his presence too loudly at the local one-runway airport. Instead, he flew commercial to St. Louis and rented a Chevy Impala, which he drove himself.

Still, Edward had more money than he could ever spend, so he tended toward purchasing small pleasures: better hotels, better food, better seats for

Broncos games. But despite sitting on mountains of money, he remained committed to acquiring more of it, in part because that was his greatest talent. Nobody ever said that Picasso had created too much art, he liked to say, and so no one should say that he had created too much wealth. Sure, it was immodest for him to imply that he was the Picasso of money-making, but at the very least he was investing's Paul Klee or Joan Miró. Still, more than simply exercising his talent, Edward believed that the acquisition and distribution of wealth would be his true legacy, especially since it had become apparent that effective child-rearing would not. As much as he had been infuriated by Jenna and her behavior, Edward knew that he would never summon the strength to completely deny her. She was his only child and he would ensure that she would have a place to live, food to eat, and, in the end, a greater inheritance than she deserved. But he was determined that her share would be only a sliver of his estate. Instead, Edward wanted to pledge his wealth to other people's children, ones who never had a chance. He earmarked millions for water-filtration systems, mosquito nets, vaccines, pest-resistant seed and school buildings in the poorest central African villages. But there was more need than he could ever fulfill, so he hoped to amass even greater wealth, many millions more, in his lifetime. He needed help to make that happen.

So he called Mike McAfee. Second to Edward's talent for making money was his gift for recognizing people who could help him make it. He had plucked Mike out of graduate school, topping offers from bigger and more famous firms, piquing Mike's interest with autonomy. He gave Mike freedom to be creative, to take EDK's business in new directions. Mike understood how the internet would fracture the gathering and delivering of news well before Edward did, and he orchestrated the low-ball acquisition of the fledgling citizen-journalist website *Muckraker* and its spinoffs devoted to sports and entertainment, properties that realized a thousand-fold increase in value before EDK sold them in another deal that Mike engineered. Edward might have been inclined to attribute that success to the kid getting lucky if Mike had not also persuaded Edward to sell almost all of EDK's real estate holdings just before the crash and then to buy them back for pennies on the dollar. When Edward calculated the amount that he had paid Mike over the years and then estimated the amount Mike had made for EDK, he concluded that Mike McAfee was the best investment he ever made.

Mike showed up at Edward's door with two cups of coffee and the binder that Edward had sent by overnight mail. It contained articles detailing seventeen start-up companies that combined technology and information in various novel ways. Mike assumed that Edward was interested in buying every last one of them.

Edward opened the door. He wore a business shirt open at the collar and a pair of slate-gray pants that comprised the bottom half of a suit that likely retailed for the same amount as a miniature European car.

"Mike, so good to see you." Edward beamed. "If I didn't make it clear enough before, I apologize, unequivocally, for everything. It was all terrible and regrettable. I hope that we can heal our relationship."

"That would be nice."

Edward handed Mike an envelope. "That's yours," Edward said. "It has nothing to do with what I'm here to talk about, but I wanted to deliver it by hand. Remember when we acquired that war game app from the guy in San Diego? You bought a one-percent share for $2,500. I just sold the app for five million. That's your payout." Mike did the math. $50,000.

"I want to make more deals like that," Edward said. "A new venture devoted to new media. Websites, games, social, apps. Maybe music and video streaming. You're better at that stuff than I am. It's intuitive to you. For me it's like speaking a second language. I have to translate in my head before I talk. I want you to run the operation. I also want you to own it, or at least part of it. We'll start you at ten percent with options to buy your way to forty-nine if you want."

"It's a flattering proposition, Edward, but I just can't go back to EDK."

"You don't have to. This isn't EDK. This is something new. It will have a different name and a different office. It doesn't even have to be downtown near EDK. It can be wherever you want. Cherry Creek, Greenwood Village, wherever."

"What about here?" Mike thought a lightning bolt might have just solved his problems.

"*Here?*" Edward hated to sound like he was disparaging Mike's hometown, but the idea seemed ill-considered on its face. "Maybe once it's up and running and successful, three or four years from now, you could have some sort of an office here. But you really need to be near a major airport most of the time. At the beginning at least, I want you to be close to Denver. I'd like to be in the office fairly often."

"How about Boulder?"

"If that's what it takes," Edward said, "but that's probably the cut-off point. I would like to be able to spend time at each office without blowing the whole day in transit."

"Edward, I'm flattered. I really am. It's a remarkable offer, better than anything that I could imagine. And I'm probably a fool to say this, but I just don't know that I'm ready to commit to something like that. I don't think I can go back there. I'd feel like I was under a microscope."

"I understand," Edward said, "but the media microscope found you here, and if it can find you here, it can find you anywhere. I don't know what other offers you're considering, but you won't escape your past in any of those places, certainly not in New York or Los Angeles or San Francisco. It may be presumptuous of me to tell you what you should do, but the sooner you start the next phase of your life, the sooner you can put Jenna and all of that unpleasantness behind you. If you stand still, it will hover over you. You and I make a good team. We can do great things. I can help you move on."

Mike sat back in his chair and rubbed his hand over his mouth, unsure of what to say.

"You don't have to give me an answer today," Edward said. "Take as much time as you need. But while I'm here, could we just brainstorm for a bit? Even if you turn me down, it will give me some ideas to pursue. Consider it a favor to me."

They spent the next hour roughing out what an ideal operation might look like. The kinds of businesses and products they would target. The number of employees they would need. Office space. Compensation structure. Time frames. A name.

Mike was struck by how good and natural it felt to talk this way with Edward. How it felt creative. When he tried to explain to others what he did at EDK, Mike could see the fog descend behind their eyes. He knew that it sounded tedious and rigorous, a slow march up a long hill. And it could be like that. Most days were defined by persistence and minutiae and slow, painstaking analysis and negotiation. But there were times – and this was so corny that he would never say it out loud, especially not to Greg – that when he was in the middle of a deal it felt like jazz, the immediate and exhilarating creation of something new.

Edward needed to get back to Denver. He wouldn't be spending a single night at the Holiday Inn, not that he would have minded. As the two men stood before the door, Edward put his hand on Mike's shoulder and looked him in the eye with the same intensity he had when making the young graduate student an offer almost fifteen years earlier. "I want you to know that this has nothing to do with Jenna," Edward said. "I'm sorry about what happened, but there's no way to paper over the past. We can only move forward. This is a chance for us to move forward in a very big way."

"You've given me a lot to think about," Mike said. He shook Edward's hand and left. As he walked down the stairs and then through the parking lot, Mike recalled that just a few weeks earlier he couldn't imagine working with Edward again. Those days seemed a long time ago.

THIRTY-SIX

Mike had never run a marathon. He
thought maybe it was time. He knew that
there were races all over the country in
October and November. That gave him at least
three months to prepare. He understood that he
would need to follow a detailed schedule if he really wanted to train for the full distance, but in the
short term he decided to start by stretching his daily runs out a bit. Even if he chose not to commit to
a full twenty-six miles, he wanted to get into the
kind of shape that would allow him to run a half-
marathon on short notice.

Since he stopped writing the book, his morning run had afforded him the chance to think about
other things, and Edward had given him plenty to
consider. Seven miles through the streets of Cameron allowed him to reflect on the details and the
possibilities. And though he felt surprisingly
strong during the final half-mile home, he stepped
into the shower still uncertain about what to do.
He got dressed and headed to Mellow Sub for coffee. He found Alyssa there alone in the kitchen
kneading and stretching the bread dough. Mike
poured a cup for each of them.

"Alyssa, I've been coming in here most days for nearly two months, and I feel like I've barely talked to you. I hope I haven't seemed rude."

"That's me, not you. I'm a worker bee by nature, not too chatty. And it's a bit of a boys club out front."

"I hope we don't make you feel excluded."

"No, not at all. I'm happy to stay in back and hide from Jenks."

"Why are you hiding from him?"

"He hasn't harassed me or anything. He's just kind of weird. I really shouldn't say that. I know he's your friend."

"That probably overstates the depth of our relationship," Mike said, and then finished off his first cup. "How long have you worked here?"

"A couple of years."

"When do you graduate from Central?"

"Already did. Last year."

"Really? What's your degree?"

"I have a bachelor's in business administration with a minor in English."

"Have you had a hard time finding a job?"

"I haven't looked for one."

"How come?"

"Because I really want to learn how to cook. I want to be in the restaurant business. And instead of paying to go to culinary school, I'm letting Greg teach me and pay me at the same time."

"Greg is teaching you?"

"He is, but he doesn't know it. I'm not even sure that he knows I graduated. He has been so closed off to people. It really helped when you got here, and it helped even more when Maggie showed up. Before that a black cloud followed him everywhere. He doesn't share a lot, but I know enough to understand that he's had some rough years. All that aside, the guy is a magician in the kitchen. I've learned so much by watching and copying him."

"Do you want to have your own place someday?"

"That's the plan."

"What's your vision?"

"I'd like to take the things I've learned here and add my own ideas in a kind of American bistro, incorporating elements that people bring here from all over the world. I want to make good food that's accessible. Sandwiches, pastas, steaks, really good fried chicken. It might sound boring, but that's what people like to eat, and there's no reason that you can't take familiar foods and make them great. That's what I want to do."

"That's not boring at all. That's just good sense."

"What about you? You're not here secretly learning to cook, are you?"

"No, just trying to figure out what to do next."

"What did you do before?"

"You don't know? I thought everyone knew every last detail of my life."

"I'm not interested in that stuff," Alyssa said. "I don't mean you, specifically, but all of that gossipy tabloid stuff."

"So you're the one."

Alyssa smiled. "There are more of us than you think."

"I was in finance. We did some traditional investing in things like stocks and real estate, but mostly I was involved in finding interesting new businesses and buying them, growing them, and then sometimes selling them. That's what I really liked to do."

"So you profited off of other people's ideas?"

Mike laughed. "That's one way to look at it, I guess. I like to think that we helped those people make the most of their ideas, both creatively and financially, in ways that they couldn't have done alone. And sometimes we paid for ideas that turned out to not to be successful. The people who developed those ideas sold high and then we took the loss."

"How often did that happen?"

"Not very."

"So is that the thing you love to do?"

"I think so. It's certainly what I'm best at."

"Couldn't you do that again?"

"I could."

"Why don't you?"

"I met this girl."

"Jill."

"Yes. I'm not sure that I can do the job and have her, too."

"Can't you try?"

"I could, I suppose."

"Then you should. It sounds like there are two things that make you happy, and you wouldn't be happy without either of them."

"I wish it were that easy."

"I can't see why it shouldn't be."

Mike met Jill at Fresco, Cameron's closest approximation to fine dining, while Liv enjoyed a night with her grandparents. Mike had hoped that his proposition would go over well but he feared that it might not. His fear was justified.

"I can't, Mike. I just can't."

"I know I'm asking a lot. But this is such a great opportunity."

"It's a great opportunity for you, maybe, but not for me, and especially not for Liv."

"Are you kidding? It's an unbelievable opportunity for her. It will open her whole world up. She could be exposed to so many different kinds of people and music and food and culture. The mountains are so close you can touch them. We could decide to go skiing in the morning and be on the slopes in the afternoon. She would love it. This would be the best thing for Liv. Denver is a fantastic city. And you said yourself that Cameron is a pothole."

Jill's eyes flared and then narrowed. "But I didn't *mean* it. This is my home. This is Liv's home. This is my parents' home. It used to be your home. And the fact that I'm sleeping with you doesn't give you the right to come in and tell me what's best for Liv. You've known her for two months. You don't get to leave for twenty years and then come back for a few weeks and tell me everything that's wrong with this town and with my life. If you don't like it, you can go. But we've made a life here. A good life. I'm not going to take Liv away from her grandparents – or her father for that matter – because you want me to. I'm not going to leave my patients because you want me to. And you shouldn't ask me to."

"Jill, I'm sorry, but I love you. I want to be with you. I want to take care of you and Liv."

"Do you really think we need anyone to take care of us? Do you think I even want that? You don't want to take care of us. You just want to have it all. But you don't get to have it all. You have to make choices. I can see the choice you've made, and I don't blame you. You and your money and your mountains will be very happy together. But don't act like you came up with this plan for my benefit. And don't even begin to act like you did it for Liv."

"Jill –"

"Don't. I'm a big girl. I understand. You said before that you were going to have to leave, and I said 'we'll see.' And now we see. Good luck in Denver. It sounds like a great opportunity."

Jill stood up and walked out. Mike sat quietly and finished his bourbon. A waiter placed two entrees on the table.

"What else can I get for you, sir?"

"Just the check. And a couple of large boxes."

THIRTY-SEVEN

Even through the phone, the slurring told Greg all he needed to know about his old man's predicament, but Jerry insisted on telling him more.

"I fell and hit my head. It's bleeding. I need you to take me to the hospital."

"Call an ambulance, dad."

"I can't afford a goddamn thousand-dollar ambulance ride. I need you to come and get me."

"I'm at work. I'm working. I own the place. I can't leave."

"Work? It's a fucking sandwich shop."

Jerry was rarely profane while sober. Greg estimated this as a D-4 intoxication event, the second-highest level of drunkenness on a scale he devised to communicate with his siblings, to the extent they gave a damn.

"Insulting my livelihood isn't going to help."

"OK, for fuck's sake, it's *your dream*. That's how much I need you right now, you see? I'm willing to ask my own son, the only one who is good to me, to walk away from the Parthenon of hoagies for an hour."

Greg bit the inside of his lip until pain shot up his face, but he didn't make a sound.

"Greg, please. *Please.*" Greg could hear this ghost of a man begin to cry. "I know I have to do better, and I will, starting tomorrow. But I don't want to die here today. There's nobody else that will help me. *Please.*"

Greg didn't want to do it, but he couldn't stop himself.

"I'll be right there," he said.

Greg looked at Mike, who was sitting at a table with a book and a beer. "I gotta go. You're in charge."

Mike stammered. "But, but, but – wait! I don't know how to do this."

"A ham and cheese is ham and *fucking* cheese," Greg said as he stomped toward the door. "You'll figure it out." Mike hoped like hell that no one ordered a muffuletta.

On the drive to the house, Greg allowed every possible scenario to float through his mind. "Occam's razor," he said over and over, an effort to convince himself that the most likely explanation for Jerry's call was just what Jerry had said: He drank himself to incapacitation and then fell and hit his head. But Greg deduced that there was a chance that it was all a set-up. He pegged it at seventeen percent. Yes, he concluded, there was a seventeen percent chance that Jerry had reached the end and was determined to take someone with him. It made him crazy that his mind worked this way. It felt like Jerry's booze was somehow killing Greg's brain cells, making him play out delusions in his head. Greg flashed on the tall safe where Jerry had long stored the implements of his former interest in pheasant hunting. Greg was pissed at himself for never having it removed from the house. But what was he going to do? He didn't know the combination, it was far too heavy for him to move himself, and he didn't have associates who were willing to bust into the house and make off with a one-ton object they couldn't open. In Greg's imagination, he would rush through the front door, through the living room, and turn the corner to the hallway only to be met by two barrels pressed against his forehead. Jerry's head wouldn't be bleeding and he probably wouldn't even be drunk. He would just be done with it all. Angry and crazy and scared, finished with this miserable life, and resentful of the one person who cared for him but who couldn't fix him. Jerry would mutter some movie cliché – "I'll see you on the other side" – and Greg's world would go black. He would be dead before his brains splattered on the far wall, unable even to enjoy the small pleasure of seeing Jerry turn the gun on himself.

When Greg parked in front of the house only basic math provided him the courage to go in. "An eighty-three percent chance it won't happen," he thought as he stepped onto the porch and turned the doorknob. Locked. He rang the bell. Nothing. He pounded on the door. No answer. "Dad, it's me! Open up!" he shouted, trying to find a volume loud enough to roust his father without disturbing the neighbors.

Greg walked around back, climbed the stairs to the deck, and found the spare key in the plastic bag beneath the potted plant. He slipped through the door and moved quietly like some sandwich-making commando in his own sad version of stealth mode. He stayed close to walls and cautiously peeked around each corner. If this was indeed the seventeen-percent scenario, he planned to bull rush the old man before he could raise his gun. Finally, Greg got to the edge of the doorway to his dad's bedroom. From that angle, he could see little but the dresser, still topped by a photo of his mom, now gone more than twenty years, plus big and empty vodka bottles, the cheapest stuff. "Jesus," Greg thought, "were they out of furniture polish?" He peered around the corner and saw Jerry lying on the bed, a wound near his left temple somewhere between a cut and a gash. Greg didn't see a shotgun, but he couldn't see his dad's right hand, either. What if he were clutching a pistol? Greg crept closer until he stood directly over the bed. There was no gun. He exhaled and rolled his eyes up to the ceiling in relief.

"Dad," Greg said.

Jerry didn't react.

"Dad," he said again, and shook him by the shoulders.

Jerry grunted but didn't open his eyes.

"Come on, dad, you have to help me help you. I can't carry you to the car."

Actually, maybe he could, but it seemed like a bad idea. What if Jerry's head injury was worse than the wound looked? What if this were some serious case of alcohol poisoning? What if it were some other medical catastrophe that Greg knew nothing about? What if he fell and Jerry pinned him to the hallway floor and they both died the saddest death right there, only to be found days later when the stench wafted into the street?

He dialed 911.

"Hi, my name is Greg Allen. I'm with my dad, Jerry Allen. He's seventy years old, maybe seventy-one or seventy-two. I've lost track."

"We know Jerry. Alcohol?"

"Yeah. From the smell of him and the looks of the room, he's had a lot to drink. He called me twenty minutes ago and said he'd hit his head, and he does have a cut. But he's not responsive now. I don't know if he just needs to sleep it off or if it's something more serious."

"We'll have paramedics there shortly. Can you stay with him?"

"Of course."

While Greg waited, he took inventory of the room. The vodka bottles he saw before. Gin. Rum. Pizza boxes. Everything empty, save for a few bits of crust. He followed drops of blood into the bathroom, and found the crimson smear where Jerry's head struck the sink. The towel rack had been

ripped from the wall. The shower curtain was wad-
ded in a corner of the tub. There was blood and
vomit in the toilet.

The doorbell rang. Greg let two paramedics in.
One looked familiar. Maybe he knew him from
school. Maybe he had been to the shop. Everyone
looked familiar in Cameron.

He led them down the hallway and into the
bathroom. "Hi Jerry, do you remember me? My
name is Rick. We've done this before. Kevin and I
are going to check you out and then take you to the
hospital so a doctor can take a look."

"You've been here before," Greg said, halfway
between a question and a declaration.

"A time or two. Who are you?"

"I'm his son."

"I'm sorry. The last time he told us he didn't
have anyone."

The paramedics checked Jerry's pulse and blood
pressure, and moved a gurney even with the bed.

"All right, Jerry, we're going to move you now,"
Kevin said.

As they secured him with straps, Jerry opened
his eyes, his pupils dancing behind a blue-white
film until they locked on Greg. He bared his teeth
like an animal and shook an accusing finger at his
son.

Greg followed the ambulance to the hospital
and then followed Jerry into a bay in the emergen-
cy room. After debriefing Greg and checking Jerry
over, the young resident said "I want to do a CT

scan, but I think he's just intoxicated. We'll want to keep him overnight, but I suspect he'll be OK to go home tomorrow. I'm going to order the scan and then I'll be back in a bit to check on him."

Jerry had begun to reclaim some of his wits. He lay still, looking smaller than before, the flash of anger gone. His eyes were clear but heavy. He was the top of an hourglass, dissolving as Greg watched.

"Thank you," the old man whispered.

Greg leaned in, and looked on the man with pity, still somehow feeling the bond between parent and child. But the bond felt different, like a shackle that had rubbed his wrists until they bled.

"Listen, motherfucker," Greg said. "I'll be back tomorrow morning. You can let me take you back to rehab or you can get on with your life without me."

Greg was halfway to the hospital exit before Jerry burst into tears.

Greg didn't go back to the shop and he didn't call. It didn't take a genius to lock up, and he knew because he locked up every night. He went home and sat in the dark. He didn't answer when Mike called or when Jill called or when they called again. He texted both of them "I'm fine. Don't want to talk now. Dad in hospital. See you tomorrow after I take him to rehab."

After a while he went into the kitchen and grabbed a banana. A bottle of Jim Beam sat on the counter. If there were ever a time when he could tear that bottle a new asshole, this would be it. But it just looked like poison. "Progress," he said aloud. He opened the fridge and grabbed a Diet Coke. He had decided to eliminate sugar, determined to stop buying bigger pants.

He pulled DVDs out of the drawer by the TV. He watched *The Godfather* and then *The Godfather Part II*. He nodded off just after Michael kissed Fredo in Cuba. He slept like he hadn't since Maggie went back to Denver.

The sunlight pried his eyes open at eight-thirty. He showered, went to Jerry's house to pick up some things, and then to the hospital, where he found his dad dressed and sitting in a chair in his room with the newspaper and a cup of coffee. His hair was neat, his posture straight. Like nothing ever happened.

"I called last night, and there's a bed for you at Serenity Springs, near Effingham," Greg said. "You ready to go?"

"If that's what I have to do."

"It is."

The two men barely spoke on the trip down I-57, but the stillness between them, with the radio as a backdrop, took Greg back to when he was just four or five, riding in the car with a father prone to long silences. That was when he learned to love music. Blondie, Queen, Springsteen. He may have been in kindergarten when a disc jockey said "here's something new. It's the Rolling Stones. 'Start Me Up,'" and little Greg asked his dad if he'd heard of this new band, and the man who was barely forty but who seemed so much older smiled and said "I believe I have." Jerry didn't seem to care much about music, but he did have a box of old 45s in good to near-mint condition: Sam Cooke, CCR, Mitch Ryder. Good stuff. Years later, Greg put some of them in the rotation for the Seeburg. He believed there was a good heart in his dad somewhere. The memory of those records supported that belief.

They pulled up to Serenity Springs and Greg carried his dad's bag inside. They filled out some paperwork and met a counselor. When there was nothing left for him to do, Greg said "you'll be OK. You'll get well."

Greg tried to embrace Jerry, but the old man didn't reciprocate. Instead he whispered in his youngest child's ear.

"You're a smug little bastard, you know? You think you're better than me. But we're the same. I got this disease from my dad, and I gave it to you. It's already in there waiting to come out. You're lucky you killed your boy. When you're old and you just need to die, there will be no one to drag your sorry ass to a place like this."

Greg dropped his arms to his side and his chin to his chest. Jerry turned and walked away.

The drive there had taken forty-five minutes. The drive back took less. Greg cranked the stereo to try to suppress his thoughts and his rage. The fact that the album playing was The Hold Steady's *Almost Killed Me*, with songs full of cautionary tales of people drowning in booze and drugs, wasn't poetic or poignant. It was just a stupid fucking coincidence. That's what was in the CD player.

Greg parked on the street in front of the shop. What passed for a lunch rush had just ended. The only ones inside were a couple of customers and Jenks and the new kid behind the counter, the one Greg always wanted to call Zach but whose name was really something else. He walked through the front door, head down and shoulders sore from trying to push everything inside. The old man's foul breath was in Greg's nose, his foul words in Greg's ears.

"Where's Mike?" Greg asked.

"He was here a while ago, but he left," Jenks said. "I don't know where he went."

The place was quiet. The new kids never put records on. Didn't they understand that this was the point of the place? They bought and sold *records*. They played *records*. Greg pulled out a copy of Public Image's *Second Edition* that Jacob had brought in from his dad's collection. Dude must have been cool, Greg thought. Fucking tragedy that he was dead while Jerry still walked the earth. Greg had never owned this album but he loved how its beauty came from an ugly place. When the singer's voice floated in on "Albatross," Jenks said "I liked Johnny Rotten better in this band."

"Cut it the fuck out!" Greg shouted.

"What?" Jenks replied.

"This bullshit rock and roll name thing that you do. Wanna call Dylan 'Zimmerman?' *Fine*. Wanna call Elton 'Reginald?' Cool. Whatever. But Johnny Rotten and John Lydon are the *same guy*. His name in the Sex Pistols was Johnny Rotten, and his name in Public Image was John Lydon. Either pick one name and stick to it or call him by the right name for the right band. Don't call him 'Lydon' in the Pistols and 'Rotten' in Public Image. Everybody knows and nobody fucking cares."

Greg stomped toward the door. As he moved past the Seeburg Select-O-Matic, he caught the reflection coming off the glass, and saw his dad staring back at him. Greg raised both fists above his head and smashed Jerry's face, spraying shards in every direction. He turned and walked out, leaving drops of blood in his wake.

THIRTY-EIGHT

Jacob came in with a copy of Bruce Springsteen's *The River* tucked under his arm, hoping to turn it into dinner. "Where's Greg?" he asked.

"I don't know," Mike said.

Jacob looked at Jill, who was leaning against the counter, coffee in hand.

"She doesn't know, either," Mike said. "And apparently Jenks doesn't care."

"I said I'm sorry," Jenks replied. "I didn't know what was happening with his dad. I thought it was just a mood. I figured he'd come back."

Six hours had passed since Greg assaulted his jukebox. It was more than a mood.

"You should have called me," Mike said.

"I've already conceded the point."

"Have you tried calling him?" Jacob asked.

For some reason, the question made Mike smile.

"Yeah, several times." Mike saw no reason to snap at a kid who was trying to be helpful.

After calling and texting for an hour with no response, Mike went to Greg's house. When Greg didn't answer a knock on the door, Mike broke a window and let himself in, afraid of what he might find. But he only found dirty dishes in the kitchen and stacks of records in the living room, the same things that could always be found there. The place told no secrets.

Mike had his elbows on the table and his thumbs pressed against his temples when Jill came up behind him and began to massage his shoulders.

"Little tight there, champ," she said.

"That feels nice," he said. "I went twenty years between back rubs."

Mike looked at the little girl across the table from him, grateful for her presence.

"Thanks for bringing your mom in, Liv," he said. "How's your sandwich?"

"Dee-licious."

"As good as Greg makes?"

"Uh-huh."

"Do you have peanut butter and banana sandwiches at home?"

"Nope. Just here. Geggy said I should eat them because they're the elves' favorite."

"No, sweetie, they were Elvis's favorite," Jill said.

"OK," Liv said. She didn't know who that was.

"Sweetie, there's some gum in my purse in the office. Could you go get it for me?"

Liv scampered out of the room.

"He wouldn't . . . you know?" Jill asked.

"I don't know," Mike said. "I don't think so. But I don't know."

Mike stood up to survey the damage to the Seeburg and his eyes locked on a single by Billy

Joel. It was no surprise to see it there because Greg secretly loved everything from *Cold Spring Harbor* through *An Innocent Man*, a fact known only to his closest friends. But as Mike looked at the jukebox, he noticed for the first time that the record had been flipped over, putting the B-side first, a sure sign that it was part of Greg's word game. The realization hit Mike like a taped fist. H8 "My Life."

Mike and Jill had called everyone they knew who might have a clue about where Greg could be. A couple of friends, a couple of bars. Greg had sounded upbeat in the morning when he called Mike to say that he was taking his dad to rehab. "There was so much fear in his eyes," Greg said. "I think he knows this is his last chance." But no word since then. Mike called Greg's sister and brother to see if they had heard anything, but they didn't even know about the hospital or Serenity Springs. Greg had just dropped off the map. Mike imagined him in Reno with Craig Doolittle and managed to summon the hint of a smile.

Jill resumed the massage and Mike closed his eyes for a minute and let his mind go. He saw himself with Greg, maybe nine or ten years old, riding their little BMX bikes on the tar-and-gravel streets of the neighborhood. If they stood up on the pedals and pumped hard heading west on the peaceful flats of McKinley Avenue, they could stop their feet and glide into the looping left towards Taft and its long, straight, gentle downhill. In the heat of the day, in the quiet of the town, they could hear the knobby tires sing as they rolled over the sticky pseudo-pavement. When they turned the next corner, they were seventeen, in Greg's first car, the crappy Corolla with the badass stereo, Mike's newest mix in the tape deck. Nirvana and R.E.M. competed for attention with Dylan and Neil Young, the new seamlessly flowing into the old. Greg and Mike rode along and sang and laughed, and later they parked and took off their shirts and sprawled on their backs and looked at the stars and cracked some beers and wondered where they would be twenty years down the road.

Mike saw his younger self and Greg from above, barely recognizable. The pounds and years and worry and wear had not yet been grafted onto the angular frames of teenage boys, with their hairless chests and visible ribs. It had recently occurred to the grown-up Mike that we are not nearly as familiar with ourselves as we think. He had been reminded that he had a small mole on his face, something visible with any glance into a mirror, but which caused no more notice than the sound of the surf to a seagull. Without looking, he couldn't say on which side of his face the mole sat or where it was in proximity to his nose and ears. He just knew that he would be able to find it if he ever needed it. But looking down on the boys from above, he remembered everything about them with photographic clarity. Between Jenna and Maggie and *The Inquisitor* and all the noise that drowned out his thoughts, Mike sometimes felt that he had lost all sense of himself. Now he remembered.

Mike jumped up and headed to the door.

"Where are you going?" Jill asked.

"To find a friend in the wilderness."

As Mike hit the edge of town, it struck him how much he missed the old Holiday Inn sign, with its gleaming star, dotted arrow and mid-century neon flair, the past's idealized vision of the future. It once welcomed people to Cameron with style, a small-scale Sinatra-at-The-Sands vibe. In its place stood a nondescript *H*, white on green. Mike fantasized about firing the corporate dolt who ordered that change.

A minute later, he turned off the state highway and on to a gravel road that soon turned to dirt. He pulled his car to the side, stopped, and headed south on foot. He had walked about a hundred feet when he saw the glow of a campfire in the Wild Prairie Outback.

On his way out of town, Mike had stopped for a cold six-pack of Schlitz Tall Boys. As he approached the man in the flickering light, Mike pulled one off the plastic ring and tossed it to him.

"I swore that shit off twenty-four hours ago," Greg said.

"You don't have to drink it."

"It would be rude to refuse a beer offered in friendship. I'll allow myself one. If you're good company, maybe two."

"So what are you doing out here?"

"Growing my beard."

"How's that coming?"

"Slowly."

"So, whatever's going on, you wanna talk about it?"

"I'm not sure there's anything to say except that Jerry Allen is one vile son of a bitch."

"I'm sorry. I wish there was something I could do."

"He's the only one who can do anything. And he doesn't have it in him. I watch him and all it does is remind me of what a terrible husband and father I was."

"I don't believe that."

"You'll have to trust me."

The two friends sat silently for a while, drinking their beers, stoking the fire.

"I've gotta get out of this place," Greg said. "I need to leave. And before you tell me I can't run from my problems, I have two things to say. First, look who's talking. And second, bullshit. Maybe you can't run from cancer, but you can run from the driveway you pass every day, the one that reminds you of how you killed your son, and you can run from a dad who is determined to die, and you can run from a sandwich shop that's the saddest dream to ever come true. When I bought Gould's inventory, I thought I was going to be the curator of some grand cultural tradition, but, really, I just collect shit that nobody wants. I can barely make my rent but I let a kid pay for sandwiches with a dead man's records, which makes me as responsible for my own problems as my dad is for his. Some things die, and there's nothing you can do to change that. You can't bring them back. Small towns and record stores are terminal, and if I stay here, I will be, too. So don't tell me that I can't run."

"I wasn't going to," Mike said, and then reached into his pocket, pulled out his keys, took one off the ring, and handed it to Greg.

"What's this?"

"My place in Denver. Great restaurants there. New ones popping up all the time. There's a place that serves seven kinds of poutine. Imagine taking the carnitas from your torta and piling it on french fries. There are no rules. You can do anything you want."

Greg gave his friend a weary smile.

"And Maggie lives close by," Mike said.

"What about you? Aren't you going back to take that job?"

"I'm going to turn it down tomorrow," Mike said. "There's a sandwich shop here in town that I'm planning to buy."

THIRTY-NINE

After putting Greg to bed, Mike called Jill, told her everything was OK, and asked if they could meet for breakfast at Charlie's to talk some things over. Mike was waiting in a booth when Jill walked in at eight-thirty, right on time, having just dropped Liv off with her grandmother. Stacy handed them menus, winked at Mike, and said "always a pleasure to see you."

They sipped coffee while they waited for their food, and Mike laid out the deal he had struck with Greg.

"You gave him $65,000?" Jill said.

"I'll write him a check today."

"But the whole shop isn't worth close to that much, and he only owns half."

"I think it could be worth more than that. A lot more."

"Well, then, aren't you taking advantage of him?"

"We'll take care of Greg when we license his image."

"What do you mean?"

"I'll explain in a minute," Mike said, "but first, do you have a dollar?"

"Probably."

"Give it to me."

Jill rifled through her purse. "The smallest bill I have is a five," she said, "but I have some change."

"Change is fine."

Jill took a handful of coins and began sorting them on the table. "There's two quarters, and three dimes, and three nickels, and – one, two, three, four, five – five pennies. One dollar."

Mike scooped the coins off the edge of the table, into his hand, and then into his pocket. "You just bought an option to buy my half of the shop. If you exercise that option, your price is five dollars. You can choose to do it at any time over the next year. Don't worry. I'll write down all the details."

"Wait," Jill said. "I can give you five dollars for the half of the shop you just paid $65,000 for?"

"Yes."

"Why would you do that?"

"Because I don't want you to be stuck with me." Mike said. "You might not want me to be your partner."

"I just want someone to handle the shop so I don't have to think about it. If I didn't have a partner, I'd close the place up. I never wanted to be in the sandwich business. I just didn't want Greg to lose the place. But if you're up for it, and if I don't have to handle it, I'm game," Jill said and then paused. "And I wouldn't necessarily mind being stuck with you."

"I'm glad."

"But what about Denver?"

"I called Edward a half-hour ago and politely declined his offer."

"Why would you do that?"

"Because you can't have everything. Sometimes you have to make choices."

"You're choosing to live in Cameron and run a sandwich shop?"

"As long as you don't buy me out."

"What would you do if I did?"

"I don't know. Maybe try to get a teaching job at the university or take up soybean farming. You know, whatever work I can find here."

"You'd stay here if I bought you out?"

"Yes."

"For how long?"

"For good. Unless you wanted me to leave."

"I might not want that."

"That's good."

"The other night, after I left the restaurant, you didn't go to a bar and get drunk and have sex with another woman, did you?"

"No. And you didn't go and make a secret plan to run away with your boyfriend from high school, did you?"

"You were my boyfriend in high school."

"Fair point. Is there a chance that we might be able to forget that the other night ever happened?"

"I've forgotten already."

"Then is there a chance that we might be able to go out some time, like on a boy-girl date?"

"Perhaps, but we can get to that stuff later. Back to the shop. Suppose I don't buy you out. Tell me how you plan to turn this money pit into a profit center."

Mike laid out the rough sketch and confessed that he hadn't yet worked out all the details. The entire idea was only about ten hours old, but it was informed by the notes he had been making all summer. The plan would begin with more competent management. There was an inverse relationship, Mike said, between Greg's ability to make a sandwich and his acumen at running a business. Also, getting a sober accountant would be a step in the right direction. But beyond more competent operation of the current shop, Mike saw a future in expansion, even franchising. Greg's face and the shop's sign had already appeared on every news outlet in the country, in print and in countless internet memes. Greg had gotten requests for Mellow Submarine t-shirts from all over the nation, and the only reason he hadn't sold more is because he never bothered to print them. People loved Greg's happy, round face. Mike had spent the night thinking about that face and its almost supernatural ability to mask deeply-felt pain. He thought that if advertising is really based on happiness as he had heard somewhere, the combination of Greg's face and a meatball sub in a television commercial ought to inspire hordes of people to stream into the shop. But not just the shop in Cameron. They would start there and move out like ripples on a pond, to Champaign, to Chicago, to St. Louis, to Indianapolis. To college towns throughout the region. And they wouldn't just appropriate Greg's face. They would also strive to maintain the vibe of the original location, the vibe that Greg had created without really trying. They wouldn't buy used records, Mike said, but they would sell new ones, and every shop would have a jukebox, preferably with vintage 45s, and they would all have a turntable behind the counter. And if it all panned out, instead of just licensing Greg's image, Mike would give him part of Mike's half, and let him operate a test kitchen in Denver where he could work every day to improve the shop's menu. Mike said that he also had another idea for Greg that we wanted to mull over.

"I also want to promote Alyssa," Mike said. "She'll be in charge of all of the food for right now. And after we've had a chance to work out the details, I'd like to give her a small stake in the business."

"Why?" Jill asked.

"Because she has ideas. I'd like to invest in them."

While Mike and Jill were discussing Mellow Submarine's expanding reach, a woman wearing aviator sunglasses walked into the Denver Public Library with her hair piled under a baseball cap. She sat at a computer terminal in a remote corner, slipped on a pair of latex gloves and typed a query into Google: *How to bypass an ankle bracelet.*

FORTY

It had been twenty-four days since Greg departed for Denver, and seventeen since the cable news channels interrupted regular programming to report that Jenna Kaye and Craig Doolittle had gone missing, and that authorities believed they had fled the country. In the two weeks after their disappearance, Edward appeared on every news network and entertainment news show in hopes that Jenna was watching. He looked straight into the camera and implored her to come home and said that there was a role for her at EDK, but she never contacted him. He knew she wouldn't, but he also knew he had to try. Though police said that they had no solid leads, witnesses from all over the world reported seeing Jenna and Craig. In one day alone, they were spotted in Vancouver, Oklahoma City, Lisbon, Kinshasa, Bangkok, Belfast, Buenos Aires and Mobile, Alabama. Mike called Edward to offer his support, but he knew there was nothing he could do. Even Lacy Nantz felt helpless. She could think of no convincing way to suggest that a man living under house arrest in Reno had kidnapped a woman living behind iron gates in Denver.

Out front, Alyssa prepared for the lunch crowd, which was growing daily as students began to trickle back into town. Mike sat at the desk in the office, examining the books and paying bills. His mind wandered and he began to sketch out a new Mellow Submarine logo that featured Greg's impish face. While he doodled, his phone rang. It had been a while since a Los Angeles area code popped up on his screen. He thought the number seemed familiar, but he had never bothered to put the Hollywood folks into his contacts.

He answered cautiously. "Hello?"

"Mike. Roger Ramsey here. Funny story that I wanted to share. I had a dream and you were in it."

"I was in your dream?"

"You were. Now hear me out, please. Just give me a minute. Please understand that this came to me in a dream and is not in any way based on something that I have any involvement with. These things never happened. Anyway, in the dream there was an idea for a show, and the funny thing is that it involves elements of things that are actually happening in the world right now. Jenna Kaye and Craig Doolittle were on the run, working their way through countries that don't have extradition treaties with the U.S. Places like Dubai and Bhutan. Places, coincidentally, with some dramatic scenery that would look great on television. And they needed money to keep going. So they called a guy in the TV business. Not me, but a guy *like* me. Call him Robert Radley. And I discovered this because, in the dream, I'm sitting in an outdoor café in Croatia. Why am I in Croatia? No idea, but it turns out that

Croatia also lacks an extradition treaty with the states. Anyway, Jenna and Craig sit down at my table. I'm reading the newspaper and I look up and there they are. I don't recognize them at first because they're wearing disguises. Then Jenna takes off a wig and fake beard and it's her. They tell me that they talked to this TV guy Robert and they came up with an idea for a show called *Love on the Run* that would feature them in these exotic locations that are beyond the reach of federal law enforcement. But the whole thing would have to be set up through some sort of off-shore operation. A production company in the states wouldn't touch it because of the legalities. And here's where you showed up in the dream —"

"Roger, don't say any more."

"But, Mike, you have to hear the rest. It's a killer opportunity."

"I thought it was just a dream."

"It is, but there was a killer opportunity *in* the dream that you should know about. I want to tell you about it in person. There's this little private island in the Caribbean. I want to take you there and tell you more. Let me fly you to Miami and then we can hop on a private flight from there."

"Roger, instead of doing that, I'm going to hang up now and call the police."

"Don't be silly, Mike. There's no law against having dreams."

"But there is a law against providing aid to fugitives."

"I would never do that, but I sure would like to show you that island. The sand on the beaches is as white as cocaine."

"Goodbye, Roger."

"Something tells me that this isn't just a speed bump on the way to Yes."

"Goodbye, Roger."

A few days later, Mike was anchored at a back table in a sea of receipts when Jill came in through the office and kissed him square on the mouth.

"I can't stay," she said, "but I was driving by and thought I would stop in and do that."

"You should drive by more often."

Jill looked at the mess laid out in front of Mike. "What's all this?"

"Taxes," Mike replied.

"I thought the beauty of a failing business is that you don't have to pay them."

"Turns out we're not failing as badly as I had hoped. And we have to fill out the forms anyway. I got a new accountant. He's on his way over. I told him I'd provide beer if we could meet here."

"Accountants can drink on the job?"

"As long as they don't operate forklifts, I guess."

Jacob had sauntered in fifteen minutes earlier, while the shop's newly-acquired copy of Elvis Costello's *Armed Forces* was playing. The kid got buttonholed by Jenks.

"Declan Patrick MacManus," Jenks said.

"Who's that?" Jacob asked, lacking the wisdom not to pose the question.

"It's Elvis Costello's real name."

"Who's Elvis Costello?"

Jenks threw up his hands. "It's who we're listening to right now! He was born Declan Patrick MacManus. Then he legally changed it to Elvis Costello. And later he changed it again to Declan Patrick *Aloysius* MacManus. He married the woman from the Pogues, and then they got divorced, and later he married that jazz singer. What's her name?"

Mike, who could not help eavesdropping, shouted "Ella Fitzgerald!"

"Jeez, no, not her," Jenks replied.

Even after the second side of the record ended and Mike put on a Diana Krall CD just to mess with Jenks, the kid remained trapped in the corner as Jenks plumbed the depths of Elvis Costello's name, discography, marriages and collaborations, including a passionate if somewhat disjointed argument in favor of the album he made with the Brodsky Quartet over the one he made with Burt Bacharach.

Jill took notice and said "poor kid."

"Better that little shit than me," Mike said. "Before Jacob got here, Jenks was trying to persuade me that Barry Manilow ranked ahead of James Taylor in the pantheon of Seventies-slash-Eighties singer-songwriters. I don't know what his argument was. I just turned up the volume."

The front door opened, and Jill saw a guy about fifty years old walk in, wearing a coat and tie, carrying a briefcase. "I think our accountant is here," she said, "but I've got to go." She slipped back out through the office.

Mike looked up. "Hey, Tom," he said, and walked across the shop to greet him.

"Hi Mike," he said, before noticing Jenks preaching to the poor cornered kid.

"Well, hey Jacob," Tom said.

The kid looked at him and stood statue-still.

"How do you know Jacob?" Mike asked.

"Met him at birth. He's my son."

Mike started to speak and then stopped. He looked at Jacob, who had closed his eyes, hoping that if he couldn't see Mike, Mike couldn't see him.

"Is that right?" Mike asked. "Small world."

"Small town," Tom replied.

"Tiny."

"So is Jacob a regular?" Tom asked. "Makes me sound like a bad parent to even ask. I suppose I should know what my boy is doing during the day."

"You must be a great parent," Mike said, "because he's a good kid. He's even cultivated an appreciation for the old records we buy and sell."

"Really? That's cool. And that reminds me. After we met in my office, I felt a little nostalgic about my old records, so I went on Amazon and ordered a cheap turntable. I haven't had one in years. And then I went into my basement to look through my old albums. But I couldn't find half of them. I must've lost some in a move at some point. Maybe I'll have to flip through the bins and restock my collection."

"You know what?" Mike said, and he walked behind the counter. "We had a record come in recently and Jacob said it was one of his dad's favorites."

Mike came back with the album tucked under his arm and then handed it to his new accountant.

"*Captain Fantastic!*" Tom said. "Oh my god, I love this record."

"It's yours," Mike said.

"Thanks so much. You're my new favorite client."

Mike took a look at Tom's clothes. A summer wool jacket with a pocket square and a perfectly knotted tie. "I like that look," Mike said. "The pocket square finishes it nicely."

"Accountants are fastidious by nature."

"Sometimes I miss my old wardrobe," Mike said, "but it's tucked away in a closet, so I guess I could visit it any time."

Mike went to the tap, drew two beers and came back to the table. He and Tom went through numbers and documents for half an hour, and then Tom put the pages into three neat stacks, put each stack into a color-coded folder, put each folder into a binder, put the binder into his briefcase, and stood up. "I'll take these back to the office and get to work," he said, "and then I'll call you in a few days."

"That would be great," Mike said.

"This is a terrific place," Tom said. "Some real possibilities here. And I'm serious about coming in to restock my collection."

"I hope you will. We have some stuff that I suspect is right up your alley."

Mike waited until Tom had been gone for thirty seconds before he shouted "Jacob, come into the office!"

Jacob shuffled through the door with his head hung low. Mike handed him the mint copy of the White Album. "You sneak this back into your house. You're entitled to no more free sandwiches. Understand?"

"Yes sir," Jacob said without lifting his eyes from the floor.

"One other thing."

"What?" Jacob looked up.

"Do you want a job?"

"A job?"

"You're a pretty shrewd kid," Mike said, "and I have a good feeling that you'd do your best not to let me down."

"When do I start?"

"Just as soon as you put that record back where it belongs. Take a picture and show me. When you do, you get an apron."

FORTY-ONE

When fall came, Mike remembered the mental note he had made back in June to run along Van Buren and through its tunnel of massive elms as they changed colors. He traversed the same route every day for four weeks to track the slow, subtle transformation, like a time-lapse film in his mind. Early on, the trees remained the same emerald green he had admired in the summer, but gradually, all but imperceptibly, the blue drained out of the leaves until they were a brilliant, translucent gold. When the sun hit the trees just right, it produced a radiant and awe-inspiring canopy, like nature's own cathedral. The first time Mike saw Van Buren's celestial glow, he stopped, looked upward and cried, feeling like he had finally found the divine in his hometown.

His mom returned in October for just long enough to announce that she was going to sell her house and move to South Carolina for good. After her balmy summer, she declared that she couldn't take another Illinois winter, nor could she take being that far from her grandchildren anymore. Time was too precious, she told Mike. She was determined to be there to watch those kids grow up. Mike remained in the house through the winter, making sure that the furnace worked properly and the pipes didn't freeze. The real estate agent advised waiting until spring to list the house. The market wouldn't pick up until April, and there was no use in starting the season with a stale listing.

Throughout those same months, in a finished basement across town, Jacob's father kept finding missing albums. One day a record wouldn't be there and the next he would spot it filed neatly in alphabetical order with the rest of his collection. Dire Straits, Dylan, Public Image, Springsteen, XTC – all where they should have been, but not where they were before. At least Tom didn't think they had been there. He began to wonder if he had contracted some sort of debilitating neurological condition. He went online and searched. There were several diagnoses that might explain the phenomenon, ranging from stress and insufficient sleep to brain cancer and early-onset Alzheimer's. His doctor couldn't imagine any persistent issues of memory loss or disorientation that would manifest themselves exclusively through the discovery of misplaced records. He didn't think that Tom really needed an MRI, but he ordered one just to be safe, and everything checked out. The doctor had no good explanation. "Maybe the album fairy," he said. Tom eventually accepted that he was fine, but he couldn't understand why his original copy of *Captain Fantastic* never showed up.

As the months passed, sightings of Jenna and Craig dwindled and then stopped. The news networks lost interest. Lacy moved on to a story about a petite blonde woman who had been abducted by Satanists before being discovered tied to a tree on the top of a hill in a national park, emotionally shattered but physically unharmed. Mike stumbled onto Lacy's show during the first week of the story. He had never seen her look so happy.

In the fall Jenks got an article published in *The American Journal of Economics and Sociology*, which demonstrated, to the surprise of all who inhabited Mellow Sub, that he really was being productive during all of those afternoons when he held down a table and sipped the High Life. The achievement raised his profile in the academic community, and in January he joined the faculty at a private liberal arts college in Vermont, where, Mike presumed, he was annoying the shit out of someone who made sandwiches or sold beer.

While Jenks was settling in the northeast, Mellow Sub was opening its second location, this one in Champaign. It only made sense, Mike thought, because so many of Cameron's kids went to college there, and they could help introduce 40,000 of their peers to Greg's creations. Jill made a point to visit the new shop when she dropped Liv off for weekends with Dan. Despite her reluctance to be a flower girl, Liv confessed to her mother that Christina had always been kind to her and had told her that she would always give Liv anything she needed, but would never try to replace her mom. Jill invited Christina to lunch at the new shop, thanked her for being so good to Liv, and expressed hope that, in some way at least, they could be friends. Christina hugged Jill, began to cry and apologized for not being warmer in the months leading up to the wedding. "It's silly, but I was afraid of you," Christina confessed. "But I've come to realize that all of the good things that Dan says about you are true."

Back at the original Mellow Submarine, Jacob proved to be a reliable employee and a willing hand in the kitchen. He had sampled as many of Greg's sandwiches as anyone, and even before Greg left, Jacob had started to make connections as he ate – the way that sweetness and spice complemented one another, the way that fresh basil made tomatoes come alive. His favorite class in school was chemistry, and he began to see cooking through a scientific lens, with discrete elements bonding together to create something new. He pressed Alyssa to teach him, and she did. Together they worked through all of Greg's recipes and some of Alyssa's, too, and the kid even created a new sandwich for the menu. Called Jake the Vegan, it consisted of roasted eggplant, pickled onions, olives, sweet red peppers and hummus on warm *naan*. Alyssa said "you're not going to believe this" when she first took a sample back into the office. Mike was so impressed that he told Jacob to stay in the kitchen and he hired a new part-timer to work out front.

In March, as the weather warmed, Mike noticed red flowers budding on Van Buren's elms, and he watched as they morphed into green leaves in April. He had not been back in Cameron even a year yet, but the completion of the seasons' cycle finally made his return feel permanent. On a Tuesday morning, while Mike was running through the tunnel of leaves, Jill was driving Liv to school and remarking that there were just six weeks left in second grade. Jill could feel her desire to freeze time, or at least to slow it, so she could enjoy these moments for just a little longer. As they approached the drop-off line, she said "OK, this is the big day. You have piano practice right after school and then soccer at six and then we'll have dinner and then –"

"I'm so excited!" Liv said before hopping out of the car and blowing her mom a kiss on the way into school.

At the end of the day, Mike grabbed some food from Mellow Sub, including a torta with extra jalapenos for Liv. The ladies returned home from soccer and the three of them sat down to sandwiches. Mike opted for a new creation by Alyssa called the Down Home, which featured fried chicken, hash browns and coleslaw on a pillow-soft hoagie roll. He had committed to a full marathon training regimen mostly so he could justify eating that delectable monstrosity once a week. Mike asked Liv about her day at school, and she said that she was building a potato-powered light for her science fair project. Mike scrunched up his eyebrows and said that a potato can't power a light bulb, and Liv said no, really, it can, and Mike asked how many potatoes Liv thought it would take to light up New

York City, and she thought for a minute and settled on a million-bajillion-gazillion.

When they finished eating, Mike cleaned up
the table and Jill took Liv upstairs and put her in
her pajamas. "You can watch," Jill said, "but after
that, it's right to bed."

Jill and Liv bounded back downstairs and
plopped down on the couch while Mike turned on
the television and checked for the fourth time to
make sure that he had set the DVR to record. The
show started right at eight. First came a montage of
scenes depicting the build-out and the food and
the frustration and the anticipation and the love,
followed by the title sequence: *Greg and Maggie
Open a Restaurant*, from executive producer Tessa
Goldstein. The episode began with some background. Greg, sporting a beard that was even more
lush and luxuriant than before, explained that
when he was at his lowest, his friend Jill saved his
shop, and when he was at his loneliest, his friend
Mike brought Maggie into his life. As he spoke, he
wore a custom-printed t-shirt that read *LIV* across
the front. His young friend squealed at the sight of
it.

Cameras bounced from Kleinsasser Capital
Management, to the condo the couple had shared
since Greg helped sell Mike's place, to the shell of
the space that blossomed into *Ethos* over the first
forty minutes of the hour. An upscale pan-
Mediterranean restaurant, *Ethos* took food from the
cradle of civilization, blended it into astonishing

new creations and dropped it into the heart of Denver. On opening night, shots of Greg dashing around the kitchen contrasted with images of Maggie welcoming guests while Moroccan music played in the background. A couple gushed over an appetizer that featured *injera*, an Ethiopian flat bread that Greg made from scratch, with *baba ganoush* and roasted vegetables. A woman rolled her eyes back in ecstasy as she tasted a short rib ragu with gnocchi. A man sat at a table, slack-jawed, after finishing a meal of *merquez* and polenta porridge paired with an inexpensive Chianti Classico. "That was, without doubt, the best thing I've ever eaten," he said.

At the end of the episode, after closing the doors on opening night, Greg and Maggie stood alone in the kitchen, exhausted but satisfied. Maggie wrapped her arms around Greg's waist and kissed him, and they held each other for a moment with their eyes closed. Then Greg turned and grabbed a pen and some paper. "Making notes on how to improve things for tomorrow," he said to the camera, and then the credits rolled.

Liv jumped to her feet and applauded, and Jill said "Time for bed. You can watch it again tomorrow if you want." Upstairs, Jill tucked her daughter in and said "Goodnight, sweetie, I love you," before turning off the light and closing the door.

After lying wide awake for fifteen minutes, Liv got up and tip-toed to her closet. She opened the door, turned on the light, and slipped into her new dress. She looked in the mirror and smiled. Her front teeth had come all the way in. She was going to be a beautiful maid of honor.

Acknowledgements

I am grateful to the many friends who have offered their ideas and support to this book. To try to name them all would result in inadvertently omitting a few, but special debts of gratitude are owed to Trip McClatchy, Kurt Hankenson, Peter Kosciewicz and Todd Palmer, who informed the text through their thorough reading and invaluable feedback, to Scott Esserman, Pat Feeney, Rick Ross and T.J. Quinn, who lent their minds when mine was unavailable, to Grant Pace, who turned some vague directions into an eye-catching cover, and to Jennifer Bartel, who rescued me at the end with her considerable formatting and layout skills. Also, as always, to Sherri, Grace and Evan, who simultaneously make this possible and impossible.

ABOUT THE AUTHOR

Michael Atchison is the author of two previous books, the novel *XL* and *True Sons: A Century of Missouri Tigers Basketball*. His writing about pop culture and collegiate sports has appeared in several publications, including *Sports Illustrated*, *The Providence Phoenix* and *Basketball Times*. He lives in Parkville, Missouri, where he is often surrounded by records and sometimes by sandwiches.

Michael is on Twitter at @MichaelAtchison.

Made in the USA
Columbia, SC
16 August 2017